MOON DYNASTY

THE WILD PACK

BOOK 2

USA TODAY BEST-SELLING AUTHOR

CARMEN FOX

Nana

WYWH

Acknowledgments

Books are written in isolation, but many wonderful people did many wonderful things to get Moon Promise from my desk into your hands. Dylan, Ana, Shaz, Kally, Carole—I thank you all.

My gratitude also belongs to you, my reader. You take my worlds and enrich them with your enthusiasm and kindness.

Garry Rodgers has helped me tremendously with his extensive knowledge of all things dead. Garry, you've been amazing. Any mistakes I made are entirely my own.

I also want to thank my mother for her unwavering support. Without her, my life would be a mess.

ONE

SOMEONE, SOMEWHERE, WAS BEGGING FOR mercy. At least this was the image I conjured as I approached Jonah's office, where he was tearing into some poor soul. Probably by phone. Strike that. *Hopefully* by phone.

I squeezed the rain from my hair, leaving a sizeable puddle on the travertine floor. Maybe I should have bought a cake. The Wild Pack's alpha loved all food, provided it was sweet and baked.

"How many times?" Jonah shouted. "I need the completed forms by tonight."

I slowed my steps, inching rather than marching toward the coat rack, and hung my raincoat on the last free hook. Until now, Jonah had struck me as the laid-back type. I wasn't sure I was ready to see my illusions shattered.

Yeah, a cake would have been a great idea.

Right then, the hottest man on the planet emerged from the door and approached with a smile that made my insides melt.

Drake's experimental fade cut, where his dark-blond hair tapered from tousled on top to barely-there at the sides, gave him a bad-boy look. But who cared about his hair or his nicely shaped biceps when the gleam in his eyes spoke of the kind of intimacy for which walls and doors were invented?

There was nothing sexier in the world than a man who knew what he wanted—especially if that something was me.

Without explaining the shouting in the background, he pulled me into his arms.

His lips gave me full-blown atrial fibrillations with a clichéd case of weak knees. The confidence in his hands, the conviction of his tongue, and his staccato breaths slayed my last inkling of reality.

"Hey," I gasped after we'd taken our fill.

His effect on my body lingered. My brain and limbs had rarely felt more disconnected.

"Hey." He peered at my lips as if considering another go.

"For God's sake, get it done!" Jonah yelled.

A massive crash sounded in the office and bounced off the walls into the hall.

I winced and pressed tighter against Drake. "Do I want to go in there?"

"He's been up and down like a yoyo all day. If anyone can cheer him up, it's you."

I glanced into his eyes—which he knew so well how to use—and let my thoughts float in their mercury shimmer. Eventually, I sighed. "Fine. Has Natalie been in touch?"

"No, she's ducking his calls. Mine, too."

"Mine, three." I shook my head, depositing more water droplets on the floor. "At least that explains his mood."

"I thought she could handle the truth."

I gave a brusque snort. "That there are werewolves out there? There's a reason we don't tell humans. It doesn't fit into their worldview."

"I *know* that." His voice tensed. "I meant Nat seemed strong enough to handle anything."

"She didn't just discover we're werewolves. She discovered

Jonah's one." I stroked his cheek, enjoying my finger's journey in the smooth direction more than in the stubbly one, and then twisted away from him. "I think she liked him."

I headed to Jonah's office, which had gone eerily quiet. "Hi, Jonah." I raised a hand.

Jonah's 'office' contained a desk, a printer, a computer…the whole shebang…but these were mainly perfunctory. As a matter of routine, the alpha conducted his meetings and most of his other work at the large dining table, on which documents, teacups, and gadgets didn't have to vie for space.

Jonah had his butt planted on the table, his phone in his hand, and got up when his gaze fell on me. "Finally. You're here."

We'd long passed the stage where he felt he had to dress up in my presence. Today, he wore khaki pants with a casual blue shirt. His right collar tip stood up, a fraction away from poking his chin, and he'd rolled up his sleeves to show lean, strong arms the color of unprocessed cotton—gray with yellow undertones.

Not everyone needed to be as healthily tanned as Drake, but a particularly hot summer, which had added a rosy glow even to my light-brown skin, had clearly bypassed Jonah.

I raised my eyebrows. "What's up? You said you needed to speak to me?"

"So much to tell you." He half-laid, half-dropped his cell on the table and crossed his arms. "First, any news about the disability center they're building on my land?"

Oh, crap. I exchanged a quick glance with Drake, who'd stayed behind by the door frame as if hesitant to enter the alpha's den.

"I haven't heard anything, sorry." I clutched the hem of my shirt, steeling myself for his reaction.

"Uh-huh." The proud alpha's cheeks deflated.

Not how I'd thought he'd respond.

"I'm sure Nat will be in touch, soon." I released my fist and straightened my top. "That center is important to her and to the people who need it."

"Right." After a small eternity, his angled jaw lifted with a proud smile. "Anyway, I've had a long conversation with your father."

"That's who you were shouting at?" I involuntarily touched my throat.

"Of course not. He's not as incompetent as—" He waved off. "No, I talked to him *last night*."

"Right."

"We were discussing future relations between our packs." He swept his chocolate-red hair away from his brow. "Especially in light of rising hostilities between Russia's royal pack and the Ukrainian free pack."

"Didn't they declare a truce?" After all, I did listen occasionally when Drake talked, even if the topic was politics.

"It's a truce, yet not a lasting peace." Jonah turned his shirt collar down and his gaze followed Drake, who silently marched past the dark-wood cabinet holding the pack's files.

Drake moved with his typical lupine grace. I liked how the fabric of his shirt moved, linen with soft crinkles was so much more fluid than stiff cotton.

Once he'd reached the other side of the room, he stretched to pull the windows shut to keep out the rain. My gaze automatically drifted to his ass, criminally obscured by his jeans.

That was what memory was for, and mine conjured a live-action video of last night's bedroom activities.

Jonah cleared his throat. "Anyway, your father and I believe it's time to be proactive about our friendship, especially since you and Drake took the Moon Promise."

I was still floundering in the dark, but the tone of his voice told me whatever he was leading up to, I wouldn't like it.

I took a step closer. "What do you mean?"

"As your mate, Drake will ascend the German throne by your

side as the king consort." Just like that, life returned to his eyes, revealing a spark of mischief.

"Sure." *Come on, spit it out.*

"First, assuming Drake agrees, he will become my pack brother."

"Really?" I swiveled toward Drake.

He'd halted mid-step, mid-room, and lifted his shoulders. A frown carved deep lines into his forehead.

I still didn't see how everything connected.

Jonah spread his arms as if laying out his entire scheme. "And at the end of the week, you and Drake will fly to Germany to attend your confirmation ceremony."

My heart gave an uncomfortable double-beat. "We what now?"

If I'd brought a cake, this would have been the moment I'd have dropped it.

"It's time, Kensi. You are to be invested as the official heir to the German throne." Jonah fell into his chair and gestured for me to join him on the opposite side of the table.

I sent my gaze from a motionless Drake back to Jonah, who looked more and more smug by the second.

"Sit." He pointed again.

I nodded but my legs wouldn't move.

Sharp invisible needles grazed my arms and neck. My eyes widened.

I forced my reactions back under control.

Jonah had every right to unleash a small dose of his dominance. As the alpha, he shouldn't have to repeat himself. As long as I lived in his pack, I would obey, no matter how much it went against my instincts.

I sat.

"You too, Drake." Jonah gestured toward the chair at the short side of the table.

For a second, Drake didn't look as if he had the stomach to join us in a conversation only Jonah was eager to have, but he consented with a nod.

Once Drake was seated to my right, Jonah's smugness exploded into an almost demented grin. "Our two packs have been the poster children of how free packs and royal packs should behave. In our high-pressure world, cooperation between packs is often lacking, and we intend to change this."

No one should sound this happy discussing candy and unicorns, let alone the sad state of our kind's social interactions.

I laid my hands flat on the table, mainly to pretend this conversation wasn't beginning to scare the crap out of me. "Yeah—"

Jonah's raised a finger to cut me off. "Aldwych's and my friendship is personal and private. Your relationship with Drake is going to go public soon. This Sunday, you will be the official crown princess and prince consort to the German throne."

I squinted. "So, because Drake and I got married—"

"Mated," they both said at once.

"Humans get married." Drake sounded exasperated.

"For crying out..." I took a deep breath. "Fine. But many werewolves do get married."

"We didn't." Drake stared daggers, which I deflected with raised eyebrows.

"Don't fight again," Jonah interceded. "You're mated either way. It makes no difference."

Taking the Moon Promise had been a spur-of-the-moment thing. The lure of finally being able to tap into my wolf and the early haze of love had conspired to make me take a step I wasn't prepared to take.

Did I need a mate to tell me I wasn't wolf enough because I preferred human company? Nope. Did I need a mate to know watching crime movies wasn't the best use of my time? Definitely not!

What had I been thinking?

"The difference is, if we were married, we could get a divorce." My gaze burning, I shot its full force at Drake.

He gripped the edge of the table and straightened, and the hurt expression on his face pierced my heart.

"Not that I ever would." I softened my voice and took his left hand in mine. "Never."

Drake didn't deserve my anger. Jonah and my dad were the ones putting pressure on our young relationship.

Drake swallowed, released the tension from his shoulders, and smiled. "Good save."

I placed a kiss on the back of his hand. "Sorry."

"Anyway." Jonah rasped, probably reminded of his lack of progress with the woman he'd had *his* eyes on. "With Drake as my pack brother, the confirmation ceremony will forever link our packs. We couldn't send a stronger symbol of unity to the world."

"That's great." I let go of Drake's hand and signaled a weak thumbs-up. "But why does this need to happen now?"

"While you were living among the humans, the voices demanding that your father look elsewhere for a successor who isn't quite so..." Jonah's eyes drifted as if looking for an acceptable term to describe my apparent disadvantage.

"Quite so female?" My pitch rose sharply.

He cocked his finger. "Yes, the voices shouting for a male successor got louder. That's the only reason you're not the crown princess already. Now you have a mate, which should shut the loudest misogynist up."

I wrapped my ankles around my chair's legs, really hooked them in, until their hard edges cut into my flesh. The night Drake and I took the Moon Promise, I met her, my wolf. *She* was everything I'd hoped she'd be. Fierce. Cunning. Proud. I was finally able to shift into my animal form and use the sharp claws of my dominance to assert myself.

Nothing could stop my ascent to alpha status.

Or so I'd thought. In truth, Drake and I were still in the phase where we used separate bathrooms, except maybe for a quickie in the shower. The extra weight of the crown could detonate our relationship before we'd had a chance to make it work.

Hell, how could Dad possibly consider this a good time for our confirmation?

"We just got *mated*." I gripped the table. "We're still in our honeymoon phase."

"Aww." Jonah's voice dripped with sarcasm. "Snap out of it. You were born to be an alpha. Time to get on that, don't you think?"

"So soon?" Drake dragged his hand across his mouth and chin.

I'd rarely seen him more out of sorts. Not that this meant a lot since we'd only known each other a single freaking month. Maybe six weeks. Crap. Why couldn't the world leave us to figure things out as a married couple before suffocating us with its social demands?

Jonah's features softened as he leaned a fraction toward Drake. "You've been my protector for years. Your loyalty, appreciated as it is, shouldn't be keeping you from finding your own pack. You were born to be an alpha. I was sure one day you'd challenge me for leadership."

"I would never." Drake vehemently shook his head.

No, he would never. In the first few days after we met, I'd glimpsed a power in Drake that had me in awe. I'd also learned this power paled in comparison to his utter devotion to those he loved.

"Maybe you won't be an alpha but becoming a king consort isn't a bad consolation prize." Jonah tapped the table's surface as if pleased with himself. "Royal succession is much less bloody than our ways."

Only one of the many differences between royal packs and free packs.

"How is this going to work?" Drake asked. "I'll continue to be our pack's protector, right?"

"Yes, for now. You'll also be my pack brother. Do you understand where I'm going with this?"

"I believe so." Drake frowned. "We'll be family. All of us. Kensi, I, you, and Kensi's father."

Maybe he didn't want to see past the obvious, but I'd witnessed great alpha minds twist situations in their favor all my life.

I let my dominance peek out for a second, not enough to defy Jonah, only enough to let on what I thought of his and Dad's plan. "We'll be representatives of both packs, the public face of your and dad's private friendship."

"Exactly." Jonah clapped. "You will be the power couple of the werewolf world and travel between the free packs and the royal packs."

"For what purpose?" I asked, even though I knew the answer.

"You will carry our message to all packs. Unite and play nice, or there'll be trouble." Jonah gave a laugh that made him sound like a Bond villain. "Don't be so surprised. You and Drake sealed your fate the second you took the Moon Promise."

Yeah, the damned Moon Promise. Seriously. What *had* I been thinking?

"Your father's people sent me an email for you with your schedule. Hang on." Jonah looked around the table. "I'll go get it."

He pushed back his chair and headed toward the desk at the far end of the room.

In the time I'd known him, he hadn't used that desk, that chair, or that printer once.

I laid my forehead on the tabletop and exhaled loudly. "You said I'd cheer him up. This wasn't what I'd expected."

Drake grunted.

"My pack's a mess," I whispered. "Is this the best time to send us on tour to spread their hippy message of love, sparkles, and rainbows? Who are Dad and Jonah to decide what we should and shouldn't do anyway?"

"They're our alphas." Drake sounded his most subservient. "We do what they tell us."

"Don't be so damn reasonable. It's our life." I jerked my gaze up, armed with a deadly glare, and immediately stilled.

His face had gone ashen, his beautiful silver eyes a lackluster gray.

"Drake?" I stroked his arm. "Are you okay?"

Jonah breezed back to the table and handed me a printout. "It is your life, but the privilege of your royal heritage comes with responsibility."

Who was I? Peter Parker?

Why didn't Jonah get it? Getting used to the fact that I was no longer single was going to take a while, and now my plans to do away with my pack's primitive ideas regarding women would have to wait, too. Talk about kicking me while I was down.

"What do you say?" Jonah leaned with both hands on the table and bore down on his protector with an intense gaze. "Are you ready to be my pack brother?"

"I'm honored, of course." Drake dropped his head. "I'll need to think about it."

"You have exactly two days to talk it through. The pack-brother ceremony is scheduled for Thursday, and on Friday, you will be going to Germany. Can I count on you to be ready?"

Drake's pale face lost its tightness, his eyes were wide and empty.

I shook him. "Hasi. Are you okay?"

His gaze cleared, and he sat straight with a start. "What?"

"I said, are you okay?" I rested my hand on his powerful chest. "What is it? This is sudden for me, too."

"No, it's not that." He fell back in his chair, laced his fingers behind his head, and gave a sigh that could blow Uncle Bexley's wig off.

"Okaaay." I stretched the word. "What is it then?"

"I'm going to meet your father." He shook his head, over and over. "Shit. I'm going to meet your father."

"I shouldn't have teased you about how strict he is."

"He's going to kill me, right? We took the Moon Promise without his permission. I should have asked him."

"For the hundredth time. I'm not an object to be passed around. If you'd asked his permission, you and I wouldn't have happened."

"And for this reason alone I wouldn't have asked him."

"Good. Then what's the problem?"

"I should have asked his permission."

I was getting nowhere. Drake was caught in a loop of horror, and nothing I said would soothe him.

I glared at Jonah to make sure he knew this was his fault. "I'd better take him home."

"Yeah," Jonah squeaked. His shoulders quietly shook but he wouldn't meet my eyes. "We've broken him."

How dare he laugh? This was a nightmare. I needed Drake—level-headed, strong-minded Drake, not a Drake who was brought to his knees at the mere mention of my dad.

"Come on." I pulled him up from the chair.

"I'm not broken," he mumbled. "It's called a moment of clarity."

"Of course." I ushered him toward the exit.

Maybe I should give him a task to distract him. He could fix his truck's air conditioner that kept breaking every five days. Then, tonight, I'd relax him. By tomorrow, he'd be back to being the strong, confident type.

How long that would last in light of what was to come was anyone's guess. Still, Drake had been right. My visit had certainly cheered up Jonah.

Two

Ten people had joined us for the ceremony that turned Drake, the protector, into Drake, Jonah's pack brother. The dining room we'd crowded into had been decorated with hand-written congratulatory banners and hand-picked flowers.

Drake had dressed for the occasion. The fabric of his shirt shimmered white with a subtle stripe, and he smelled glorious in the new cologne he'd bought especially for today.

He jiggled his eyebrows, and a smile lit up his face. "Like what you see, princess?"

"Always." I kissed him and then slapped his ass. "Now go. Jonah's waiting."

Once he was off, his brother, Colt, came to stand by my side, stiff as a pole and with his arms crossed. What was running through his mind? Being related to the alpha presumably came with certain benefits, but he wasn't exuding enthusiasm. Was he worried he'd be losing his brother, first to me and now to Jonah?

Of course, Colt hadn't been consulted.

What else was new? That was how werewolf society worked. Ours was an instant, granulated life that came prepackaged with instructions, much like coffee. No thinking required. Except, I was a fan of coffee. Loved it. Couldn't get enough of the stuff. Werewolf politics, on the other hand…

Maybe Drake was right and I'd become too human to feel at ease among my own kind.

The ceremony was over quickly. Drake and Jonah had whispered words they'd read from a book. I stood too far away to hear them, or maybe they were not meant for my ears in the first place.

Finally, Jonah and Drake hugged it out and grinned, as if newly in love. The brotherly bond between them seemed already up and running.

When Drake and I took the Moon Promise, the true change occurred on the inside, unseen by anyone else. With the ritual's last word, my hopeful confidence that Drake was *the one* cemented into an absolute certainty, without a single magical sparkle in sight.

Werewolf magic wasn't flashy.

"I'm so happy for you." Fawn, a former teacher of Drake's, pulled him into a hug that lasted.

And lasted.

In many ways, I'd come to love the Wild Pack more than my own. Under Jonah's leadership, people came together to celebrate and commiserate, to build each other up and to protect. The only reason members of my Boroughs Pack would gather as one was to make it easier to stab each other in the back.

Jonah zeroed in on Colt. "Come here. Brother."

Colt smiled timidly and allowed his alpha to embrace him, yet his stick-up-his-buttishness remained. Whatever transformation had overcome Drake and Jonah clearly hadn't extended to him. At least not yet.

I was next to hug Jonah.

"I'm happy for you," I whispered into his ear.

And I was. The alpha had struggled over the last few weeks, maybe because his relationship with Nat never got off the ground or maybe because of business or political strain I wasn't aware of. All of that was forgotten today, and he allowed himself to grin without restraint.

"Be happy for all of us." He set his forehead against mine, one of the highest honors he could bestow on me.

"I am." Then I snickered.

He lifted his head. "What's so funny?"

"Basically, you're now my brother-in-law-in-pack, which sounds ridiculous."

"How about we say we're family and leave it at that?"

"That works." I squeezed his hand, a gesture that only yesterday would have seemed too intimate.

"Let's drink!" Jonah's voice rang out as he laid his arm over my shoulder. He glowed from the inside out.

Two women and a man entered the dining rooms with trays carrying champagne and fruit juice. They wore black suits with white gloves, an unusual note of elegance in a pack that didn't value glitz and glamour.

Jonah waltzed off to mingle with his pack, and the embraces and encouraging slaps on his back spoke of the love his friends held in their hearts.

My dad's pack didn't dare get close to their alpha. The only hugs he got were mine—and I hadn't seen him in well over a year when he'd visited me in Chicago.

Drake came up behind me and slung his hands around my waist. "It feels like he's my brother. Isn't that the weirdest thing?"

I reached back with my hand and cupped his neck. "My mother's cousin told me our rituals are more powerful than they seem. Guess you witnessed a prime example of that power today."

He kissed my earlobe, and an exquisite shiver ran down my spine. In moments like these, my body ached for him.

Rowel, who'd only recently become head of the Moon Festival Committee, clinked his glass with a spoon.

"Many of us have watched Jonah and Drake grow up from unruly pups into the alpha and protector they are today." His words earned him a few laughs. "Both suffered personal tragedies under Marlon's rule, and together they pulled themselves, and each of us, out of the darkness. Now they're forever joined in pack. Ladies and gentlemen, please raise your glasses to Jonah and Drake."

The warmth in his voice nearly brought tears to my eyes.

The entire room, I included, raised our glasses. "To Jonah and Drake."

Drake lifted his head a fraction and otherwise stayed glued behind me. I sipped champagne, crinkled my nose at the bubbles that invaded my nostrils, and then laid my head back on his shoulder. He was marginally taller than me, barely two inches. The perfect height to accommodate any kind of PDA I wanted to lay on him.

Someone had found the sound system's on-button, and a song from the 1970s rocked the room. The volume of the conversations went up to compensate, and Drake and I watched in silence, body on body, slightly swaying along.

No one had told me I'd one day live in a tiny town, surrounded by werewolves, in a committed relationship, and subject to an alpha who wasn't my father—and yet be mostly content.

Jonah waved in our direction.

"The boss wants to talk to us." Drake's breath tickled my ear.

"I choose not to see that." I shifted my gaze away from the alpha. "He'll want to talk about our trip, won't he?"

"That seems to be his favorite topic at the moment."

"If Natalie ever speaks to me again, I'll blame her for this mess. If she'd kept him occupied, the idea of sending us away wouldn't have entered his head."

It probably would have, but I was okay placing blame elsewhere.

"You're moving a step closer to your dream." Drake kissed my cheek. "Besides, aren't you excited about seeing your dad?"

"Don't confuse my happiness of seeing my dad with the dread about going back to court."

"Shouldn't you be reassuring me, rather than raising my terror level to DEFCON one?"

I grinned. "You'd think, right?"

"Come on." He kissed my ear again and then slapped my ass. "Let's not spoil Jonah's mood."

And yet Jonah was about to spoil mine. One of the many perks of being a fully-fleshed alpha.

Jonah was waiting by the door to the hall.

Once we'd caught up to him, he laid one arm each over our shoulders. "Two court administrators have arrived from Germany. I've set them up in the empty room next door. You should go and see them."

I shot an evil look at the wall he'd pointed his chin at. "Um. Do you know their names?"

"Stirling and Brent."

My fingertips dug into my hand. "Stirling? Seriously?"

"You don't like him?" Drake asked. "That means I'm going to hate him, right?"

I hung my shoulders. "He's okay, I guess. He's my dad's Lord High Chancellor and does his job, whether it suits you or not."

"Don't make them wait." Jonah pushed us forward to get us moving. "When you're done, we'll eat."

As if I needed an incentive to get this over with.

Drake and I entered the room next door, holding hands, afraid to let go.

Stirling and his partner bowed deep before me.

"Your Royal Highness," Stirling said in a resonant tone. "It is good to see you well."

"Please." I waved him off with both hands. "You don't need to bow here. At least not while we're in America."

For Drake's benefit, I kept our conversation in English. Most

Germans knew enough English to get by. Those at court were educated in the finer points of English grammar. Stirling's accent was nearly perfect—and very British.

It had taken me years to acquire a generic American pronunciation.

Stirling straightened. "Your Royal Highness. Sir. If everything goes according to plan, by this time on Sunday, you will be the official heir and consort to the throne. I suggest you become accustomed to royal courtesies now and learn the appropriate responses and mannerisms."

I shot him a sheepish smile. "Yeah. All right. Guess that makes sense."

"I'm glad." Stirling stood straight as a rod, with his neat mustache at a ninety-degree angle. Only his mouth moved, and only if a hard consonant required it. "You release your subjects from a neck bow or a curtsy by a single nod of the head."

It wasn't as if I didn't know what to do. I just didn't want to.

"How will I see the nod if my head is bowed?" Drake asked.

Stirling shot him a snobby glance. "A nod will be expected, which is why our gesture of honor lasts no more than a second or two."

His stiff movements, know-it-all tone, and the total lack of pink under his white skin only reinforced the notion that my father's High Chancellor could only benefit from letting his hair down once in a while.

"Right." Drake's hand tightened around mine. "Gotcha."

I totally felt for him. Stirling's apparent superiority intimidated me, too.

"Next, I would ask that you speak in complete sentences, such as, 'I understand.'" Stirling creased his nose. "'Gotcha' is—"

"American?" I suggested.

"Gotcha is a colloquial expression not suitable for court. Now. Brent is his majesty's new tailor." He pointed at the man to his right. "He will take measurements needed to adjust the traditional gowns. Meanwhile, it seems prudent to refresh your memory about royal protocol. Or to induct you." He singled out Drake with a glance. "As the case may be."

I exhaled sharply, resigned to the fact that this was happening.

Stirling pushed out his chest. "You will address the king as 'Your Majesty' and 'Sir.' Do not shake his hand unless it is offered first, in which case you will greet him with a 'How do you do.'"

"I understand." Drake's voice remained firm, even though I detected a note of sarcasm.

Good. Stirling hadn't beaten him yet.

"When dining with royalty, place your napkin on your lap." Stirling continued to lecture us from his spot, which happened to be the center of the room. "Keep wrists and elbows off the table while eating."

"Drake knows how to eat." I pursed my lips.

Stirling's expression likewise turned sour.

The last thing I wanted was for Drake to feel he'd made a mistake marrying me. I'd accepted at an early age the rules and conventions accompanying royal life. He shouldn't have to.

"Your Royal Highness?" Brent gestured for me to step toward him. "If you could stand with your arms out?"

I obliged.

"Thank you."

"Let us move on to the ceremony itself." Stirling positioned himself closer to Drake, yet remained within view, and clasped his hands behind his back. "Two hours before the confirmation ceremony begins, two ladies-in-waiting will assist with your attire. Brent and his—"

"No way." I spun my head in his direction. "We don't need help getting dressed."

"Your Royal Highness, please stand still." Brent tugged on my pant leg.

"Protocol must be followed," Stirling boomed.

I clenched my hands into fists. Painful ones, and hard enough to pummel his stupid, rule-abiding face.

Drake coughed.

His subtle hint helped me focus. I relaxed my hands and gently pushed Brent aside before aiming a healthy dose of dominance at Stirling.

My dad's faithful Chancellor started, his mouth gaping. Even though I eased the uneven swell of the pheromones that transmitted my dominance, I held his gaze, unblinking.

His face paled, his jaw trembled, and finally, he bowed. "As you wish."

Growing up, when dominance had not yet been an option, I'd learned to hold my own with facial expressions, posture, and sheer stubbornness, but none of that had worked on Stirling. Seemed I'd finally turned the tables.

"Good." I stretched out my arms again, so Brent could keep on measuring. "You may continue, Stirling."

"Thank you, Your Royal Highness. When the fanfare begins, you will enter the throne room with your hand supported by your Schutzherr's arm." He took a breath. "Although not protocol as such, it might be visually appealing to move with the sound of the trumpets."

"Trumpets?" Drake scratched his forehead. "Jeez. And what's a Schutzer?"

"Schutzherr means protector." I eyed Brent's swift motions as he measured and noted numbers. "It's the title of the claimant's husband."

"Her mate's title," Stirling corrected me and immediately winced, even though I'd refrained from disciplining him again. "To be precise, *Schutzherrin* is the usual title, since, traditionally, the claimant's mate is a female."

"Welcome to the twenty-first century," I mumbled, then frowned as Brent ran his tape measure between my legs. Wholly unnecessary, considering the traditional gown for me would be a dress.

"In the throne room, her royal highness will announce her claim to the crown. If everything proceeds as planned, his majesty will declare her the heir to the German throne. Her Royal Highness, Crown Princess Kensington of the Boroughs Pack, of the House of Berg, and her Prince Consort, Drake of the Boroughs Pack, Protector of the Wild Pack."

"Sounds pretty straight-forward." Drake's tone relaxed. "Although signing my name is probably going to give me carpal tunnel syndrome."

"If I may make a suggestion, sir?" Stirling shifted an inch to the side, away from me.

Drake had mentioned a few times that my dominance packed quite a punch, and it was satisfying to see he was right. I'd waited long enough to finally prove my alphahood.

"Of course." Drake gestured for Stirling to get on with it.

My man valued directness, not a pompous beating around the bush.

"Drake is an appropriate name for the Wild Pack." Stirling attempted a smile. "Would you perhaps consider choosing a name more appropriate to the Boroughs Pack? We have a fine selection of—"

"No, he won't." I whipped around again, nearly taking poor Brent's head off with the swing of my arm. "He's not going to change his name for you."

"Of course." Stirling's nasal tone punctuated another curt bow. "Forgive me."

Brent peered at me one last time and then walked across the room to turn his attention to Drake.

Kings and queens across the world had changed their names and birthdays, but I had no intention of inconveniencing Drake more than I had to. For all his alpha power, taking the throne by my side wasn't what my gentle country boy had dreamed of all his life. Yet he'd accepted the burden for me. I'd be damned if I watched him being eaten alive by the crown's machinery.

By the time Stirling dismissed us, the sun was setting. Luckily, he and Brent had turned down our dutiful invitation to join us for dinner, claiming they had far too much work ahead of them. As if we were slackers.

"Are all your father's courtiers like Stirling?" Drake asked. "He's pretty intense."

"Some are worse." I produced a sloppy smile. My heart simply wasn't in it. "Already wondering how to undo the Moon Promise?"

Even though I knew what his answer was going to be, my breathing stilled.

He leaned over and kissed my forehead. "Not on your life."

THREE

DRAKE'S CABIN, OR RATHER, *OUR* cabin, lay miles away from civilization. My years in Chicago had turned me into a city girl but living smack in the middle of the woods was wonderful. Trees, with their unmistakable scents and tranquility, had felt like home even before I'd been able to release my inner wolf.

Drake turned off the truck's lights just as the first flash of lightning struck.

"We're home, and safely I might add." He stared ahead, unmoving.

"Are you saying I would have wrecked your truck?" I squinted at the rain, which hit the windshield like strings of spaghetti.

"Your track record isn't great. You've totaled two cars since I met you."

I bit down on a bitter taste. "The first one happened a few hours before we met, and it wasn't my fault. The second one was deliberate because I was trying to escape from a murderer."

He shrugged. "Doesn't mean I'm wrong."

"Oh, I'm sorry." I dramatically clutched my hand to my chest. "Maybe you would have preferred it if I'd let him kill me?"

Thunder cracked through the air, promising a wild and noisy night.

"Of course not." He banged his head against his headrest. "I don't like other people driving my truck."

"I'm not other people. I'm your wife."

"Mate, Kensi. You're my fucking…" He blew out air. "You're my mate."

I crossed my arms and stared through my window into the darkness. "You should have promised yourself to your precious truck then."

"My truck doesn't answer back. Where's the fun in that?"

I peered at him. "Yeah?"

His lips had relaxed, hinting at a smile. "Yeah. And while it's a mighty fine truck, you look better. And you certainly smell better."

"Okay. Keep going."

He unbuckled his seatbelt and leaned toward me to undo mine. "It's also dense as a pile of metal. You, on the other hand…"

He swept my hair away and nuzzled my neck.

"What about me?" I asked, suppressing a sigh.

"You have an amazing mind. That's what made you one of the best private investigators in the world."

I coughed. "One of?"

"What am I saying? *The* best private investigator in the world."

I turned my head and moved in for a kiss. Drake had a knack for redefining my moods. Tonight, we shouldn't be arguing. We should be making love because sleep wouldn't happen for either of us.

Although the pack celebrations had been joyous and distracting, my mind couldn't entirely leave things alone. How the Boroughs Pack would react to our arrival worried me, but worse were the minor questions that kept gnawing at me. Would we stay in an ambassadorial suite or in my old bedroom? Would Dad and Drake hit it off? Would Drake like the Black Forest, or would he miss Marlontown, Colorado too much?

"Race ya?" Drake cocked his head toward the door.

The circle where he'd parked was mostly gravel. A myriad of puddles peppered the way to the cabin. Still, I wasn't made of sugar.

"On three." I took a deep breath. "One."

We leaped out of the truck and ran toward the front door. Within two steps my neck was wet, and two steps after that, there wasn't a dry fiber left on my body. I jumped over a puddle to close the distance between me and him. He laughed and side-stepped me. I gripped his belt and yanked him back.

"Hey!" He, in turn, grabbed my sleeves and pulled before shoving me aside. I flailed my arms, lost a few precious seconds… and he beat me by five feet.

"You cheated," I said, gasping and chuckling at the same time.

"You cheated first." He pulled me tight to keep the rain away from me.

The new lock, installed after Drake had lost his keys a week ago, withstood his efforts at first, and eventually succumbed.

Teaspoons, socks, even sweaters. He had a habit of misplacing things. The keys would turn up sooner or later—everything else did—but he wouldn't take any risks and had the locksmith out that night.

He was a protector through and through.

Giggling like kids we ran into the hall. Drake picked up a couple of towels along the way and we dried each other's hair, kissing all the way into the bedroom while somehow kicking off our boots.

"Hasi?" I held his face between my hands and looked at him earnestly.

"Hmm?" He was working on drying my locks, which naturally took longer than his short cut.

"How are you doing with this whole thing? Going to Germany,

becoming the prince consort, doing Jonah's and my dad's bidding? That's a lot to take in."

He dropped his arms, letting his gaze drift past me. "I knew it was coming. I knew it the moment I fell in love with you. I just didn't expect it to happen so soon."

"Yeah, me neither." I tightened my hold on his face, forcing him to look at me. "I'll make it as easy on you as I can. Promise."

"You don't have to protect me." He tapped my nose with the tip of his.

"Yes, I do. This is my burden. My heritage. I've been preparing for this all my life."

"Then why are *you* so tense?"

"Because now that the moment is within reach, I'm terrified. Returning to the place where I grew up comes with many emotions. I love my dad and can't wait to run with him, to show him my dominance, introduce you." I kissed him gently on the lips. "On the flip side, I will come face to face with the ones who taunted me growing up."

"You had a tough childhood, but kids are cruel everywhere. Your bullies have grown up, too, maybe have children of their own, and understand what their behavior did to you."

I snorted. "As if. They're now royal guards or courtiers, even Marshal of the Pack, with all the privileges that come with their positions."

"And you're a princess. Their crown princess in a matter of days. You've won."

"I guess." I unbuttoned his shirt, starting at the top. "Besides, once I'm the queen, they'll get what's coming to them."

He raised an eyebrow. "Really? That's your priority once you're queen?"

"Maybe not my first priority, but it's on the list." I tapped my fingers against my temple. "Like an elephant, I don't forget."

"What *is* number one on that list of yours?"

I brushed his shirt aside to look at the chest that, like now, never failed to make my heart beat faster. "Give women equality, of course."

Drake didn't have a six-pack. He didn't have manly hair carpeting his chest either. What he did have was well-built pectorals, a steely stomach, and a strong V leading my gaze to his groin like a neon sign I couldn't resist.

He weaved his fingers through my hair and watched as I undid his belt, opened the button, and unzipped him.

I let out a fortifying breath, realizing only now I'd been holding it.

Slowly, gently, I pulled down his pants. He stepped out of them, leaving me with a view of his powerful legs and tight-fitting shorts that hid none of his excitement.

Damn, I'd definitely married up.

"My turn." He slipped my short-sleeved shirt over my head.

His gaze zeroed in on my cleavage, and he licked his lips.

Who cared if the twins lifted and fell fast, giving away my exhilaration? This, right here, the touching, the undressing, and the making love, these were areas without friction. And I was aching for him.

Within seconds, I stood in front of him in nothing more than my underwear and socks.

He stepped closer in his distinct way, where he trapped the heat between his chest and the silky fabric of my bra—a glowing heat of bubbling lava as if we were creating our own world between us. Warmed by our private volcano, we kissed.

My thoughts focused on that kiss, zeroing in on every nuance of it. The hesitant brush of his lips, the short intake of air before his mouth landed for good.

Each of his caresses added a layer of spine-tingling anticipation. It took a nudge, no more than a move of his head, to open my lips.

Notes of champagne zinged my taste buds, although the flavor I was after, the taste of Drake himself, lay deeper.

He guided me to his well-worn but oh-so-bouncy mattress and supported me as I lay down on the bed. His weight followed, covering me with his naked skin.

I pushed his shoulders to shift him off me, to take control of our next moves.

"My turn tonight, princess." His dulcet voice softened my resistance.

All my life I'd fought to be on top. To prove my alpha chops to kings and leaders. This country boy, with the body of a grizzly and the soul of a teddy, had the power to mellow me, if only for a night.

And he made it worth my while every time.

Somewhere in the blissful haze that followed, we'd rid ourselves of our remaining clothes, and yet I could swear he didn't break contact between his lips and my skin. Only now did his head wander down my neckline as he dabbed kisses across my shoulder blade, inching closer to my breast.

"You tend to go for my left breast first." I ran my foot up along his leg.

"Are you saying I'm predictable?" He slid a hand behind my ass and squeezed.

I squealed and playfully pulled his ear. "I'm saying you're playing favorites."

"It's a perfect breast." He cupped it from the side and licked the pinkish-brown circle around its protruding center "Look how it fits into my hand. And then there's this."

He flicked his tongue to give my nipple a quick tap.

I sucked in air.

He chuckled. "I love it when you do that."

To prove his point, he did it once more.

Even though I knew it was coming, he got me again.

"It's like your remote control. Look." He tightened his lips around it and sucked.

I pressed my leg against his, felt my pelvis move under his groin and fill with sweet delight.

He shifted his body to between my thighs and his finger into the wetness already waiting for the main show.

"See?" He grinned triumphantly. "Your other breast does the same thing, only slower."

"Some people like taking their time."

"Princess, have you seen you? It takes willpower to put my pants on in the morning when I'd rather park inside you all day."

His breath hovered over my shoulder again, too far from the *remote* for my liking.

"Park?" I pulled his head up.

"I'm telling you, getting dressed, leaving the house, working, it's all a waste of time considering I could be inside you."

I tapped his chin with my thumb. "And yet you're still talking."

He raised both eyebrows. "You make a valid point."

He returned to his favorite button, using nothing more than his tongue to turn up my volume, as my breathing sped up and my insides burned for him.

The teasing circles he described only intensified my longing. I crossed my ankles over his ass and forced him down, and within seconds, he slid inside me in one smooth, mind-spinning stroke.

I let out a gasp.

Until Drake, I'd never made a sound during sex, but then, I'd never been made love to. Because even though the mechanics were the same—the long, hard drives, the stretching of my walls, the inching closer to my all-rockets-are-go spot—what he and I did, every night like a well-rehearsed play, was to turn lust-driven sex into an expression of our love.

I sighed into his ear, using my arousal to speed up his movements while clinging to him for dear life.

We might not have worked out how to live together, how to communicate, but this, this rough ride through my emotions and needs, was everything I'd yearned for. Every hard thrust became a caress, every deep pump tangled my insides, coiling the fabric of my core, linked my nerves to my brain, teased me…

tickled me…

rocked, drove, and stroked me.

"Drake," I shouted, held my breath…and rode out the climax that crashed over me.

Three seconds later, maybe ten, my limbs eased up, and he took his final nudge inside me before lowering himself onto my sweaty, shaking body.

"Wow," I whispered.

His performance deserved a standing ovation, and a three-letter word was all I was capable of. Typical.

He rolled off me and wiped his forehead. "That was our best one yet."

His face after we made love was the sexiest thing. His cheeks were flushed, his hair a perfect mess, and his lips were swollen enough to make me want to bite them.

Drake was a talented protector, but a lesser-known skill made him a whiz in the bedroom. Even when, like tonight, I was stressed and my thoughts whirred, he usually pushed my body to its heights, no matter how long it took.

I shifted onto my side. "We work."

"That we do."

I leaned into him. "We'll be okay, won't we? With all the changes that are coming?"

He gathered me close, my nose against the crook of his neck, and slung his arms tight around me. "We'll be fine, princess."

Outside, a flash of lightning split the night, followed one Mississippi later by thunder. The rain attacking the window and Drake's calm, strong breaths lulled me to sleep.

Four

THE ROCKY PLANE RIDE IN the Gulfstream G650 together with Stirling's repeat reminders of royal protocol had wrecked any chances of catching even two winks, let alone forty. The flight wasn't a complete bust, though. Drinks that could grow hairs on my chest had put Drake and me into a playful mood. In fact, his whispered commentary on Stirling's efforts often had me in stitches.

After a late dinner, or early breakfast, considering the time difference, Stirling had finally seen the pointlessness of his explanations and retreated to the part of the plane that was partitioned off.

I leaned into the aisle, making sure he couldn't hear me. "Guess we can stop drinking."

"We'd better." Drake, who sat opposite me, gave a happy grin. "I don't want to slur when I meet your father."

"Yeah, that would not make the best first impression." I nestled back into my seat and closed my eyes.

The engines droned in dull monotony, swaying my body without doing a damn thing to tire my mind.

"Why can't I sleep?" I clawed into the upholstery. "I'd be happy with an hour. Just one lousy hour."

We'd left Denver on an overcast afternoon, and watched the sunrise over a blue German sky from the panoramic windows.

"Nerves?" he suggested. He was usually Mister Confidence, but not today. He kept biting his lower lip and frowning, too.

His anxiety came courtesy of his copy of "Pack Relations, Volume III." Chapter ten detailed how the last visit by a free werewolf—more than two centuries ago—had resulted in the poor guy's untimely death.

He found it tough to banish this new-found knowledge from his mind.

I'd told him times had changed, which was true, but had they changed enough?

For the pack's sake, I hoped they'd find a way to adapt because I was no longer an alpha-wannabe who only relied on her sharp tongue to assert herself.

"His majesty has talked to the pilot and organized a surprise." Stirling stood in front of us, his mouth every bit as straight as his mustache. "If you would like to glance out of the window?"

Drake and I turned our focus to the outside. Below us, as far as the eye could see, the Black Forest covered this precious piece of Earth in countless shades of green.

"There." I pointed. "Oh my God. These are the All Saints Waterfalls. And here, this is our castle. Look, Hasi."

The mighty building where I'd grown up stood on a knoll overseeing the town below. Round towers connected two irregular wings, with a large ornate garden to the back.

"That over there is the bell tower, although I'm not sure it still works. I've never heard it ring." I didn't even try to contain my excitement. "One half of the castle is open to the paying public, and the other half is private."

"It's huge." Drake, who lived in the land of the giants, where roads spanned the width of some German villages, sounded impressed. "And the Black Forest goes on forever."

"Yup. It's not all trees, though. We also have bogs and tarns. I stay away from them, though. Snakes, you know."

"Tarns?"

"Mountain lakes in hollows that were carved by glaciers a long time ago. Here's a fact that will make you smile." I gestured into the distance. "The river Wolf flows not far from here."

"That's a cool name. And where's the airport?"

"In Karlsruhe." I stretched my neck to catch another bird's-eye glance at my home. "It's not long now."

"You sound like something's weighing on you."

"What?" I set my hand flat against the window. "No, just wishing my dad could pick us up."

"Maybe it's a good thing he's not. I did have too much whiskey." He popped one of his favorite peppermints into his mouth. "Besides, I'm not at my best when I'm tired. It would have been nice if we'd been able to catch a few minutes of sleep."

"Oh, Hasi." I dashed over into the seat next to him and moved his hair into an approximation of a side parting. "Worried you're not going to look pretty for my dad? You know I love you for your mind, right?"

He laughed and pushed a peppermint in between my lips, too. "*You* might. Will your father?"

"He'll love you every bit as much as I do," I whispered and kissed him. "This is the part you don't need to worry about."

The seatbelt signs flashed, and we followed the flight attendant's instructions, although it would take another half hour for us to land.

For once, my excitement pushed my worry aside. When I'd left home, I'd done so because it had become harder and harder to keep my secret: that I was a dud, unable to shift into my animal form. My return, on the other hand, felt like a triumph. I was finally every bit the wolf my former bullies were.

Hopefully, Dad would find the new, improved me a worthy successor.

I sat wiggling my legs, tapping my feet, until my second peppermint candy had melted away in my mouth and we touched down. The pilot wished us a happy day and then declared it was safe to get off.

I was home.

We gathered our belongings as quickly as we could.

I pointed at Drake's phone, which he'd left on his seat, next to his travel pillow. "Don't forget your—"

The wave of a figure on the tarmac outside stole my voice. Then I beamed. "Dad's here. He's come to pick us up after all."

I ran toward the stairs, and just as quickly turned around to grab my laptop bag.

"Go, run." Drake shooed me away. "Stirling's gonna give me a hand, won't you?"

Stirling winced, possibly at Drake's inconsiderate use of American vernacular, but nodded nevertheless.

I planted a hard kiss on Drake's cheek and practically flew down the stairs into my father's arms.

"Da bist du, Schatz," he mumbled.

"I han di vermissd," I mumbled back. 'I missed you.'

Dad kissed my hair, then held me a few inches from his face to study me. "You look thin."

I pulled my shoulders straight. "You look funny."

In fact, he looked exactly as I remembered him. Well, almost. My skin got its natural tan from my Roma mother, whereas Dad had always been a rugged light-beige. But like Jonah, he was starting to look unhealthy.

"Are you taking care of yourself?" I smushed his face.

"Don't fuss." Dad gently brushed aside my hand and let his features flow into a smile. "Now, where is that mate of yours?"

I turned toward the plane and sucked in a deep breath.

The sun bore down on *my mate*, bathing his tanned skin in coppery tones. Sure, he was tall by most standards, yet he descended the stairs looking like Zeus himself—if Zeus had ever traveled by plane.

My father's dominance shot out, as harsh and painful as any I'd witnessed.

"Dad!" I flinched.

The rush of his pheromones had nothing to do with me and everything to do with Drake.

Drake's alpha genes were evident in his posture, in his walk, in everything he was. When he entered the room, people noticed. When he spoke, people listened.

Despite decades of practice welcoming kings and their queens, my dad's alpha wolf responded instinctively. He had to prove his superiority to this powerful intruder.

Hadn't I told him over and over how gentle Drake was?

As if to prove me wrong, Drake let *his* dominance out of the box. His alpha pheromones, the chemicals that could sooth pack mates as well as administer a hell of a shock, scattered through the air and caused my father to huff.

"Enough," I whispered. My skin itched and burned as their dominance clawed its way across my arms, then my neck and my face.

My tolerance for alpha powers was unmatched, yet being pelted from both sides was taking its toll. Perspiration covered my forehead, and my muscles weakened to the consistency of tapioca pudding.

They were both behaving like children. Drake wasn't even an alpha leader, so by rights, he should be the first to give in. Then again, it had been Dad who'd started this pissing contest.

The people around us, bystanders who only caught the outermost barbs of the battle, broke away toward the limousines. Each to their own. Running wasn't how I rolled.

"Stop it, you two." I unleashed my own arsenal of pheromones, one sharp stream of Kensi magic.

Both men recoiled as if bitten by a snake. Their dominance was gone in an instant.

"Was this really necessary?" Hands on my hips, I bore down on them with my gaze.

"My daughter has truly found her wolf." Dad rubbed his arm. "And he has teeth."

I extinguished my powers and sidled up to him. "*She* has teeth, you mean."

Drake patted the side of his neck and gave me side-eye. "If you don't toe the line, she also has claws and an impressive arsenal of swear words, not all of them in English *or* German."

"You're a man to be envied and pitied at the same time." Dad laughed heartily and finally relaxed his shoulders.

In the old photos on his living room walls, Dad's hair was dark. A proud chest and a slim waist gave me an inkling of what had made him such a catch in his twenties and thirties.

Now, his hair was almost white. And, like the Earth's magnetic poles reversed every three hundred thousand years or so, so had his proportions. Now it was his belly that determined his shirt size.

His smile was the only feature that hadn't changed. It rarely made an appearance, but when it did, it warmed anyone's soul.

He offered Drake his hand. Drake shook it and belatedly remembered to bow his head at the neck.

Stirling's advice and reminders of 'how do you do' had got lost between the drinks and the pheromones.

Strictly speaking, as Jonah's pack brother and member of a free pack, Drake was under no obligation to demonstrate any respect to our king. After all, shedding royal rule was what had made his pack 'free' in the first place. Yet as my future Schutzherr and prince consort, he would soon stand under my dad's command.

He would be a man with two masters. Three, if we included me.

"How was the flight?" Dad draped his arm over my shoulders and pulled me tight.

He was about the same height as me, but his stature depended less on physical height and more on his alpha genes. Not unlike Drake.

"Long. At least we didn't have a layover." I scanned the area to make sure we wouldn't be overheard. "It would have been a blast without Stirling onboard."

"I could have sent Glendale." Dad swept a strand of hair out of my face.

"I misspoke." I gave a double thumbs-up. "Stirling was a delight. I love hanging out with him."

Dad gestured for me and then Drake to get into the vehicle before climbing in after us.

"Where's my laptop bag?" I checked Drake's far side, which was empty, before putting on my seatbelt.

"One of the guys outside took it off me." Drake also strapped himself in. "It's in the trunk."

"Jeez, are you serious? You know I like to keep it in sight. The computer has all the confidential material about my old investigations, let alone my case notes and my recorder. If any of it were to fall into someone else's hands—"

Dad knocked on the glass behind him to signal the driver we were ready. "There are no thieves in my pack."

"Sorry." I lowered my gaze.

The limo took off, one in a column of four vehicles, and we were finally going home.

"I enjoyed seeing your castle from above." Drake's fingers clamped around his seatbelt as if afraid Dad was going to steal it. "The architecture's impressive."

"It is." Dad smiled, and I appreciated his effort. "Wolfstein Castle sits on a mountain ledge overlooking the town of Wildbach, a community that's about half werewolf, unbeknownst to the humans who live there, of course. The first alpha king made the castle his home before there was a Germany, or at least the Germany of today."

"The castle was built in the eleventh century?" Drake dropped his question as if it were no big deal, when in fact he'd been cramming for days, eager to impress my father with facts and dates.

"Yes, although it's changed since then. As the town grew, the castle received a leafy terrace, a botanical garden, and, a stone's throw away, a water park. We also grow our own wine. The vineyards, too, started small and were built up row after row up the hill."

"Like the ring seats in the Colosseum," I weighed in. "And the wine's to die for."

Dad smoothed his pants and glanced at his lap. "We don't currently sell it, but we do serve it on special occasions. There should be a copious amount on the table at your confirmation feast."

"What's wrong?" I leaned forward as far as the belt let me. "Something's on your mind."

"To be honest, I was hoping to start selling wine on a larger scale by the end of next year, but there are logistical problems."

"You would have to log trees," Drake said. "And that will get you into trouble with the human authorities."

Dad looked up. "Yes. Exactly. And our town, especially the pack, is demanding a sustainable approach to the environment. I support this, naturally, but it's a balancing act."

"Because the pack doesn't want to give up pack loans or subsidies either." Drake nodded grimly. "Jonah's dealing with the same issues. How to get money without sacrificing land or upsetting the pack."

"Selling our wine to exclusive collectors would help us make ends meet. The quality's certainly there." Dad cast his concern aside with a wave. "We'll work it out, I'm sure."

I took Drake's hand, which quickly relaxed into mine. His life as a protector had prepared him surprisingly well for his future here. My father would be thrilled to kick around ideas and concerns with someone who had a better aptitude for admin and management than me.

Life was going to be tough for Drake at any rate. After my coronation, he'd have no say in where we'd live or how we'd spend our weekends. Was he the fool for following me willingly, or was I the fool for believing I had what it took to be the queen my country needed *and* the wife he deserved?

"This is Wildbach," I said, my tone hushed. "If people still sent postcards, this is where you'd go to buy them."

"The castle gift shop also has a good collection." Dad stared at the people in the streets who peered back at us through the tinted windows, probably attempting to figure out what celebrity was passing through their town. Dad didn't leave the castle often, so the appearance of a limo was bound to pique curiosity.

"I hardly recognize it." I slumped into the seat and gave a little-girl sulk. "The shops are all wrong. Everything's different."

"For someone who constantly tells me off for my aversion to progress, you spend a considerable amount of time complaining about change yourself." Dad cocked his head. "Care to explain that?"

I wrinkled my nose. "Maybe I like the idea of change more than change itself."

Or maybe I was so reluctant to embrace it because my life had taken too many unexpected turns recently.

"A rare moment of introspection." Dad tapped my leg with his foot. "I'm proud of you."

I stuck my tongue out, and both men laughed.

A few minutes later, the castle rose from between the trees. "There," I shouted.

The castle, at least, was as I remembered. Its gray stones were shaped evenly, set with perfection by the original builders and by all those who'd added to the structure over the centuries.

"Look." I squeezed Drake's hand.

These walls had been built not just for safety, but also to be filled with love, and I'd make sure he'd feel both. This would be his home, too.

I leaned across his lap to take in the view as our limo puffed and panted its way up the hill like the train-that-could, past the vineyards and the conservatory, until we'd reached the parking lot.

I climbed out of the car and stretched, both arms above my head. "It's good to be home."

"The castle missed you, too," Dad said solemnly.

I stepped aside as Brent and Stirling walked past, with a courteous nod to my dad, followed by the footmen who carried our luggage.

"Hang on," I shouted and ran after them.

The taller of the men glanced at me with large eyes. "Your Royal Highness?"

"Sorry. You're not in trouble." I wrapped my hand around the tote's strap, which he'd slung over his shoulder. "Could I have my bag, please?"

"Of course." He quickly handed it over. "I'm so sorry."

"It's all good." I clutched it under my arm. "Thank you kindly."

I returned to my dad and Drake, who both looked like I'd lost my mind.

"Such fuss over a bag." Dad gestured, his smile gone. "What did you think he was going to do to it? Kidnap it?"

"My files are important. He could have dropped the computer or thrown it onto a table."

"He's not a delivery driver." Dad aimed a glance at the sky before addressing Drake. "It was nice meeting you. Unfortunately, I need to get back to work."

"Thank you, Your Majesty." Drake remembered to bow.

My father waved goodbye. "I will see you both for dinner?"

"Hang on." I caught my dad's sleeve. "Where are we staying?"

"In your room, of course." Dad dropped his voice. "You're not a visitor. This is and always will be your home."

"Thanks." I slung my arms around his neck. "I hoped you'd say that."

Dad gently let go and walked toward Glendale, who was already waiting for him at the castle entrance. I gifted my father's Marshal of the Pack a mildly toxic glare, which he returned. If I'd had any hope I'd be welcomed back by him or any of his friends, his facial expression dashed it.

"I like your dad." Drake's voice was, for once, untroubled.

"I knew you would. He likes you, too. He's not usually this friendly to people. Most strangers consider him a pretty serious guy."

"He's a king, which makes him a heavyweight."

"Come on." I slipped my hand through his arm. "Let's take the scenic route."

"Everything around here seems like the scenic route."

I guided him past the defunct greenhouse that had stopped housing our tomatoes when our old gardener died, and along the stream that had been my playground when my best friend and his brother came to stay.

"This is like a fairytale." Drake laughed as he spread his arms. "Meeting a princess. Becoming her mate. Finding a new home inside a castle."

"You didn't even have to prick your finger on a spindle or eat a poisoned apple."

He tipped my face up toward his and kissed me. "Better than a fairytale, then."

We pushed through densely planted bushes onto the faint path that seemed to go unused now that I no longer lived here.

"This is not only the side entrance, but it's also my preferred shortcut to my rooms." I pushed the bronze door handle and needed my weight to gain entry into the small foyer.

Maybe foyer was too fancy a description for the tiled square inside, although its size was impressive for a staircase.

"Rooms?" Drake looked at me funny. "Plural?"

"Study, living room, and bedroom." I climbed the steps ahead of him.

"The two of us had vastly different upbringings." He ran his finger along the mosaic window as if to check it was real. "Vastly different."

"We did." I waited by the next window for him to catch up. "I had the privilege of discipline, protocol, and loneliness, and you had to make do with friends and all the spare time in the world." I tsk-ed sarcastically. "Poor baby."

"Okay, I see your point." He leaned over the banister and glanced down, then up, and whistled. "I'm not saying you had it easier. Just that your life was different."

"I guess, although it didn't prepare me for the real world. I didn't know how to use a range until I moved to Chicago. I had to pay my neighbor twenty bucks to explain how a washing machine worked."

"There you go." He resumed walking. "Despite everything, you survived. You learned, became self-sufficient, and didn't kill yourself in the process."

"I know, right? I'm a natural."

"Except for cooking." He sprinted up a few stairs to the top floor and stared out of the tallest of the windows, which was the main source of light in this part of the castle.

"What are you talking about?" I gestured with my arms, nearly knocking my laptop bag against the banister. "I cook the best cereal."

"Princess, whatever you're doing with cereal isn't cooking. I'm not sure what it is, but I do know the correct ratio is not one part cereal to five hundred parts milk."

"I thought you liked it when I make breakfast." I placed my hand on his shoulder. "I make it with love."

"You're right." He wheeled around and kissed me. "Your love's the ingredient that boosts it from palatable to downright fantastic."

"A compliment. Are you all right?" I touched his forehead. "You poor man. You've made it more than twenty-four hours without sex. You no longer know what you're saying."

We headed along the corridor, decorated with paintings and plants and dainty lights I'd got for Christmas when I was eight.

"Now that you mention it, it's been a while, yes." Drake unleashed a long, suffering sigh.

"You're in luck. Here we are." At the threshold to my door, I raised my hand and let it hover over the handle.

"What's wrong?" he asked.

"I've never had a boy in my rooms."

"You're kidding."

"No, of course not. At least not since I was about fourteen. My father would have gone mental."

"I'm not just any boy, though." He stood close enough behind me to warm my neck with his breath.

"True. You're *my* boy." I opened the door. "Okay, no judgment, please."

It was immediately obvious, I'd also opened the door to my past.

Drake let out a long whistle.

Except for maybe the fine grain in the wooden floor, my living room, or rather living room/dining room combo, looked like it came straight from a costume drama. A small seating arrangement with a TV, hidden inside a sleek cabinet, had been pushed into the corner. The couch was big enough to comfortably seat two people. The room's main feature, though, was a mahogany table that shone under the light of a modern chandelier. A large basket of chocolate bars and assorted candy stood at the center.

"I promised you German candy." I angled my elbow at the basket and then set my laptop bag next to the suitcases the footmen had already dropped off. "What do you think?"

"Love the candy bars, but this doesn't look like the room of a young woman. Are you sure this room's yours?"

I gave a dry chuckle. "My governess claimed it was perfect for a young lady."

"Fit for a princess." His smile looked frozen in place.

"Quite." I pointed to the open door to my right, which gave a view of my bed. "And this is the bedroom."

He walked solemnly toward it, like a worshipper moved through a church, and then stopped by the door frame. "Do I have reason to be jealous of all these plush toys?"

"See Lulatsch there, the tall blue thing?" I sneaked past him and cradled my plush childhood friend against my chest. "He's going to eat you if you aren't nice to me."

Drake approached. "Aren't I always nice to you?"

"Most of the time." I kissed his cheek.

"Seriously, are you hanging on to them for our kids, or will I have to get used to an audience in the bedroom from now on?"

"Kids?" God no. We were so not there yet, buddy. I laughed, my voice too high.

"We are going to have kids eventually, aren't we?"

"Yeah. I mean, I think so." I dropped onto the edge of my mattress, holding Lulatsch tight against me. "Sorry. Your question took me by surprise."

He frowned. "Don't you want any?"

"A few months ago, I wasn't sure I'd ever be queen because I wasn't able to shift. Yet it was all I'd ever wanted. And husband and kids, that was for other people."

He sat next to me. "Things have changed."

"Understatement." I brushed Lulatsch's blue fur straight. "It wasn't like I didn't want a relationship. Neither did I not want a relationship. How about you? Have you always known?"

"Like you, it wasn't a matter of *wanting* anything. I had a vague idea that in the future, I'd have a mate and pups. Everything came together when I met you."

I leaned against his shoulder. "We found each other without looking. And yes, I do want kids."

"Good." He kissed my head. "That's a start."

"Um, is there a time frame?" I caught his solemn expression through the curtain of my eyelashes.

"Sometimes I want them right now. Then I remember there are so many things I want to do before we have kids."

"Me, too."

He laid his hand on mine.

"Not this year." I waved Lulatsch in his face. "Right?"

"Definitely not. We'll know when the time is right. Until then…" He grabbed my stuffed animal from me. "Looks like we'll have all the company we need."

"You're right. They are a bit much. I'll move them to the chair." I got up and heaped my teddys and grumpy cats and Lulatsch into my arms. "Or we could ask for one of the ambassadorial suites instead. Dignitaries get fancy rooms with big beds and high-falutin' security on their doors."

"I'm a simple country boy, princess. High-falutin's not my style." He scratched his nose as he watched me move to a wooden chair in the corner. "These fancy rooms you mention is where you'd put your visiting kings?"

"Kings, but also diplomats." I unloaded my stuffed animals into the chair. "During their stay, their quarters become a fortress, an extension of their country. Off-limits even to our staff, unless they request housekeeping services or whatever. But mostly, they travel with their own people, which we'll house in rooms on the ground level."

"I assume you don't clean *your* own rooms?"

"No. We have someone who cleans when we're not in our rooms. We trust our staff, which is important if you allow them into your sanctuary." I looked at my toys again and frowned. "Seriously, if you don't like this room, we can ask for another. It doesn't have to be an ambassadorial suite."

"Hey, I love this insight into who you are. Toys, photos, posters of your secret crushes—I want to see them all." He studied my walls. "Where are the boyband posters, by the way?"

I laughed. "The last time I was here, I was twenty. Besides, Dad let me keep toys on my bed. The only other decoration he allowed were books and photos. Protocol, you know."

"Protocol sucks." He stood and checked the book spines on my shelf. "These are all detective novels and anatomy books."

"We have plenty of history books in the forbidden library. Once you're the prince consort, you won't be bored."

"There's a forbidden library?"

"Yes, the Royal Library."

He grimaced. "Libraries are tempting enough. When you add the word forbidden…"

God, I loved that guy. I wagged a finger. "Too tempting?"

"Definitely."

I pulled him back toward my bed, which offered room enough for us now that it had been cleared. "Speaking of forbidden things, my father would probably prefer you and I didn't have sex in this room. A young woman like me inviting a man into her bedroom— it's very much frowned upon."

"Frowned upon?" Drake laid his hands on my ass and drew me close.

"You might even say scandalous."

His eyes sparked with a particularly intensive shade of silver. "Now she tells me."

Lunch could wait, and dinner was hours away.

"Stop talking," I mumbled and melted into his kiss.

Five

INNER WAS SERVED LATE, AT eight-thirty, mainly because that was the time my father had been able to claim for himself. It mattered little that he was the alpha king. His schedule was almost entirely in Glendale's hands. As his majesty's Marshal of the Pack, Glendale was responsible for the organization and affairs of the court—and he knew how to wield his power.

"This tastes great." Drake struggled with his Käsespätzle, a Swabian dish consisting of local pasta covered, or rather drenched, in cheese and topped with fried onions.

He was using both fork and knife to attack the cheese strings, careful to follow the instructions Stirling had given him.

Dad leaned forward and eyed Drake's efforts with obvious confusion. "You don't eat pasta dishes in Colorado?"

"We do." Drake kept his gaze anchored on his plate. "It's very cheesy, and with my hands hovering…"

"Maybe the hovering is the problem." Dad shook his head before shoveling another bite onto his fork. Both he and I kept our wrists firmly on the table, like normal people.

Drake's gaze darted to me. "Stirling said no wrists or arms on the table. Didn't he?"

"He did." I swiped a strand of my hair to the side. "Did you notice he's not here watching you?"

"Could have told me," he mumbled and finally arranged his hands so he could eat.

The poor guy's head had to be all over the place with all the conflicting ideas he'd been fed. Hopefully, he'd soon realize my father, the dad, was an easy-going man. My father, the king, on the other hand… In his official capacity, this werewolf alpha had quite a bite.

That was an issue for another day.

"I love having you home, Schatz." My father stared at his half-empty plate as if his food was poisoned. "But not everyone's thrilled with the development. Your mate was supposed to cut off the critics' cries for a male crown prince. Instead, we must now convince them it doesn't matter that your Schutzherr is a member of a free pack. Not even an alpha leader in his own right."

"Drake could eat most alphas for breakfast." I wrinkled my nose.

Drake certainly *could* have them for breakfast. Trouble was, he didn't want to. Luckily, as a prince or king consort, he wouldn't be involved in disciplining the pack or pushing our agenda. His job would be to support me, more or less the way he'd been supporting Jonah.

"That's hard to believe if you need to speak for him." Dad glanced expectantly at Drake.

Turns out, my father, the king, had made an appearance after all.

With a shrewd look, Drake set his fork down on his plate and moved his glass to the side. "It doesn't matter if she's buying a car or claiming a throne. People speak to me before they even acknowledge Kensi. For her to claim the position she deserves, she must be louder and brasher. And she does this well. Luckily, I'm confident enough in my dominance to let her speak for me when she wants to."

I glanced at him, my mouth open, which probably made the smile I was developing look awkward.

My dad chewed, swallowed, and finally gave a nod. "I'm happy with that answer, as long as you two understand you're not picking the easiest route."

"What do you mean?" Drake picked up his fork again. "Does my background make Kensi's life really that difficult?"

"Of course not," I said forcefully.

"He's a *Reig'schmeggdr*," my father said forcefully. "An outsider."

"Easy, Dad." I held up my hand. "That's enough."

"It's a fact we can't ignore. Those who feared being ruled by a woman found comfort in the fact that you'd find a strong wolf one day."

"I did. He is." I glared.

"But now you've presented them with another reason to object to your rule." Dad leaned toward Drake. "Haters will hate, and you will become the object of that hatred. Be prepared."

I ground my teeth. "They'll accept us, both of us, because they'll have no choice."

"This is the purpose of your visit." Dad tapped his plate with the forked end. "The ceremony will lock you in as my heir and her prince consort, and the pack will have no say in this matter. Then the hard work begins because attitudes won't change overnight."

"That's why Jonah and you want to send us on a goodwill tour." I swallowed and reached for my glass. "It's not just to spread your message of unity around the globe. You also want to raise our profile as a couple in the hope that our celebrity status will force the Boroughs Pack to finally accept us."

"I'm not worried." Drake gave a thoughtful look. "Kensi and I have each other's backs whatever they throw at us."

I briefly touched his arm. "Yes, we do."

He glanced at my fingers and smiled.

"Don't underestimate the opposing voices." Dad pushed away his plate and patted his stomach. "Putting Drake on the throne needles our people. Especially with so many eligible princes around the world."

I made a gagging sound before putting my fork down, too. "I've met most of them and, eww! Also, no one knows the history of the werewolves better than Drake. Seriously, Dad. His encyclopedic knowledge is epic. He understands the mistakes made in the past and the importance of cooperation."

"It sounds like you've picked up knowledge since I last saw you yourself." Dad laid a hand on the table. "I'm pleased."

I pointed my thumb at Drake. "Encyclopedic knowledge. Many, *many* hours alone in a cabin in the woods. It makes a girl wonder if she's not attractive enough."

Drake shot me an intense glare. "I have no way of responding to that with your father here."

"I appreciate it." Dad didn't smile at our banter. No doubt it had been a long day for him, too. "In any case, once the ceremony is over, everyone will have time to get used to the situation. Hence the urgency."

"Okay. I get it," I said. "Now that we got that out of the way, can I ask you something, Dad?"

"Of course."

"Do you think you'll have time to run with me soon? It doesn't have to be tonight, if you're busy." I didn't dare meet his gaze. A rejection would crush me.

"I've wanted to run with you since you were born, Schatz. How about now?"

"Yes." I looked at Drake. "You don't mind, do you?"

He was about to touch my cheek but picked up his glass instead. "I'll find a way to occupy myself."

"Have more food. I've also retrieved the minutes that chronicle my own confirmation ceremony for you to read." Dad pointed at two journal=sized books lying on a table. "It should give you an idea of what to expect tomorrow. We can't afford to screw this up."

"That's very thoughtful." Drake leaned back, drooling over the cheesy meal, yet refraining from heaping another portion onto his plate. "Thank you."

"Here." Dad grabbed a couple of sheets from a cabinet and handed them to him. "Read these, too."

"Come on, Dad." I was already by the door.

Dad gripped my shoulder and steered me out of the room. "Show me what you've got."

Six

"H OW OFTEN HAVE YOU SHIFTED?" Dad asked once we'd passed the guards' rooms.

"As much as I can." I hooked my hand around his arm as we took a side exit out of the castle. "The first one hurt like hell. It's been manageable since then. As you say, pain's all in the mind."

I hated lying to my dad, but admitting my weakness would have been worse. In fact, every shift caused as much agony as the one before. Maybe a little less, but when I found myself in the throes of "shit, that hurts," I didn't grade my pain by degrees of intensity.

"I remember your mother's first shift." Dad's gaze trailed into the distance. "She thought she was dying. Actually, *I* thought she was dying. Took her a while to get the hang of it."

"My dominance is still unfocused. I know how to use it, but I don't always find my target. Good thing Jonah's the forgiving type."

"Only you could attack a pack alpha with dominance and live." Dad laughed.

When we entered the rugged trail leading through the vineyards toward the tree line, the light had already faded into a dull twilight.

"How are you, though, really?" Dad briefly pulled me tight. "And don't fob me off with a 'fine,' the way you do on the phone."

Nothing got by my father.

"Marriage will take some getting used to. I love Drake. Like, crazy love him. Definitely more than I thought possible after such a short time. The difficult part is getting to know him."

"Remember, the Moon Promise isn't like human marriage. It's a bond." He quashed my objections with a gesture. "The important thing is how you relate to each other. Clearly, you two had to weather a few challenges."

"Being hunted by the police. Mortal danger. Sure, sure." I sarcastically waved off. "But what drives him crazy? He says he wants children, but how does he want to raise them? Is he going to discipline them when they're naughty or will I have to do that? That kind of stuff."

"A relationship's about discovering each other for the rest of your lives. A *good* relationship comes from accepting what you discover."

Soon, the castle behind us was no more than a dark silhouette against the moonlight.

I gave a quiet cough. "Then there's the confirmation."

"Is there a problem?"

"No, nothing like that. But am I doing right by Drake? Becoming a king consort wasn't what he wanted he had in mind for his future."

"He's not alpha material?" His voice sharpened.

"Of course he is." I kept my gaze away from his knowing eyes. "But as a king consort, he'll be neither alpha nor independent."

"He knew who he married. Don't invent problems when there aren't any." Dad tightened his hold on me. "I'm sorry. I'm not being terribly empathetic, am I? I wish…"

His sigh nearly broke my heart.

"Me, too." I patted his arm. "In moments like these, I miss her most. I once dreamed I was walking down the carpet to recite my claim to the throne and Mom was sitting next to you, smiling."

"I couldn't say for sure if she'll be sitting next to me, but I know she'll be there in whatever form she can. She wouldn't miss your big day for anything. Maybe she's watching us now."

"Maybe." Yet I believed neither in Heaven nor in reincarnation. My focus was firmly on *this* life because it was the one I could control.

Once Dad and I were surrounded by trees, their canopies shutting out most of the moonlight, we were alone. My steps had gone silent. Only the rustling of the leaves resonated in the gusty wind.

"You can leave your clothes up in that tree." Dad pointed at a tree perfect for climbing. "That's where your mother used to leave hers."

A fitting place, then.

Allowing my wolf to meet my dad's wolf was a moment that would stick in my mind for the rest of my life. I'd been waiting for so long, I nearly tripped over my socks in anticipation.

One might think releasing my wolf from her human prison would earn me brownie points, but *she* had other ideas. Even though the door was wide open, *she* scratched and clawed her way out.

The shooting pain and stomach-twisting burn in my chest and throat subsided as soon as the shift was complete. *She* and I were one.

For a few seconds, I stood, drinking in my surroundings' softer colors that my wolf vision afforded me. There were new sounds, too, and it took my ears a minute to disentangle the bird calls overhead from the small mammals in the undergrowth. Somewhere among these sounds bobbed the in-and-out of my father's solid breath.

I emerged from behind my tree.

Dad's broad, short ears moved forward. His magnificent white-brown fur caught the moonlight that snuck through the trees. What a figure he struck. Many years ago, I used to hide my hands in his thick pelt. Found solace in it while he surveyed the surroundings, ever vigilant, ready to disembowel anyone who dared hurt his daughter.

Now I was grown up enough to fend for myself.

Dad padded around me, then came up and rested his muzzle on my neck. I returned the gesture.

As a man, my father had a unique Dad smell. The cologne he'd been wearing since I was a child, the fabric softener of his clothes. But now that we were both wolves, I caught an earthy scent coming from his fur, filled with strength and power. This was the dad I'd have met as a kid if my stupid genes hadn't played such a cruel trick on me.

A new truth dawned on me.

All this time I'd felt the absence of a mother. Never had I understood I only knew half of my father as well.

If my wolf eyes could produce tears, I'd be crying. And if my mouth could shape words, I'd most definitely cuss at life's injustice.

Instead, I licked Dad's face.

I didn't just lick his face, I also tasted his fur, nudged his neck, and told him 'I love you' in every wolf way imaginable. This was the father-daughter moment I'd been waiting for my entire life.

He took my outpouring with patience and a glint in his eyes.

Until he nudged me away with his head.

I tapped him with my front paws, almost climbing on his back. I was far from done showing my affection.

He nosed my stomach to stop me and then trotted away.

So much for our special father-daughter bond.

A few steps later, he glanced over his shoulder.

He hadn't brushed me off. Rather, he wanted to run.

With a yip, I skipped after him. We sprinted through the woods I'd grown up in and leaped across narrow streams. We hopped over logs and crawled through bushes, and with Dad by my side, the woods I knew so well became a new world.

Silky smooth leaves brushed against my shoulders, and when I glanced up, small patches of the clear gray sky peered through trees as tall as giants. Exploiting our extended range of vision, we chased a squirrel, scared a few rabbits who didn't know our stomachs were stuffed with cheesy pasta, and sneaked past unsuspecting humans out for a late-night hike.

Too soon, we'd circled and returned to our starting point at the edge of the woods, where I ran full-speed into his flank.

He whirled around.

I stood, panting. *Play with me, Dad.*

He sat, waiting, his tongue lolling. *Play what?*

I took two steps. *You'll see.*

He growled. *Bring it on.*

I pounced. *Boo.*

He leaped aside, and my paws landed next to him in the grass. He grabbed my neck fur between his teeth, then held still. *What now, little one?*

If he shook his head, he could hurt me.

I stayed where I was.

He pushed from above onto my head, but I wasn't going to submit easily and pushed back up.

He moved his chin across my head and neck. *You're beaten.*

I steeled myself against the pain I'd feel and coiled out from under him. Twisted my head. And laid both my front paws on his shoulders, mouth open. *Take that.*

He shook me off, and his dominance flared. *You want to play rough?*

Oh yeah. I'd forgotten about that.

However, taking the brunt of an alpha's dominance was my wheelhouse. Until the Moon Promise had connected me to my wolf, I'd had to rely on arrogant looks and impassive smiles to counter other people's aggressions. Things had changed, though.

I rolled out my dominance, the power to subjugate and

discipline my werewolf enemies, and drove my dad into retreat. This was the legacy my mother had left me. The blood of the First Ones ran inside my veins, making me a force that could no longer be ignored. *See, Dad?*

His body slammed into me. *See what?*

My dominance faltered, and my front legs buckled.

Dad grabbed my muzzle with his mouth and held on, his dominance whipping me like a cat o' nine tails.

Maybe I could have rallied my pheromones again. But I was beaten, subdued—and wholly and utterly happy. *You got me, Dad.*

He let go, gave a satisfied sniff, and padded off to where we'd hidden our clothes.

"That was fun," I said once we'd shifted back into human form.

"Your dominance is almost as strong as your mother's," he said wistfully and kissed the crown of my head. "I'd forgotten how much it stings."

"And I'd forgotten you're used to withstanding a fair amount of punishment." I grinned. "I won't make that mistake again."

"Haven't I taught you relying on dominance alone won't be enough?" He slung his arm around my waist as we walked back to the castle.

"You did. Guess I've grown lazy over the past two months." I leaned my head on his shoulder. "Tell me honestly. Do you believe I'll make a good queen, or are you pushing for my confirmation because I'm your daughter?"

"I hope your mate can make up for your many shortfalls."

I prodded his waist. "I'm serious, Dad."

"Very well." He took a few breaths. He wasn't a man that could be rushed. "I'm proud of the woman you've become and of the alpha leader I know you will be. Your mother was a remarkable queen, filled with compassion and strength. I have no doubt you'll rise to the challenge of being the alpha I've raised and a queen in your mother's image."

His words pinched my throat. For the sake of my composure, I shouldn't be thinking of Mom tonight. Of her smile that came not from memories but from wishful thinking. Of her voice that I couldn't recall but had heard many times in my imagination.

Dad kept his grip on me, didn't allow me to miss my step on the uneven trail.

The castle lay in quiet contemplation, even though the resident pack members wouldn't have gone to bed yet. The moon, peeking through two clouds in the sky, reflected off the rounded windows, giving them a milky sheen.

When I was little, I often saw faces in these windows. Faces of friends I didn't have. Faces of people I hoped were waiting for me. Mostly, the face I saw was my mom's. Maybe Dad had been right all along, and she'd been here, waiting for my return.

Dad pushed open the side door and, arm in arm, we squished through the frame.

"You've been quiet," Dad whispered, probably to keep our approach secret from the guards patrolling the area. "Did I say the wrong thing?"

"No." I pressed my head against his shoulder. "You didn't. Thank you."

"You're welcome."

I kissed his cheek and ran up the stairs before he could stop me. He'd never seen me cry. And even though no tears had made it onto my cheeks, it was because the knot in my throat kept them at bay.

Seven

DRAKE AND I TOSSED AND turned all night. He kept criticizing the mattress, the shape of the pillows, the fact we were using two blankets instead of one. Yet I rarely acknowledged his complaints. My mind had been soaring like a butterfly, unable to stay with one flower—or rather, one thought.

I finally turned toward Drake, who lay on his side, and watched the even rise and fall of his chest. Had jet lag got the better of him and finally offered him a well-deserved nap?

I stroked his cheek and smiled. "Hasi, wake up."

A smile made his face appear younger.

"Hey." I pulled his earlobe. "Wake up."

"I'm awake." His mouth moved, words came out, but his eyelids remained glued shut.

"Why am I so nervous?" I covered my eyes with my arm to block out the light peeking through the blinds. "It's only going to be us, my dad, and a few pack members, I think. No biggie, right?"

"*You* are nervous?" He gave a raspy laugh and turned onto his back. "Imagine how I'm feeling."

"We could run away. Forget the whole thing ever happened."

"I hear Iceland's nice and remote this time of year."

I chuckled. "Iceland's remoteness doesn't depend on the season as much as you may think."

"Who knows more about geography? You or I?"

"I wonder." I sat up, clutching my cover.

"Are we in agreement?" Drake pushed himself up, too, and kissed my ear. "You're going to look ravishing in snowboots and one of those knit caps with a ball on top."

"Naturally." I caressed his jaw, losing myself in the shimmering gray of his gaze.

A forceful knock on the door to my bedroom yanked me out of my happy place.

I hitched up my blanket to cover my shoulders. "What?"

Stirling entered, a thick folder in his hand. "Your Royal Highness. Sir. His majesty asked you be woken two hours before the ceremony."

He surveyed the room in one smooth pivot and then opened the blinds. The sunlight's glare highlighted the lines of his elegant suit as he stepped back into the center of the room.

"Thank you." Drake acknowledged our Lord High Chancellor with a nod.

"Your breakfast is being served in your front room now." He clapped twice, giving permission to two women to enter my bedroom.

While I appreciated the fact that they didn't ogle my husband's bare chest, I didn't like that they evaded all eye contact. Any form of submission from women, even the professional type, upset me.

The two ladies carried the dress my mother had worn at her confirmation ceremony. It was made from a silken pale-pink fabric, with a skirt section that barely fit through the door. With luck, its width and length would hide the ugly white closed-toe shoes that completed my outfit.

Drake, meanwhile, was provided with a tailored black suit and an elegant burgundy robe, last worn by my father.

At least we'd both look pompous.

"Thank you, Stirling." I gestured to indicate I was ready for him to leave.

"In one hour, Brent and his team will arrive to make you presentable. Makeup, hair, and the fit of your clothes must be perfect. At ten to eleven, I will come and escort you to the throne room."

I hid my misgivings under a yawn. "Did Dad invite many people?"

"His majesty invited our social and political leaders, plus a few of our international friends. I am sure you have been informed of the larger importance of this ceremony?"

"You mean that Dad and Jonah want to pimp us out to spread a message of peace, love, and harmony?" Suddenly uncomfortably aware of my bladder, I wiggled closer to the bed's edge. "Sure."

Stirling relaxed his glare for once. "May I speak freely, Your Royal Highness?"

"It's no secret you disapprove of many things I do," I said in a slightly irritated tone. "But you may always speak freely around me."

"Very well." He gave an audible sigh. "I don't disapprove of your lifestyle as much as you may think. However, this confirmation ceremony is important to the future of our kind."

"Whoa. Aren't you being overly dramatic?" I asked. "How bad can the situation be?"

Stirling's nod was almost a bow. "The situation is, in fact, critical. Collectively, our kind is running out of money and land. We therefore need you two to foster a sense of unity among packs, and our campaign begins at home. This confirmation ceremony will not merely be an event, it will be a spectacle. The dignitaries started arriving last night, and his majesty has been up since six o'clock to greet them."

"Oh." I clutched my throat and stared at Stirling.

"See?" Drake's cheerful tone didn't seem entirely appropriate. "And you thought you had reason to be nervous."

I stuck the tip of my tongue out, and only my sudden blind panic prevented me from laughing hysterically.

Stirling coughed. "Your Royal Highness?"

"Okay." I swayed for comfort. "What you're saying is it would be good if I didn't trip on my way through the throne room?"

Stirling gave a slim smile—an expression I hadn't thought his face capable of. "That is exactly what I was saying, Your Royal Highness."

"Fine. Okay. One perfect ceremony coming up." I fixed him with my gaze. "Don't say I never do anything for you."

He gave a bow and then hustled the two women away before following them out.

Drake and I got showered in record time and sat in our pajamas at the dining table, obsessing over the ticks of the wall clock that kept nudging us ever closer to the big event.

I forced myself to eat a bite. Cast a nervous smile at Drake. Drank the mild Italian roast I loved so much. Every action was another step toward the moment my destiny would come true.

At 9:40 a.m., Drake stood. "We should get dressed. I don't want to give your father a reason to dislike me more."

I flinched and leaned my head to the side. "What do you mean? He loves you."

"That's not been my impression." He waved me off. "But let's not worry about that. Maybe the nerves got to him, too."

"You may not have realized this because I'm such a delight to be around, but most Germans will let you know where you stand with them. Dad totally would. So, whatever vibe you got from him, I'm sure it's nothing."

"Right."

"Come on, today's all about the confirmation. Which reminds

me, I might need help hooking up the back of my dress. Yes, you heard right. Hooks." I rolled my eyes. "What's wrong with zippers?"

"Hooks can be fun." He gave me a smile that looked innocent but, as experience had taught me, was fueled entirely by dirty thoughts.

"If only we had the time," I said, even though his lips did look in desperate need of a good kiss.

He slapped the tabletop with both hands and adjusted his shoulders. "You're right. Come on."

Unsurprisingly, forcing myself into the dress took a while. The fabric wasn't as restrictive or bulky as I'd feared. Neither was it as flexible as I'd hoped. In the end, he had to help me put my shoes on.

So much for being a strong, independent alpha-queen-to-be. Why I couldn't wear a suit and robe like Drake was a question for another day.

Was Drake right and Dad hadn't been the welcoming father-in-law I'd promised? If so, it was too early to panic. Once they got to know each other, things would fall into place. At least that was the kind of thinking that had kept my marriage alive so far.

The jewelry laid out on the dresser had once been worn by my mother when she became my father's Schutzherrin, his lady protector. One piece had been forged especially for me, to wear on this day: the ring that marked me as a member of the royal family of the Boroughs Pack.

I'd barely arranged Drake's tie when Brent and his team appeared. On his instruction, we were prodded and straightened, our faces powdered, my hair stiffened, until Brent finally clicked his tongue to signal his content. As quickly as he'd breezed into the living room he was gone again.

"Is that you, Drake?" I walked toward the handsome man with gelled-back hair and touched his shoulder. "My, you look pretty."

"As do you." He gripped my hand. "What is your name, milady?"

"You can call me whatever and whenever you wish, kind sir."

He blew a kiss near my cheek. "You look like a picture from the cover of a magazine. To be honest, I can't wait until I see your real face again."

"You told me you married me for my brain." I gave a flirtatious smile.

"I didn't marry you at all."

I briefly closed my eyes. "Not today, please."

"You're right." He pulled me toward him, but not so close that I'd smear my makeup onto his suit and robe. "Hey. I like your dangling curls."

He flicked one of the two twirled strands that Brent had taken pains to arrange artfully on either side of my face.

"Brent's going to kill you." I lightly kissed him, ensuring that my lipstick wouldn't stain his lips.

Then Stirling's knock came, and playtime was over.

&Eight;IGHT

&Drake; and I entered the throne room, which was decked out in temporary decorations and velvet curtains. Two glittering statues of wolves put even the blinged-out throne to shame. Flags carrying our pack's royal coat of arms—three fir trees on a gold background, with two crown-wearing wolves standing between them—hung from the gold-leaf ceiling behind the throne.

My ring displaying the same emblem felt heavy, as if it carried the weight of the entire pack.

I clung to Drake's arm, watching my steps in my peripheral vision, keeping my chin high. Right foot front, left foot front. My shoes pinched, making my walk awkward. Right foot front, left foot front. The hem of my dress toyed with my toes, threatening to trip me. Right foot front, left foot front.

The faces looking upon us from the gallery were familiar ones. My father's lawyers and their wives were in attendance, as were Lords and Ladies whose names I'd forgotten, and a handful of businessmen that had bought their way into our nobility. Many smiled at us, a sign that Dad's plan was working. The pomp and circumstance of the occasion was wowing them.

But not everyone had been convinced yet. Crown Prince Bayou of the Dutch pack stared at us from the benches lining the gallery. He wore a suit and a shirt with a collar so stiff, it could be choking him. Not that style was important to him. In his mind, he was God's gift to women, whatever he wore.

Right foot front, left foot front.

My king sat on an elevated deck on his throne, which was padded in purple corduroy. He wore a robe and his crown, a monstrosity decorated with enough jewels to make the human monarchy shake with jealousy. Even though he wasn't smiling, his eyes shone with pride.

Or maybe, pride was what I wanted to see in them.

We approached the designated line to the sound of trumpets. When we'd reached the end of the carpet, I curtsied deep before the king. Drake timed his bow with my curtsy.

My father gave the signal for Glendale to kick off the ceremony.

Glendale, who only vaguely resembled Stirling despite being his brother, unrolled a scroll and began reading the ritual in his nasal voice.

Drake stood beside me, ingesting the German language with his typical impassive expression.

A short while later, Glendale repeated the paragraph in nearly flawless English. On he went, swapping between languages. A wonderfully sterile occasion, scripted to perfection.

How weird was it that, on the day my childhood dream came true, I missed the personal touch? Back at Jonah's and Drake's pack-brother ceremony, they hadn't needed fancy speeches or bling. Everything had been warm and welcoming.

A confirmation had to be cold and impersonal, though. This was business, after all. The beginning of a year-long marketing campaign Dad and Jonah had concocted.

Then it was my turn to speak. I licked my dry lips, closed my mouth, breathed through the nose.

My life had been building to this moment as my first stepping stone toward becoming queen. Dad had trained me as best as he could. Would it be enough? Could I lead a country?

I pushed out my chest to project my words. "Your Majesty. I have come before you to stake my claim to the most exalted position of *heir* to the German throne."

Glendale's nose twitched.

I aimed my gaze firmly at my dad. "I am of your blood and of your forebears' blood, and like our forebears, I shall command this kingdom by prudence, by strength, and by sword. Like you, I shall rule by wisdom, by mercy, and by reason. To these qualities, I will add fairness, foresight, and steadfastness."

The rustle from the gallery grew louder.

I took another deep breath and felt my heart slow. "I appear today with my mate, a powerful man and wolf in his own right. With him by my side, I ask for and will accept your promise to pass on your kingdom to me, your rightful heir."

The trumpets played a fanfare, once, twice and—

One by one their notes died. My father's gaze traveled past me. His jaw slackened, and he shot to his feet.

"What is the meaning of this?" he shouted.

A wolf with striking red, black and white marking slunk across the red carpet. It wasn't one of our local wolves, yet I felt I knew it. Under its chin hung a black clothes-tube, a container reminiscent of a large quiver of arrows. All wolves owned one, of course, to carry their clothes with them on runs, but this one was of the finest quality, sturdy yet decorated with delicate gold lines and symbols. One by one, the wolf's limbs lengthened. Its snout shortened as it shifted into the figure of a tall black man, with muscles that spoke of many hours in the gym.

Before anyone could protest against his nakedness, he'd retrieved clothing from the tube and, without missing a step, put on dress pants and a white shirt. His muscles rippled beneath the cloth with a life of their own, and by the time he was level with us, he'd added an aggressive red tie and a jacket to his outfit.

It was the smoothest shift I'd ever witnessed.

He bowed deep before the king and then stood with his chest puffed out. "Your Majesty. I am Scimitar, second son of King Lance of the Warrior Pack, your pack brother."

My dad took a threatening step forward. His skin shone like a waxy layer over ash.

The party crasher tucked the last of his shirt into his pants. "The laws enshrined by our common ancestors extend the right of succession to pack family. It is on this basis that I, your pack nephew, claim to be named your heir today." He offered me a condescending smile before steering his attention back to my father. "Your daughter is a strong and proud woman, but this kingdom requires a male heir. A male *royal* heir."

My gaze flitted across my dad's open mouth, past Glendale's frozen figure, to Drake's wide, silver eyes.

This wasn't a prank. This was happening for real.

I unleashed my dominance, or rather, it unleashed itself. Most of my pheromones flew off into the ether, but enough of them struck my target. Scimitar's legs buckled and he fell to the floor, arms outstretched.

I hitched up my skirt and stalked toward him, glaring, to say the only thing that came to mind. "What the actual fuck, Scim?"

Nine

Drake gently nudged me away from Scimitar's treacherous grimace, and my dominance dwindled.

What had I ever done to him? This was supposed to be *my* moment. After everything I'd been through, after a rollercoaster life of will-I-won't-I become the Boroughs Pack's alpha queen one day, my future had been dealt another knock.

I glanced helplessly at Drake, then my dad, then Glendale. Their postures dashed any hope of salvaging the situation. The ceremony was over.

While the trumpeters and our guests mumbled and pointed fingers in our direction, Glendale sprang into action.

"Ladies and gentlemen, honored guests. Please, if you could make your way into the dining hall?" He snapped his fingers, and the guards opened the tall wooden doors of the throne room.

Where had they been when I needed them? Scimitar used to enjoy free run of the castle when he was a teenager and could conceivably have been a guest at my confirmation, but didn't it strike the guards as even a little odd that he'd strolled in in his wolf form?

Footmen arrived to usher out the guests.

"You will be kept abreast of any developments," Glendale promised.

While our visitors vacated the room, thrilled rather than upset by the interruption, Dad hovered in front of his throne, his eyes shooting daggers. My heart burned alongside his.

"Scimitar! I am waiting for an explanation." My father leaned forward as if struggling to keep himself from charging.

Scimitar got to his feet and dusted himself off.

"I have a right to claim my place in your line of succession, do I not?" His faint South African accent gave his words a gullible innocence I knew he didn't possess.

"Granted to you by ancient law." My dad's voice echoed. "A law that, until today, hasn't been invoked."

"I'm invoking it."

Scimitar had always been a wily asshat. The German crown stood head and shoulders above the others. In fact, it was the best-prized metaphorical headgear in the world. And it was mine. Always had been, always would be. Why would he do this to me? Why would he do this to my father, who'd welcomed him many times with open arms?

"Kensi?" My father's look demanded a reaction. "What do you say?"

"I'm speechless. Wordless." I tilted my head, trying to widen my vision beyond Scimitar. "Not entirely wordless, but the words I do have aren't suitable for polite company. Not that I've ever considered Scim polite *or* company."

"Thank you for that," Dad mumbled. "Glendale?"

Glen took a demonstrative step forward. "Yes, Your Majesty?"

I'd bet my last candy heart he was enjoying the show. Yet, he was too conniving to betray his emotions.

Dad's hands rolled into fists, and his dominance was beginning to swell. "Can I rely on you to have words appropriate to the situation?"

"Scimitar's claim is lawful, Your Majesty. Although her royal highness, Princess Kensington, is the presumptive heir, Scimitar, as your pack brother's youngest son, may challenge her claim. It's perfectly legal."

"Challenge? As in a duel?" When did we start settling conflicts like free packs? I knew how to use a foil, an epee, and a saber, but throw me in a hand-combat, one-on-one kind of situation against a man, and I could lose everything. As a matter of fact, I'd lost to Scimitar in countless disciplines growing up.

"The choice of the challenge lies within the king's discretion." Glendale's neck was bright red, as was his face.

The foil, Dad. Pick the foil.

"If I may make a suggestion, however?" Glendale gave a curt smile. "The Black Forest Cup is starting tomorrow. It offers a variety of challenges, physical and mental. If our two stakeholders participate, the winner would surely make a worthy heir."

A worthy heir? That damn throne was mine. I hadn't woken up earlier to study or trained harder than the rest of my peers to see my future stolen from me in a flashy stunt.

"What if another participant wins the Cup?" I squeezed the words from between gritted teeth. "It's not just individual competitors but entire groups that enter, including humans."

"Afraid you'll lose to a human?" Scimitar laughed. "Your life among them may have softened you, Kens, but I'm not afraid to prove myself."

The onset of his dominance toyed with me.

Gripping the folds of my ridiculous dress, I stomped forward and shifted my face close to his. "Bring it on."

Drake coughed, and I belatedly released about fifty percent of my dominance.

Scimitar stumbled like a plastic toy in the wind. Even though he stayed upright, my aim had been true this time. Ish.

He quickly regained his composure. Rather than retaliate, he—hell, did he wink at me? Damn, he was figuring me out. Testing how far I'd be willing to go, and how far I could take my powers.

Jerk. When the time came, he'd feel their full strength.

"So it will be." My father's voice vibrated out of control. It took a lot to make him lose his calm. "You will be entered into the Cup anonymously to compete for the rightful succession. I will remain impartial, but know this, Scimitar. You've set back relations between me and your pack by centuries."

"Your Majesty, I have a legitimate claim."

"Legitimate, perhaps. But ethically, your tactics are highly questionable." Dad's head had sagged from the weight of his crown or the strain of the unexpected challenge. "If you lose, and I have confidence that you will, I will dissolve my relationship with your pack. Is that clear?"

"Your Majesty." Scimitar turned pale.

Nicely done, Dad.

"Now go." My father extended a finger toward the door. "Will you need help with your preparations?"

"I've brought my mother and my brother, Claymore." Scimitar's confidence had rebounded. "With your permission, we will be staying in our old quarters."

My head snapped up. "Clay's here?"

Scimitar smiled a movie-star smile, all teeth and charm. "He's excited to see you, too."

Then he bowed before my dad and shuffled backward for a few steps before walking out, swinging his empty clothes-tube by his side.

"Why do you look so happy?" Drake furrowed his brows.

My smile widened. "Clay's here."

TEN

DRAKE AND I RETURNED TO my living room. We didn't talk on the way. I could only guess as to what was going on in his head. As for me, I found it tough to balance my emotions.

The warm, fuzzy memories from my childhood fought against a cold-hearted reality in which Scimitar had betrayed me. Had Clay known? Had anyone? There had to have been red flags. Why did my dad pay a network of spies if they couldn't flush out a kingdom-shaking plot like this?

I took off my ring and placed it in the bookcase near the windows. If I wanted to wear it again, I'd have to fight for it.

In the living room, everything had been straightened and cleaned. The table sparkled, and everything had been reset as if we hadn't left it in a state of near chaos this morning. The chocolate bars had also been replenished. Order was good. If only someone could tidy up inside my brain, too.

"So." Drake pulled me into a chair opposite him. "How are you doing?"

"I couldn't say." My head was spinning, and I felt physically sick. "This wasn't how I'd imagined this would go."

"Are you worried? I mean, can Prince Scimitar seriously take the crown from you?"

I shrugged, suppressing any sign of my emotions. "Until an heir has been confirmed, succession isn't ensured."

"I refuse to let anyone take this from you."

I watched him take my hand, without sensing his touch. In fact, I wasn't feeling much of anything, other than the twisting sensation in my gut.

"Are you listening?" He used the crook of his finger to lift my chin. "We're going to beat him."

I closed my eyes for a second, and the absence of visual stimuli brought the sensation of the hard back of my chair and Drake's soft touch back into focus.

"Maybe," I said.

"Definitely."

His confidence didn't allow dissent. And maybe I deserved his optimism. Not everything was lost. The Black Forest Cup would prove to Scim and to my pack that I was worthy to be their alpha queen. A win from me would silence the nay-sayers.

"Why is he doing this to me, though?" I gave a shrug fueled by a shudder. The kind of whole-body shudder that started at my shoulders and went all the way to my toes. "Don't get me wrong, he's always been a pain in the ass, but he's not evil."

"Do you know him well?"

"Yeah. At least I thought I did." I stretched out my legs.

"And what about this Clay?"

"Clay's Scimitar's older brother." I gave a bitter chuckle. "We were six when Clay and I decided we'd be friends forever. The few months he and Scim spent with us every year were my happiest. Clay was special, and besides my dad, there was no better guy out there."

"Until you met me, right?" Drake coaxed me into his lap.

"Until I met you." I wrapped my arms around his neck. "You're my life. I'm more in love with you now than I was when we took the Moon Promise. That ritual clearly isn't just a bunch of words."

He tenderly kissed the corner of my mouth. "No, it's not."

"And I'm sorry for this mess. Coming to a different country, to court, no less, was always going to be hard for you, but this isn't what I expected at all."

"Me neither." He averted his eyes.

My chest squeezed tight around my heart. Was he wondering if he'd made a mistake entering the Moon Promise?

Without a doubt, I'd benefited more from our bond than him. Not only had the Moon Promise helped me shift into my wolf form and set free my dominance, but it had also bound Drake to me for eternity. And he was quite a catch.

In exchange, he got a woman who shied away from fulfilling a female werewolf's stereotypical role, a royal title he never asked for, and now this disaster.

Who could blame him if he wanted to bolt?

"What's Glendale's story?" His gaze was back on me. "It's clear he's not a fan of yours, but I'm impressed by his knowledge of ancient laws. He knew what to do immediately."

"He did, didn't he?" I frowned. "He's a crafty guy. Glen and I grew up at court. If you've heard me talk of bullies, picture him. Stirling's his older brother and more than once had to punish him when he'd gone too far."

"How did he go too far?" He lowered his voice. "Did he hurt you?"

"Nothing physical. No, it was his mental cruelty that haunted me. He spread rumors about me being stuck up and putting people in our dungeons when I didn't like them. You know, kids' stuff. Our relationship could have improved when it became clear he was being groomed for the role of Marshal. Instead, he became the guy boys wanted to be and girls wanted to date while he continued to exclude me."

"I'm sorry."

"He didn't dare do any of this when Scim was around, though. Don't get me wrong, Scim's as brazen and ruthless as they come. He's also loyal to a fault." I took a deep breath. "He used to be loyal to me, too."

Drake gathered me close, and I laid my head against the crook of his neck, soaking in his calming scent. No doubt, the royal machinery was buzzing with activity, but in this part of the castle, everything lay quiet.

"Listen, princess. Nothing's going to be accomplished in this getup." He pulled on the collar of his robe. "What do you say we change into normal clothes?"

"That's the best thing I've heard in a while." I kissed him, then wiped my lipstick off his mouth. "Come on."

I slid off his lap and dragged him up from his chair.

Fifteen minutes later, we'd changed into formal pants and shirts. 'Casual' meant something else when you were a princess. The number of jeans I'd owned while I grew up could be counted on the fingers of one hand.

We took a seat on my couch and snuggled, neither of us speaking. What was there to say? Until I'd talked to my father, I was in the dark. Was I seriously expected to compete for the Black Forest Cup?

A footman interrupted our quiet reflection with a loud knock. Dad had summoned us to his office.

I immediately shot up from the sofa. Finally, we'd have answers. Maybe even a plan.

With Drake by my side, I hurried after the footman, who led the way as if I hadn't spent the major part of my life in this castle.

My father's office had changed since I'd last been here. The white wall had been wallpapered over with a gray pattern, and white curtains framed the two arc windows. His dark-gray desk, the only piece I recognized, featured a computer, a notebook, and a stack of papers, with everything at neat angles.

My father's anxiety typically manifested in him straightening his clothes over and over, so a neat desk meant he was under a great deal of stress. And who could blame him? I wasn't the only one who had something to lose.

"Hi, Dad." I didn't hug him.

He stood behind his desk, supporting himself on one fist, his face creased by every wrinkle he owned.

"Kensington. Good." He rarely called me by my full name. "Sit."

"Your Majesty. Sir." Drake guided me to the chair without pulling one up for himself. "I imagine you and Kensi have things to discuss."

Dad looked at him as if he'd lost the ability to understand English.

"I'm confused about a number of issues," Drake continued. "Instead of bothering you with questions, is there a library that has appropriate reading material?"

"That's considerate of you." Dad straightened, his face less ashen. "Our Royal Library is out of bounds, but my staff and I use a private library, which holds a number of English books that should answer your questions."

"I appreciate it, sir."

"Turn left outside this door. At the end of the hallway, you'll find a room marked *Bibliothek*. That's our personal library." Dad scribbled on a piece of paper and handed the note to Drake. "Show this to the lady behind the desk and tell her what you're looking for. She's highly knowledgeable."

"Thank you." Drake bowed, squeezed my shoulder, and walked off, hugging the note as if it were a prized autograph by his favorite teen super-crush.

As soon as the door fell into the latch, I rose from my chair. "So, Scimitar's causing trouble again. I feel I should be less surprised."

Dad smiled grimly. "This time, he's gone too far. I will be talking to him and his mother this afternoon to see if I can understand his motivation. Maybe you could have a chat with Claymore?"

"You can count on it. Can Scim really take everything from me?"

"Schatz, I've invested the major part of my life in training and preparing you for your future. No one is going to take this from us."

I edged around the desk until I was within touching distance, but the time hadn't come. Now more than ever I needed to be strong and prove he hadn't made a mistake grooming me to be his successor.

"Remember all these years we've been saying the Black Forest Cup is a great tourist attraction?" I chuckled without amusement. "I kind of wish I'd taken part at least once, if only to see what it involves."

"If it should come to this and I fail at dissuading Scimitar from going through with his scheme, you will compete and you will win. Every year I get to sign off on the individual challenges, and not once has there been a task you couldn't win."

I stared at the bookcase in the corner, which was bursting with books. "If Scimitar wanted a throne, you'd think he'd go after his father's."

"Claymore's the presumptive heir. If he's about to be confirmed as the Crown Prince, Scimitar might feel left out."

"Clay hasn't been confirmed yet?" I frowned. "Don't tell me. It's because of his limp, isn't it?"

"Royal packs aren't so different from free packs. We, too, want our alphas to be strong. That's why so many of ours object to a female successor. Claymore's facing the same uphill battle."

"It sucks."

"Yes, it does. Only one of many reasons why Jonah and I decided to get the confirmation ceremony over with. Once you and Drake have been confirmed, our pack can start coming to terms with the situation. Besides, it's only prudent. Who knows how long I've got left on this planet."

"No, you don't." I raised a hand. "I don't want to talk about that. Especially not today."

"I'm planning to nag you for many more decades. Don't you worry."

"Good." I took down my hand and made a vague gesture. "Maybe King Lance should follow suit. And while he's at it, he should adjust Scim's moral compass."

Dad inserted a pen into his pen holder and straightened his keyboard. "That's not our business. It's bad form to suggest tactics to other kings."

"You're King Lance's pack brother."

"Oh, Schatz." He gravely shook his head. "We became pack brothers at a different time, long before either of us had been named crown prince. Since then, we've grown up to be different men."

"Do you believe he put Scimitar up to this stunt?"

"No. He wouldn't dare. No royal alpha would." Dad rubbed his chin. "I have to admit. Scimitar's been an ambitious boy. Never thought he'd be this brash, though."

"Naturally, I have every intention of winning the Cup." I bit my lip. "At the same time, it's not going to be easy. Scim's a single-minded guy who takes no prisoners. I haven't won many challenges against him in the past."

"I know your willpower." Dad's words carried conviction. "No one's better equipped to win than you."

It wasn't my willpower I doubted.

After a brief knock, the door to the office opened and Drake returned, clutching a book under his arm.

"What is it?" I stepped away from my dad. "Bad news? Did you not find anything to read?"

"No." He approached, his chin high. "I mean, good news. In fact, I'm allowed to enter the Cup with you."

Whether it was fear of my father or the historical surroundings, his strides never faltered, his voice never broke. He was a rock in this storm.

"About that." I pressed my lips together. "They do allow couples to compete for the Black Forest Cup, but this isn't that. This competition is about the throne."

"The book lays out the situation in which several claimants compete for the throne." He tapped the cloth-bound cover. "If the claimants have Schutzherrins, which I'm guessing are the female versions of me, they're allowed an active role, whatever form it may take."

"How progressive of the ancient packs." I glared at Dad.

"I raised you with all the opportunities I would have given a son." My father's expression softened. "However, your mate brings wonderful news. You will compete together."

"Hang on." I crossed my arms and eyed Drake. "You don't think I can win by myself?"

His dominance flared for a second. "Did I say that?"

I clenched my teeth. "Not in so many words."

"I certainly wouldn't bet against you." He made himself larger, blocking my field of view. "Our future is shared. Why, then, shouldn't we also overcome this challenge together?"

"Your mate raises a valid argument." Dad tapped the desktop. "You claim Drake is one of the advantages you bring to the throne. It stands to reason he will also be of benefit during the challenge. If Scimitar had a mate, the situation would be the same."

"You're right." I ran my fingers over Drake's arm. "Sorry, Hasi. And you know what? We're going to win. About time, too. I've been waiting to get another opportunity to wipe the smug grin off Scim's face."

"That's settled then." He gave a terse smile.

Had my stupid outburst hurt him deeper than I'd thought?

"I mean it." I laid my hand against his cheek. "This is great news. Why aren't you happy?"

"Actually, I'm building up to another issue. Of course, I'm not a private investigator, but this struck me as odd. Look here." He leafed to the front of the book, where a ruled sheet of cardboard had been attached to the title page. Drake was the last name on a short list of three.

"Huh," I said. "Dad?"

"Yes?" He stooped to catch a glimpse. "What is it?"

"Why did Glendale borrow this specific book four weeks ago? Did he know something we didn't?"

Eleven

IT DIDN'T TAKE A HUGE leap to understand what had happened.

"Glendale doesn't consider me alpha material." I slammed the door to my living room and began pacing across the polished floor. "No doubt he was the one who put this bug in Scimitar's ear to begin with."

Worse, Dad had refused to accuse his Marshal outright. As if his name in the book hadn't been proof enough.

Drake pulled out one of the high-backed chairs and sat. "You said your dad's closest confidants knew you weren't able to shift or dominate for the longest time. Maybe he based his opinion on outdated information."

"Glendale wasn't aware I couldn't shift."

He waved for me to come closer. "Okay, you're the private investigator, and I'm merely the sidekick, but would he collude with another pack to take you down?"

My shoulders relaxed as I arranged myself on his lap, one leg on either side of him. "You're not my sidekick, Hasi. You're my Schutzherr. My protector. I'm a weak woman and need you to look after me."

"I'll settle for being your mate."

I playfully gaped my mouth. "You'll *settle*?"

"Not now. My mind's swimming." He rested his head against the back of the chair and took me in, starting from my eyes and then to my chest, and back up again. Then he sighed. "Tell me about the Black Forest Cup."

"That I can do. The Black Forest Cup started out as a local event in the 1980s, a way for the pack to integrate with humans. Over time, the Cup's reputation spread first nationally and then internationally. Not everyone can enter, though."

He moved my hair behind my ears. "What are the criteria?"

He had a tactile personality and wasn't always aware of his actions.

I was. His unintentional touches brought a smile to my lips and a skip to my heart.

"The committee is run by werewolves with the support of humans." I ran my finger along his neck, where his collar ended, and opened the top button. "If you're human, you must prove a certain level of fitness, for example submit certification of a recently completed marathon or triathlon or better."

"And the wolves?"

"As a wolf, you must have been submitted by your alpha. An alpha can submit more than one competitor, which themselves are not usually of royal stock like Scim."

"How come I haven't heard of the Cup?"

"Because it was never meant for you. In free packs, you establish your hierarchy by fighting and physical challenges. For royal packs, there's less opportunity to stand out and be celebrated. The Black Forest Cup is one of those opportunities. Bragging rights go to the alpha who sends the best-performing competitor. Dad's content keeping a close eye on the challenges, without nominating a pack member."

"He knows the path in advance?" Drake grinned.

"Sure, but he's not going to share this with us." I wagged my finger. "Dad wouldn't cheat. In fact, all the royal alphas are briefed on the course in advance, so they understand the terrain and can send their best pack members."

"How can you be sure the alphas won't tell their competitors?"

"Trust." I drew a quick breath. "It's a matter of honor."

"Do humans ever win? Sounds as if the wolves have an advantage."

"You'd think. I mean, we're naturally faster and stronger. Even though we expect alphas to play by the rules, the participants don't need to." I counted off on my fingers. "You can't physically harm or injure competitors and you must register at the campsite every night. In the morning, you'll leave camp with your time advantage intact. Those are the rules, and they're the only rules. Usually, the best cheaters win. And believe me, humans are every bit as sneaky as werewolves."

He laughed. "I don't doubt it. What about women and men? Any advantages there?"

"Again, no. Over the past fifteen years, we've had a few female winners, both human and wolf." I undid two more of his buttons. "Humans are luckily more verbal about equality, and my dad's pretty progressive. Or at least as progressive as he can be. He insists the obstacles are geared toward testing a variety of strengths and talents. Brain and brawn."

"Okay then." His fingers ran to my chest, a pretty good sign he was done talking and his interests had wandered to an activity of a different kind. "Anything we won't be able to handle?"

I leaned in to nuzzle his neck. "There's nothing the two of us can't handle."

TWELVE

A S THE SUN WENT DOWN, Drake sought permission to return to my dad's private library to dig up more information about the Cup. I was glad he was going to join me in this challenge. Scim would just have to suck it.

While Drake was out, I headed toward the Warrior Pack's quarters, but it wasn't Scimitar I'd come to see. I'd promised Dad to talk to Clay, although I'd have gone without my father's insistence.

Was I going to recognize Clay? He'd been a stocky kid with a patch of curly black hair, only a few shades darker than his skin. More than a decade had passed since then.

He'd first visited with us from his native Pietermaritzburg as a kid with a clubfoot. His mother claimed German physicians would do a better job than South African ones, yet everyone knew his father, King Lance, wanted his son's weakness out of the public's eye. Every time Clay needed surgery, he stayed with us for months.

As did Scimitar.

Clay's cast and my inability to shift made us outsiders at every turn. While Scim could be found where the action was, Clay and I stayed on the outside, missed the annual Mooning—the time when kids shifted for the first time—and soon had built our own world. In that world, we'd forever be friends.

The Clay who'd opened the door looked like a stranger.

"Hi." I smiled.

"Kensi." He sounded thrilled and held out both his arms, then reconsidered and went for a handshake instead.

Awkward.

His figure had smoothed into a man's, and he carried his surprising height as if he'd been born with it. His hair was cropped close to his head, which made him resemble his father more than his brother.

"Come in." He walked practically without a limp into his living room. "I was wondering when I'd get to see you."

I closed the door behind me and followed him in.

Yes, his movements were almost smooth. Why would his pack consider him weak because of a clubfoot anyway? If I told Natalie about this, she'd be pissed. She didn't let her wheelchair get in the way, and no one would dare suggest she was limited by it in any way.

"You've changed." I took the chair Clay had gestured to and set my elbow on the polished dining table. "I mean, you're still you, but…"

"I'm no longer a kid?"

"Yeah."

"You too. I mean, you're a woman now." He stuck his hands into the pockets of his dress pants and lifted his shoulders. "I'm not saying you used to be a man, of course."

I laughed. "I know what you meant. Don't worry."

"I should have known I'd forget my grown-up maturity the minute you walked back into my life." He slumped into the chair opposite me and ran his hand through his short hair. "Story of my life."

"Yeah, you're still a dork, but for the first thirty seconds, you were fantastic." I gave a thumbs-up. "Some first-class adulting going on."

"Shut up." He gave me a light kick with his foot. "Although I missed your sarcastic cheers."

My smile remained, but the expression behind it lost its joy. I felt it seep out of me as if someone had pulled the plug.

Not someone. Scimitar.

Clay's quarters appeared uninhabited. The counter with the coffee maker hadn't been used since he'd arrived. The dining table showed no stains. Not even the throw-pillows had been disturbed.

Hopefully, he'd settle in soon. Our castle would forever be his second home, even long after I became queen. Assuming that was still in the cards.

"I'm sorry about my brother." Clay leaned forward. "Never took him for such an unscrupulous guy."

"He didn't tell you?"

"I was under the impression we'd come to watch your confirmation ceremony. Like, surprise, look who's here to witness your moment." He puffed up his cheeks before letting out a stream of air. "This morning, he told me about his plan."

"And you had no idea?"

"I'm telling you, I didn't." He inclined his head. "Though he's been acting weird for a few weeks. Constantly arguing with my dad. Whispering with Mom. Mood swings." He beckoned me closer with a finger. "I think he's entering puberty."

"Funny." I rewarded his attempt at humor with a chuckle. "Scimitar's ambitious, but he isn't power-hungry. If that's all this was, your father would appoint him to be his representative in charge of one of your smaller packs. I mean, South Africa's a big place."

"I know. It's almost like it's a whole country." Clay scratched the corner of his mouth.

I blew a raspberry. "I'm serious. Going after the German crown? That's a big deal. Why?"

"You would have to ask him." Clay averted his gaze.

He'd grown into his skin, which wasn't as brilliantly ebony as his mother, yet a shade darker than his father's. He occupied adulthood with a poise that seemed natural, but a poise *my* Clay from back-when hadn't possessed.

"Remember our plans for our future? The promises we made." His gaze drifted across my face and back into the distance. "The lists we kept like some demented Santa Claus?"

"One column for the kids that were nice, and the whip for the rest?" I let my wolf pick my smile: stern with a flash of predator. "I still have my list, yeah."

Clay's trip down memory lane seemed more wistful and less cruel than mine.

"Have you changed your mind?" My tone was without judgment. "My dad says he expects your confirmation to be around the corner."

"Maybe." Clay's spine shot straight and his eyes regained focus. "And yes, I'm committed to justice, all the way."

I'd dealt with enough liars during my career as a private investigator to know when I was being served a platter full of half-truths.

Had he lost his appetite for revenge? I totally understood that. Or had Scimitar told him about his plans after all? If he had, I had no right to blame Clay for his silence. Caught between me and his brother, he'd have to put family first.

Clay checked his watch and got up. "I have to go meet Mom and Scim for dinner. It's going to be an odd evening."

"I can imagine." I rose and shook his hand again. No way would his dinner table conversation be more uncomfortable than the one we'd just had. "It was nice to see you again."

"You, too."

I lifted my hand before taking off.

"I mean it," he said when my hand clasped the handle. "It was nice catching up."

I forced a sad nod before leaving his living room.

Whatever my mind had hoped for in terms of Clay's and my reunion, I'd have thought it would have involved more emotions. First, unbridled joy at seeing my best friend. A sense of familiarity as we talked. Common ground while we discussed Scimitar. And finally, regret about having to part ways again so soon.

Instead, a cloud of white noise filled my chest.

Everything in my life was changing, and it was changing too fast. A hurricane raged inside me, spinning me one way and the other. There was no post to grab. No anchor to drop.

Tomorrow, I'd enter the most important competition of my life.

THIRTEEN

MORE THAN A HUNDRED OF us assembled at the starting line of this year's Black Forest Cup. Many of our competitors would resign after the first day. I wasn't going to be one of them.

The Black Forest offered thousands of miles of walking trails, marked and equipped with information points, signposts and maps along the way. Pushchairs, wheelchairs, the old and the young, the fit and the gasping—everyone found a morsel of information or a standout feature they liked.

On paper, the Black Forest Cup course would take us exactly along those signposted paths. Newbies would undoubtedly stick to them like Germans clung to their beer, but those in the know understood that to win, outside-the-box thinking was required.

From my position at the front, I scanned the field behind me.

"He's at the far back." Drake indicated the place with his thumb, without taking his gaze off the woman carrying the starting pistol. "I assume you're looking for Scimitar, aren't you?"

"He's so smug." I clenched my jaw. "Probably trying to provoke us."

"Is it working?" He raised his eyebrows.

Both of us wore a stretchy material that wouldn't weigh much once stuffed into our clothes-tubes. Even our sneakers were the most lightweight Wildbach's one sportswear outlet sold.

I crossed my arms in front of my chest. "I don't care that he's starting the race behind us, as long as that's where he stays."

"Look out." Drake nudged my shoulder. "The fun's about to start."

About six of the approximately fifteen runners ahead of us carried backpacks. Another six had clothes-tubes similar to ours strapped to their backs, marking them as fellow werewolves. Humans were more concerned with food and drink, while our priority was not to be left naked after a shift.

A minute later, the starter pistol went off, and Drake and I started running.

For the first fifteen minutes, our group moved slowly. There wasn't much in terms of shade, but after surviving the hottest summer in Colorado on record, the sun didn't worry me.

Tree branches hung over the path, their large leaves—larger than my hand—brushing my shoulders and head as I ran past. The noise from the main road not far from here was hardly noticeable among the murmured conversation from our fellow competitors. If they could speak, they weren't working hard enough. Despite the fire inside my belly, it was too early in the race to kick off a stink, so I stayed quiet.

The path comfortably allowed four people to jog next to one another, and the frontrunners hogged their pole position, following the blue arrows that had been sprayed onto trees to get us on our way. And so it went. Fifteen minutes in, the Black Forest Cup was a pleasant, polite activity, with trails that might sooner or later lead us to castle ruins and waterfalls.

Well, I wasn't here for pleasant and polite. My hopes for this event went beyond beating Scimitar. Quite simply, I was here to win.

Drake, by contrast, had deeply immersed himself in the home of the Black Forest cake, the land of the cuckoo clocks, and Grimm's fairytales. As much as I'd wanted him to fall in love with my home, this wasn't the time for open-mouthed appreciation of the ancient trees that had survived kings and battles or of the perfectly upright rocks cleverly arranged to mark our path.

Our route snaked at a moderate incline through the hills, separating the steep ascent to our left from the even steeper gorge to our right.

Ahead of me, the blue arrows stopped. From now on, we'd have to find checkpoints and camps on our own. A faintly trodden trail branched off, leading up the hill. There was every reason to believe this shortcut would lead back to our path on the other side, potentially far ahead of the rest of the field. The climb would be exhausting, though. The trees uphill grew fairly dense, with low-hanging, long branches waiting to slap my face, and ferns and dead leaves underfoot eager to trip me up.

Despite this, I smelled an opportunity.

"Let's go that way." I subtly stretched out my finger. "It'll be faster."

"Shouldn't we stay with the others?"

I scrunched my face. "They're too slow."

One of our fellow runners, a tall lanky werewolf man carrying the Dutch pack's coat of arms, turned to shoot me a poisonous look.

I smiled sweetly. "Sorry. You weren't meant to hear that."

Distracted, he bumped into the woman ahead of him, who pushed him aside without losing her stride, making him stumble.

"Let's stay with the group for a while." Drake jerked his chin. "I don't want to miss our first checkpoint. Besides, I want to get a feel for the terrain."

The tall Dutch guy, meanwhile, veered off to make his way up the rocky slope. If he was going to get to the first checkpoint ahead of us, Drake and I would be in for one hell of an argument.

The slow pace continued. A soft breeze caressed my bare shoulders and stomach. A large sheet with the number 178 had been pinned to my front, while Drake wore number 176.

Scimitar was number 177. It didn't take a huge leap to guess that Glendale had entered us into the competition. Separating Drake from me seemed in line with his sense of humor.

Would Scim take the opportunity to scramble up the hill, too? He could be halfway up by now. Once he shook us, we'd never catch him.

"Push him out of your mind," Drake whispered. "We'll get him later. Let's concentrate on *our* race, okay?"

"Yeah. Okay." I wasn't out of breath.

But as usual, he'd made a good point. Scimitar's game plan was known only to him. We, in turn, could only control *our* pace, *our* path, *our* race.

I breathed in deeply as if inhaling the entire forest into my lungs at once. Even in human form, I loved running underneath the rustling foliage, with birds singing in the air. Whether it was here in the Black Forest or back in the woods in Colorado, nature's ancient soul bled into every leaf, every branch, and every rock, connecting my two homes.

Something fluttered far in the distance to my right, a jostling movement high above the ground. A red flag, the sign for our first checkpoint, had been strung up between two branches. Humans wouldn't yet be able to spot it, although werewolves might if they were paying attention.

At any rate, this was our chance. If only we weren't cocooned inside the throng of frontrunners.

"Drake, hang on." I pressed my hand against my ribs and leaned forward, as if unable to breathe.

"What?" He pulled me out of the way of the complaining runners. "Are you okay?"

"I need to sit down." I gasped as if I'd been deprived of oxygen and weaved into the brush to our right.

He had little choice but to follow me. "Don't tell me that light jog was too hard?"

Once I was sure we couldn't be observed by our fellow runners, I held my hand over his mouth and dragged him further away from the other runners.

"There." I indicated across the gorge that opened in front of us. "That's the mark for our first checkpoint. I don't think anyone has noticed it."

He checked over his shoulder, then squinted at the flag. "You're right. The distance to that point along the main path is going to be what, four, five miles. Now that we know where we're going, we can sprint the distance at a sustainable pace, maybe look for a shortcut to carve out a lead."

"I already have a shortcut in mind. Let's climb down the rock face, then run across the river, and climb back up on the other side. We'd be shaving at least fifteen minutes off our time, possibly more. Worth a little bit of effort, huh?"

"Our clothes-tubes won't make climbing easy."

"If they get in the way, we drop them and pick them up once we're down."

"They might become a problem on our way up."

I waved into the distance. "You can't see it from this angle, but behind the thick line of trees, the hill isn't all that steep. We can do this."

Drake looked one last time at the shrubbery separating us from the main field of runners, then hitched up his clothes-tube. "Lead the way."

Taking care of our steps, we approached the edge of the bluff. A few small rocks loosened under my tread and clattered down, each clang serving as a reminder of what would happen to us if we weren't careful.

At least he was finally recognizing the need to hurry. We'd have to press every shortcut and every advantage if we wanted to beat Scimitar.

The rock face was too steep to climb at first. A few minutes later, though, a relatively safe way down popped into view.

"Here." Without waiting for his approval, I sat at the verge, turned around to grab the cliff's edge with my fingers, and lowered myself onto the uneven platform below.

From there, I took three sashaying steps to my left and repeated my earlier maneuver.

The gorge was deeper than I'd remembered. All that stopped me from being pulverized upon impact was the goal in front of my eyes and the certainty that Drake was with me. His mere presence infused my veins with courage.

"Are you all right?" I didn't dare take my eye off the rock protrusion I was dangling from.

"I'm fine." He had more bodyweight to haul down, but he was also stronger than me. "Don't worry about me. Just be careful."

"Okey—" My right foot slipped, kicking free a loose rock. As luck would have it, that opened a decent hole, large enough to find a more solid hold. "—dokey."

With a combination of speed and caution, I fumbled my way down the uneven wall, once or twice hanging by the tips of my fingers, at other times balancing on my tiptoes. The scratches and bumps I picked up along the way would heal soon enough.

About four feet from the ground, I jumped—and landed on my ass.

I cursed. "If you're going to jump, don't fall."

Drake leaped off and landed two feet next to me, without a wobble. "I see you don't take your own advice."

He pulled me up by my hand, into a deep kiss.

My man. My woods. My home.

My perfect moment.

The telac, telac, telac of a grouse rang in the distance, and he lifted his gaze. "Ready for part two?"

"Bring it on."

He'd managed to distract me again. Hadn't I made it clear we couldn't afford to hold hands and see the sights?

We sprinted over the bumpy ground along the river, which followed its natural path with quite some force, splashing and gurgling when it struck the banks. I pushed with my legs, pumped with my elbows, to make up for the time we'd wasted on our moment of romance.

The trees here stood every bit as dense as those above, with branches too high to reach. The temperatures had dropped, too. Nevertheless, the rich, brown earth remained moist in places, at least underneath the mosses and woodland plants.

"The bridge." I approached a simple wooden structure that didn't look terribly sturdy. "Don't fall into the river."

"Another good, although unnecessary, safety tip."

I turned and skewered him with a glare. He simply wasn't getting it. My future stood on a knife-edge, and he was joking.

"Whoa." He raised both hands. "Lighten up."

My dominance whipped toward him. "I don't have time to lighten up. Get your shit together."

Drake gave off a rumbling growl. "Don't push me, princess, or you and I are going to have a problem."

I took a deep breath and shut down my pheromones pronto.

"How many times?" His voice sounded pressed. "Dominance has no place in our relationship."

The tangible effects of my powers on others were new territory for me, yet that excuse had run its course. On the occasions where I'd let myself get carried away by anger, he'd shown incredible patience. Each time, I'd vowed not to target him again. It was a tool of subjugation, a symbol of superiority, and he deserved better.

"I'm sorry." I held on to the railing and took a deep breath. "Winning the Cup is important."

"I get that."

"I don't think you do." I added a smile to soften my words. "This might look like an adventure to you, but my future is at stake. I can't afford to stare at squirrels or smell the roses today. If I don't win—"

"We will." Drake took my chin in his hand and kissed my cheek. "Of course we will, but arguing isn't going to get us to the finish line faster."

I let my gaze drift for a second before settling firmly on his confident eyes. "I will try to stress less. Okay?"

"That's all I ask. Now come on. This bridge is going to be fun."

He bounced past me to take the lead again, testing every plank before declaring it safe and pointing out the ones that seemed to give.

Arms stretched out for balance, I followed him across.

"You're right. That was fun." I leaped onto the ground and glanced back at the river. Despite its uneven surface, it shimmered a dark green, reflecting the trees too high for me to make out as anything other than dark silhouettes.

"Look." Drake raised his hand to his forehead to form a peak against the sunrays making it this far down. "Guess we've been found out."

Among the dozens of runners filing onto a stone bridge high above, a few stretched their fingers toward us. The red flag couldn't be visible from their vantage point, so they had to be wondering what we were doing.

The front two added speed to their jog, but not everyone was disgruntled. Three runners waved at us, and I waved back.

At their pace, it would be another thirty minutes at least before the front sprinters arrived at the checkpoint.

We were going to be there in ten.

"Race ya." I bumped Drake with my shoulder and took off.

Finally, my lungs were pumping. We leaped over fallen logs and skidded across exposed rock slabs until we got to the slope on the other side.

I dug deep and attacked the hill with everything I had, using tree trunks to take the effort off my legs where I could. The terrain was looser than I'd expected. Once or twice, I went on all fours if a lower center of gravity prevented me from sliding back down. Perspiration clung to my face, to my armpits, and to my back, and every drop was worth it.

Drake overtook me halfway up. His tattoos moved as his muscles did, a ripple of waves that could happily carry me away to distant shores.

"You should wear this gear all the time." I shot him a predatory grin as we emerged on top. "It shows off your best assets."

He straightened into a standing position and slapped my butt. "Ditto."

A wooden hut stood not two minutes from us. I shook the earth from my hands until only a brown layer remained. My bare calves, between the bottom of my three-quarter pants and my socks, hadn't fared any better. Of course, cleanliness wasn't my goal today.

We stepped up to a line that had been carved into the path and marked with a laminated sheet that read, "*Hier warten.* Wait here."

"Willkommen." A man in his late thirties greeted us with a smile, carrying two cups of water, which he held in outstretched hands.

He wore a yellow visibility jacket over a slim body while keeping a clipboard clamped under his arm. His steady footwear, camouflage jacket, and Aussie-style hat indicated he was no stranger to the woods.

"Thanks." I grabbed a cup and downed it in one gulp.

Water had never tasted so fresh or clear as in this moment.

Drake had no sooner finished his drink than he eyed the other cups lining up along the porch's wide banister. He, too, had given his all, as the dirt and scratches on his face, arms, and legs confirmed.

"Help yourself." The man, whose nameplate read 'Mark,' said in heavily accented German. "We have plenty of water."

We gulped down another cup each before chucking our empty cups into the yellow recycling bag.

"Thank you, Mark. We're ready for our first challenge." Drake eyed a log on the far side of the hut. It was too square and smooth to be lying there as nature had intended.

"You're eager." Mark gave a rattling belly laugh.

Drake checked over his shoulder. "We want to maintain our lead."

Mark's nose twitched.

"Are we not the first?" I asked, incredulously.

"No, but you're in second. That's wonderful. I don't expect the other runners for another fifteen minutes."

"Who beat us here?" My voice grew urgent because I had a nasty feeling in the pit of my stomach.

Mark checked his board. "Number 177. He left about five minutes ago."

Scimitar had beaten us? "So 'ne Scheiße," I whispered a German curse.

"It's okay," Drake said, not entirely convincingly.

"Don't worry." Mark tapped his clipboard. "Let's do the task fast and then you can catch him."

I bit my lip to stop myself from swearing again. We'd used a risky shortcut, and Scimitar had nevertheless beaten us. How was that possible?

"The task is simple." Mark led us toward the log, which was only one of dozens arranged in the manner of a maze. "Walk on the posts to reach the tankard on the other side. You cannot turn around. If you go the wrong way or step off the logs, you must start again. On the way back, you must also stay on the logs. Understood?"

The tankard, which was, in fact, a simple beer glass with a handle, stood about three hundred feet away from us, too far for anyone other than the most eagle-eyed of humans—or a werewolf—to spot.

"Do we both go, or only one of us?" Drake pointed his thumb at each of us in turn.

"Both. I mean yes." Mark chuckled. "You can go together or alone."

We mumbled our thanks.

Two seconds later, Drake stepped on top of the first log and heaved me up. "We're in this together, remember?"

"I remember."

Hand in hand, we walked, with our free arms jutted to the sides for balance, until we reached the first junction. The trees around the hut had been trimmed, allowing the sun to take full advantage of the thinned canopy and remind us why we'd slathered on sunscreen before we'd left home.

Mark watched us like a hawk from the main path. Although the rules didn't forbid cheating in terms of getting from point A to point B, the tasks had to be performed as instructed to obtain the clue that would get us to the next stop.

"I'll take the right path, you take the left." Drake gestured ahead, separating our halves.

Since when did I take orders from him? Yet in the spirit of 'lightening up,' I kept my complaints to myself.

It immediately became clear that, even though a maze was simple to follow from the bird's-eye perspective used in magazines, it wasn't so easy when your vision extended at a level only about six feet above the path itself.

"My side's a dead end." Drake glanced at me.

"I can't see all the way through to the tankard. At best, I can get us safely halfway without getting lost."

"Okay, you lead." He helped me past his body, copping a feel as I slid across the beam.

I took a large step to get ahead of him, and from there we ran where we could, slowed where the logs appeared slippery, until we reached the point where I'd lost track.

Once again, we divvied up the task, and a few minutes later, we reached the tankard without earning any penalties.

Drake picked up the jug and sprinted back the way we came, leaping from one log to the other. Steadily I dashed after him, giggling like a schoolgirl at the pure triumph of our first passed checkpoint.

When we returned, Mark applauded. "Well done, you both. That was wonderful. Really wonderful."

I glanced to my left, where the first runners were rounding a bend. They'd be here in less than five minutes.

"Don't worry." Mark took the tankard off us and handed us a piece of paper. "This is the hint you need to find the second task. The other runners must do the maze one after the other, while the others wait behind the line so they can't see."

He jerked his chin toward the line across the path.

"That will spread out the field, giving us a chance to carve out a decent lead." Drake smiled at the man and shook his hand. "Thank you very much, Mark. You've been great."

"You also." Mark laughed and slapped Drake's back. "Good luck, you both."

We waved and took off, and then ran until we were out of sight. We stopped and unfolded the paper, on which two sentences had been printed.

"The first riddle is in German," I said. "It reads, ,Welcher Baum singt wie ein Traum?'"

"Meaning?"

"What tree sings like a dream? And the English riddle is, 'What tree can you carry in your hand?'"

"Man." Drake scratched his temple. "I know that one."

I balled a fist. "What is it?"

"Give me a minute." He took tiny steps to his left as if looking for a clue among the trees. "It's on the tip of my tongue."

"Maybe a twig?" I kicked a thin specimen lying at my feet. "It's part of a tree, and it fits into my hand."

"Got it. It's a palm." He jerked his fist in triumph.

"In the Black Forest? Seriously? Not a place famous for its rich harvest of coconuts."

"I know that, Klugscheißer." He'd been picking up German words from me at an alarming rate and had shown a talent for remembering insults and expletives. Klugscheißer, meaning literally "knowledge pooper," or "smartass," was one of his favorites.

I punched his arm as my only response.

"Anyway, I'm sure that's the answer." He gave a helpless shrug. "So, how do we get to the beach?"

I rolled my eyes. "Now you're copying my jokes. At least be original."

"No, no. You used sarcasm to show me up. I was the one who made it funny." He bared his teeth in a superior smile.

"You keep telling yourself that." I dismissed him. "Anyway, the beach isn't the only place you can find palm trees. They make attractive decorations in many homes. Or maybe—" I snapped my fingers. "I've got it. Come on."

I started running at a steady pace.

"Care to fill me in?" He fell into a fast trot by my side.

"The tree that sings like a dream is a larch. In German, a larch is a Lärche, a homonym with Lerche, meaning lark."

"There must be loads of larches here."

"Two miles from here, there's a place called Lärchengarten. It's a botanical garden or, more specifically an arboretum, you know, where they grow all types of trees in one place, and not just the ones native to the Black Forest. There are worse places to look for a palm tree."

"Well done." He adjusted his clothes-tube without losing his stride. "How are competitors who don't live here supposed to guess that?"

I lifted my elbow toward an encased map of the area that stood at the edge of the trail. "They can look it up. I expect most hints will direct the runners to locations that can be found on any tourist map. The Lärchengarten arboretum should be clearly marked."

"So, Scimitar will be headed there, too?"

"He's almost as familiar with the area as me. The question is, did he get the same answer?"

"If he did, we could be in trouble." Drake upped his speed, his breathing labored now. The race to the top had finally ensnared him, too.

"I know a shortcut." I put speed into my run so as not to fall behind. Whatever it took, I wasn't going to be the one letting our team down. "Let's hope Scim doesn't."

Fourteen

Not many people knew the area as intimately as me. Without allowing myself to get distracted by memories, I guided Drake far away from any trail, through dense undergrowth and ferns, back into the silence of the forest, the place where tall trees reigned.

A strongly spiced scent was my first warning of danger. Blood rushed to my head, and I stopped dead in my track. A wild boar stepped into our path, roughly a hundred and fifty feet from us. It had a long, blunt snout, beady eyes, and enormous tusks that could slice open my thighs and skewer me in five different ways.

It snorted menacingly.

I reached for Drake's hand. Except, he wasn't where he was supposed to be. He kept on moving with purpose, stomping loudly toward the grunting animal.

"Breathe, Kensi." He beckoned for me to follow. "It's a pig, and you're a goddamn werewolf, not a chicken."

The animal ran off, back into the underbrush.

"Yeah?" I said belatedly. "These things have literally killed ten people in the last decade alone."

"I doubt the number's that high, but in any case, we have a race to win. Remember?"

We soared over the soft ground with its treacherous rocks and half-buried branches and made impressive time—in human terms. Unless we reassessed our strategy, catching up to Scimitar would be a pipe dream.

"Let's shift over there, behind those trees." I pushed the branches aside and handed them to Drake as I passed him so they wouldn't knock him in the face.

Once I'd reached a place with decent coverage, I removed my clothes-tube from my back. "I'll take this tree."

"You don't have to hide every time you shift." He wagged his eyebrows. "I've seen you naked."

"I know, but let's keep the magic alive, huh?" I disappeared behind a thick trunk and quickly stepped out of my clothes.

Once I was as nature intended, I stuffed everything, including my sneakers, into the tube, which was about the size and width of a rolled-up yoga mat. The clothes-tube came with an elastic band, which I eased over my head and tightened under my chin.

I took a deep breath and called forth my wolf. *She* was already waiting, her claws sharp as ever. My legs shrank, my back distorted, then my face lengthened, triggered by an unbearable pain at the center of my stomach. A pain that spread until it coursed through my upper body from my lungs to my waist, filling every capillary and fiber with angry heat.

Shifting wasn't fun, nor was it easy. Drake had taught me breathing techniques to take the edge off, yet I hated every second of my agony.

My lungs had shrunk and worked hard to compensate. Eventually, the heat lessened. I sniffed the air and then padded out from behind the tree, my wolf ears pricked.

Drake's brown-red fur vibrated from his inability to stand still. He took a few steps on the spot, ducked and stretched, then approached. We spent a minute nuzzling and smelling each other, then I licked his face and dashed off.

We sprinted through the densest areas, avoiding the musky scent of wild boars. Overhead, the sun broke through the gaps between the trees, lighting up twisted roots, dead branches, and fallen leaves that crunched beneath our paws.

Once or twice, the clothes-tube around my neck got tangled in twigs, causing the strap to dig into my flesh. Soon we arrived at the botanical garden.

Two larch trees framed the gated entrance, and in the center stood a five-foot palm tree in a planter.

We disappeared out of view and shifted back into our human forms before getting dressed. If anything, this time, the pain was worse. I ground my teeth and powered through. What was a moment of discomfort now compared to sweet victory later?

Back on two feet, we entered the botanical garden through the gate.

"Guess that's one way to get a palm tree into the Black Forest," Drake noted with a nod at the interloper. "Look, it says it's not a tree."

The sign that had been erected next to the planter read, in both German and English, "The Arecaceae, commonly known as palms, are a family of flowering plants typically found in tropical and subtropical climes."

We headed into the garden, paying little attention to the surrounding greenery. I applauded the effort that had gone into gathering the variety of species, but they'd still be here after the Cup took a perfect spot in my trophy cabinet, which I'd have to ask Drake to build.

We found our second checkpoint in a clearing near the end of the garden. The booth manned by the volunteer was situated at the end of an obstacle course. One way across was to wade through a vast water-filled pit.

"Let's avoid the brown sludge." I grimaced. "I don't know if the camp has showers, and a crust of mud won't make us run faster."

"Agreed." He stepped onto a rock and pulled me up next to him. "Go on then, princess. Show me how it's done."

From the rock, I climbed onto the broad, sturdy branches of a tree, and then swung on a rope, which I released to dip onto a trampoline located in a gap between two trench sections. I angled my jump to grip another rope strung between two large poles. Moving one hand over the other, I dragged my weight across to the other side, dropped onto a log, and ran toward the booth.

I panted and needed a second to catch my breath, yet my flawless effort lifted my mood. My clothes were drenched, and sweat glued my hair to the back of my neck, but every bead had been earned.

Two minutes later, Drake came up behind me, sweaty like me and grinning from ear to ear.

"Hallole," the woman greeted us in a cheerful tone. Her dark hair fell in luscious waves onto her shoulders.

"Hi." I put on a smile to overplay my hair envy. "Please tell us we're the first ones."

"No, but you're second." She scratched her head, probably in sympathy with our unkempt appearance. "Very good."

I swiveled toward Drake, who pressed his lips together.

"Would you like water?" She gestured to the dozens of filled water cups on the table in front of her.

"Thanks." Drake's breathing was returning to normal, and he passed me a cup before helping himself.

"These are the instructions to get you to camp." The lady, whose name was Kim, handed us a piece of paper containing the second clue.

"Have you been working hard?" it read. "You've only had to labor twice thus far. I had to overcome twelve labors."

"That's Hercules, right?" Drake grinned. "And you said reading history books is a waste of time."

I laid my lips on his for a salty kiss. "All I said is between us, only one needs to memorize the history of our planet, leaving my brain free for important things."

"Uh-huh." The silver in his eyes flared. "Like what?"

"Like the fact that about an hour from here, there's a large rock the locals lovingly refer to as Hercules. It sits in a huge clearing."

"Which would make a great place to set up a camp accommodating about a hundred tired competitors."

"Exactly."

He nodded at Kim. "Thank you. This was a fun obstacle course."

"You're welcome." She waved us off, giggling.

As soon as we'd left the botanical garden, Drake headed back into the denser woods and reached for his clothes-tube.

I touched his arm. "It's not worth it."

"Are you sure?" He let go of the tube. "We run faster as wolves."

I averted my head. "I don't shift as fast as you."

A welcome breeze brushed across my shoulders, alleviating the late-summer heat while bringing with it a shiver shooting down my spine.

Drake gathered me into his arms, moved my sticky hair out of my face, and looked into my eyes. "I'm sorry. I forgot. It's the pain, isn't it?"

I rested my forehead against his shoulder. "It's getting easier every time, but I've already shifted twice today."

"Wow, aren't you sweet?" Scimitar's voice dripped with sarcasm.

Damn. He must have waited for us. His clothes were dry, or at least not dirty from ditch water, although he'd broken a sweat, too, giving his skin a varied brown shimmer.

Drake and I let go of each other, and I widened my stance to steel myself against the competitive banter that was bound to come my way.

Scimitar wore similar clothes to Drake, and he filled them nearly as well. He was about my height and wore his hair slightly longer than his brother. His skin tone differed from Clay's, though, as it was lighter and more like his father's. After all, the boys did have different mothers.

Except, Scimitar was no more a boy than Clay.

"I didn't expect you to solve the first clue so fast," I said. "So, why stick around? We're not going to help you find the answer to the second one."

"I don't need the clues to find my way." He waved a folded sheet at us, jutting his flat chin. "It helps to have friends in high places."

I stepped toward him. "What does that mean?"

"Wouldn't you like to know?" He gave a toothy grin and touched his forehead in a salute. "Race you to camp?"

"Show me that." Drake ripped the paper from his hand and held it so I could see, too.

"It's a map, with all the checkpoints and camps marked." Drake folded it back together with force. "How did you get it?"

That conniving bastard.

Scim snatched the paper back and threatened Drake with a finger.

"Don't try that again." He tapped his ring, which sported the emblem of his pack. "Do you understand what this means?"

Drake wasn't easily intimidated. "It means you're a prince of the Warrior Pack. Big whoop."

"Big whoop?" Scimitar gave a grim laugh. "You won't say that once I've been confirmed as the heir to the Boroughs Pack and you have to crawl back to America as the no one you are."

A fire seed grew in my belly, from where its biting heat flooded my throat and ears. Who the hell was this guy, and where did he come off dissing Drake? He wasn't in the same league as my husband.

"Since when do you use your station to bully people?" My dominance built steadily, seething and urging me to unleash it. "Especially using a station that isn't yours by birth."

I felt dirty as soon as the words were out. It was only after King

Lance had officially acknowledged his mistress's son as his offspring that Scimitar gained a royal title. A sore spot, understandably, and not one I'd ever pressed before.

"There was a time when I'd have agreed with you. Well, times change." He wrinkled his nose as if disgusted. "This map will put your crown onto my head. Sure, it will pinch and itch, but each time I scratch I'll think of you two."

"You only think you're going to win." I gritted my teeth. "We'll prove you wrong."

"I don't think I'll win. I *know* it." Scim tucked his map away inside his clingy top. "For what it's worth, I'm sorry. I really am."

"Why are you doing this? Have I hurt you?" I tried in vain to keep the whimper out of my voice. "I thought we were friends."

"We are. We were." For once, his shoulders slumped, and he turned away his head. "Sometimes we must do things that aren't pleasant or fair because life isn't fair."

"No one's forcing you to take this challenge. You could drop out, head held high."

"No." He barked the word. "This is how it has to be. Get over it."

He unleashed a strand of his dominance, which smacked me right around the head.

Drake immediately retaliated, his power more measured than Scim's attack on us.

"Shit." Scimitar winced and stumbled backward. "Anyway, I'd love to stay and fight, but I have a Cup to win. See ya at camp."

He turned and ran, holding his clothes-tube's strap tight.

"What a jerk." Drake's posture was tense. "Still waiting to see that stand-up guy you told me about."

"You and me both. Do you know what really annoys me? Cheating competitors I can deal with. That's the name of the game." I sounded calmer than I felt. "But how are we going to win against cheating organizers or kings? Someone gave him a fucking map."

Drake crossed his arms, glaring at the trees where he'd last seen Scimitar.

"Think Glendale collaborated with Scim?" My fingers curled tightly around my clothes-tube's elastic band.

I should have punched Scimitar. Should have made him eat his words.

Even without perfect focus, I could bring him to his knees and watch his sorry ass squirm. The genes I'd inherited from my mother would have made a light meal of him.

Why hadn't I? Did my memories cast such a shadow I could no longer distinguish between my former friend and the asshat challenging me for a throne that was rightfully mine?

Dad had refused to ask Glen about the book he'd borrowed from the private library and whether his Marshal played a role in this disaster, but he couldn't overlook this breach of trust.

Of course, whispered oaths of vengeance wouldn't help me win. I needed a plan.

"Let's not focus on Scimitar." Drake's voice remained calm. "Can we beat him to camp?"

"I know a shortcut. If we shift, we have a chance."

"You want to shift?" He lifted his eyebrows. "Are you sure?"

"Whatever it takes." I clenched my teeth to counter the heaviness in my chest, this ingrained fear of pain.

He needed to understand the agony I'd suffer to confirm my inheritance. That damn throne was mine, and Scimitar wasn't going to steal it. Not now. Not when I was so close.

Drake and I shifted in record time and took off running at full speed. With every leap and every step, my helpful brain reminded me Scimitar was ahead of us. The only question was, would my shortcut beat his route?

Our destination came into view about forty minutes later.

Set in a large clearing surrounded by tall pines and trees I couldn't name to save my life, the campsite began with a yellow banner marking the finish line of our first day.

A woman noted our numbers and time in a folder and waved us through into the spacious clearing around the stone known as Hercules. Ten white tents, each capable of housing more than ten people, had been erected in the shape of a circle, with plenty of tables and benches filling the inside. The organizers had even hauled in portable toilets and a makeshift shower area.

So where was Scimitar?

After a thorough wash, Drake and I headed for the bar to rehydrate and then to the barbecue, where a big-bellied man with a gray beard and a Santa-like disposition threw a couple of steaks and sausages on the grill for us. He also confirmed we were the first to arrive.

Drake and I high-fived. My painful shift had been worth it.

The next runner arrived as the sun sank beneath the treetops, yet it wasn't Scimitar who waved at us. Had the impossible happened and he'd got lost on the way? Even with a map, wrong turns happened. Once surrounded by brush, far away from any landmarks, anyone could lose their bearings.

By the time we'd finished our food, our postures relaxed. We already had more than an hour on Scimitar, a lead we'd take into day two.

The next single runner jogged into sight, followed by the first group of participants, and so forth, until the campsite teemed with people. Still, no sign of number 177.

Was he okay? Something had been going on with him, as his challenge and his unhinged ramblings had proven.

When the camp had filled, a steward welcomed us by means of an electric megaphone. He gave the fastest time, aka ours, upon which a cheer erupted. Then he shouted out the slowest time, and an even louder cheer sounded. Sour grapes weren't allowed. By day we'd been competitors, but the night connected us. Language gaps were bridged by alcohol, and music made us move to the same rhythm.

Drake and I found ourselves among a small group of humans. We were hogging a long camping table and its two benches and chatted and waved our arms about as if our sodas had been beer to help us overcome our inhibitions. Our new friends—two German women in their twenties, one Italian man in his fifties, and a Swede who tore into his sausage as if he hadn't eaten in days—didn't hide their competitive spirits. Despite this, no one openly resented our interim first place. They'd catch us up tomorrow, they joked.

The one voice I kept expecting to hear didn't make itself known. Scimitar had to have arrived by now, too. Losing one's bearings was one thing, but he was too familiar with the area to stay lost. Besides, in wolf form, he'd have picked up the scent of a human runner sooner or later. Maybe he was hiding from us, ashamed to have lost his lead. Or maybe he'd taken my advice and dropped out of the race.

If wishes were horses.

Drake listened intently to the German couple, who—like us—had only recently gotten married. The two women were sweet together in the way they finished each other's sentences and kept touching the other's hands or arms.

Why hadn't Drake and I melted together like them?

Our alpha genes often got in the way, with blazing challenges ending in fiery make-up sex, but common ground shouldn't be that hard to find for two people in love. We needed to work harder.

I needed to work harder if I wanted my marriage to succeed. What would happen if the Moon Promise failed? Our love would remain—this was an immutable law of the ritual we'd undertaken. Could love turn to hate or even be overshadowed by it?

At least we were in sync about our attack plan for tomorrow. We'd shift as often as we'd have to, no matter the cost. The prize of the crown would be worth any amount of pain.

With a map at his disposal, Scimitar had the upper hand. However, he'd still have to check in at the checkpoints and do the trials. This was how Drake and I would even the odds. That, plus the time advantage we'd take into tomorrow, meant we stood at least an equal chance of being crowned winners on Friday.

In any case, today had been a good day, and I found myself smiling for no reason other than the joy of being in the present. The air was rich with the fragrance of leaves and clay, of the dozens of torches lighting the site, and of the barbecue that had been going all night, grilling steaks and sausages.

People had gathered around the tables and between the tents, speaking, laughing, and offering encouragement to those who'd been struggling. On the bench opposite us, Susanne laughed in a high-pitched tone so infectious I joined in, without having the foggiest idea what they'd been talking about.

Drake smiled at me briefly before turning back to her. "Then what did you do?"

"I waded the remaining distance through the trench, with Anne cheering me on." She kissed her wife's cheek. "Although her support died the second I asked for a hug."

We broke out in another round of laughter.

By the time it was ten, the chatter slowly quietened. Those who preferred to sleep inside were moving into the tents. Others wandered off to find a clean, soft spot on the ground. Drake and I had decided in advance to sleep under the star-studded sky, away from the crowd.

But with jet lag and a messed-up circadian rhythm, we weren't yet ready for sleep. The six of us remained seated, telling tales of future glory and past failures.

"I haven't laughed this hard in a long time," I confessed and snuggled closer to Drake, who'd laid his arm around my waist.

"I'll be winning tomorrow and the day after that and the day after that, and then you'll be crying." Paolo, the Italian guy on the other side of the table, beat his chest. "Good to get laughter in now."

Since he wasn't competing to win but to raise money for cancer research, we took his unrealistic boasts in the spirit in which they were intended and chuckled.

"I mean it." His smile flickered as he nodded toward something behind us. "Uh-oh. You were too loud and someone called the police, huh? Naughty, naughty."

Two policemen stalked across the ground, hands near their belts. They wore blue uniforms, with guns holstered at their waists. One had a bushy beard with a wisp of hair peeking from his hat, while the other was clean-shaven. Both looked too serious to be following up on a noise complaint.

"Numbers 176 and 178?" The bearded guy checked a notebook.

"Here." I raised my hand. "Why?"

"We must speak with you."

"With us? Um. Sure." Drake got up and wagged his finger at his friends. "We'll be right back. Don't let anyone steal our seats."

"Never," Susanne and Anne said at the same time and promptly dissolved into laughter.

The cops steered us away from the tables and the torches, which flickered in the background and made people appear as mere silhouettes. The unmistakable odor of mushrooms lapped up at us as if the ground were bathed in them.

"We're told you registered together with number 177. Can you confirm this?" The officer with the beard looked and sounded as if he wouldn't disgrace his face with a smile.

Had Scimitar got so lost they were now sending search patrols?

"Scimitar, yes." Drake coolly crossed his arms. "He's competing on his own."

"When was the last time you spoke to him?"

Werewolves weren't the only ones regarding equality as nothing more than a word in a dictionary. Some women might be okay with that. Not this one.

I stood tall. "Around the second checkpoint, at the arboretum."

"He was ahead of you then, but you were the first two to arrive at camp, correct?" The guy without a beard spoke English with confidence. "Didn't that seem weird?"

His voice hit a sharp edge, and a flash of icy cold washed over me.

"No, we were fast. What's this about?" My stomach sank, leaden and off-kilter, and I grabbed Drake's hand. "Is Scimitar okay?"

The men exchanged a quick glance, and it was the guy without the beard who answered. "We're sorry to inform you that your friend's body was recovered approximately three kilometers from here."

"Scimitar's dead?" The two words stole the last wisp of air in my lungs.

An invisible force pushed against me like a mighty gale, pounding my chest to prevent my next breath. My teeth, my stomach, my neck—all locked up tight to let nothing inside.

There I stood empty, waiting for a punchline that wouldn't come.

Fifteen

Not long ago, Scimitar had been as alive as any werewolf could be, running through the woods and being one with nature. Now he was supposed to be dead?

Laughter and music drifted from the campsite while Drake and I held each other. The race hadn't strained my lungs, but at this moment, breathing had become the hardest task in the world.

A police officer called Max took our statement. She repeated each question and followed up on our answers with a questioning look as if giving us the chance to revise our statement one last time before she committed it to her notebook.

Once she'd left, a Cup coordinator quietly ushered us to a car, where clothes had been laid out.

"Most likely, he tripped or fell down a gorge or into the river," Drake whispered while we got changed in the cramped back of the vehicle.

"You think that's possible? He was as fit as any top athlete."

"True, but accidents happen. Or maybe he was sick? Something could have affected his brain, which would also account for the challenge, which you say was out of character."

The drive to the castle dragged. For most of it, I held on tight to my seatbelt, its rough edge cutting into my palm. Scimitar being compelled to his actions by sickness was such a tragic concept, I wasn't ready to contemplate it. An accident, on the other hand, was one I found easier to believe.

The car's engine stopped humming, and the doors opened. Ten other cars stood in their parking spots, lined up with ruler-perfect precision. Order was good. Order was what my disheveled mind craved.

On our way into the eerily silent castle, I grabbed Drake's sleeve. "What if his death is the action of a deranged person on a rampage? Or of a serial killer?"

He gently removed my hands from his arm. "In real life, not every death has a sinister cause."

The stairs seemed steeper tonight, as if reluctant to be climbed.

Outside Dad's office, I was struck by another possibility. "Maybe all of this was a prank? Scim's challenge. Making us take part in the Cup. His supposed death. What if none of it's been real? I mean, it's possible, right?"

His lips parted. Rather than agreeing, he knocked on the door. "Let's find out."

Dad's office was filled with people trying to make sense of madness. My father worked hard to help us. He made phone calls and bellowed instructions to ensure only our pack coroner would examine the body. Glendale and Stirling, meanwhile, did their best to answer his stream of questions with what little information they'd gathered from the police.

None of their actions changed the facts. Scimitar was gone.

Every past moment with him played like a song in my mind. Hard beats pounded over his calls to be pushed higher on the swings, while mellow notes accompanied his acts of kindness, like the summer when he carried me and his brother piggyback for weeks after I'd sprained my ankle and while Clay was recovering from surgery.

I arranged myself rigidly in my chair, afraid any movement could startle these precious images away like a flock of birds.

Was I selfish in my grief?

There were others who'd known him better; people with whom he'd had a connection that went beyond the fuzzy memories of a long-ago childhood. But the ache in my chest was real. The tightness in my throat was real. The stiffness of my bones, the fire burning my eyes, the chill in my hands—all real.

I'd never fret over Scim riding a unicycle again. Never again fall for his stupid dares to scale unscalable trees. And who knew how many dirty jokes had died with him.

The part in me that treasured these memories sat numb.

Queen Nimcha's red-rimmed eyes stared at a spot on my father's desk. Her skin was the hue of rich soil, almost glowing in its rosy undertones. She sat like a doll, with a blank expression fixed to her face.

Clay stood apart from the rest of us, outside of the sun's rays that were only just beginning to creep through the windows. His clothes were the same as yesterday's, now sporting sharp creases. He appeared to be lost in thought, not listening to my dad's orders, not seeing the manic rush of people in and out of the office.

At that moment, not a day had passed since I'd first met him, a four-year-old visiting his father's pack brother in a foreign land. He didn't have Scimitar's easy likeability or confidence, but the two boys had been close.

With heavy steps, I approached Queen Nimcha.

When I was a shy thirteen-year-old, I was obsessed with her beauty. I'd slathered my face in her brand of face cream to give my skin the same smooth complexion. For Christmas, I'd wished for her brand of perfume, which made men shower her with compliments. Later, I had Clay send me the types of dresses she wore. Colorful and slender, giving her walk a subdued sway. I'd hold them against me in front of a mirror, waiting for the day I'd be tall enough to put them on.

"Hello, Kensington." Queen Nimcha's voice was as sonorous as I remembered.

"Your Majesty." I curtsied. "I am profoundly sorry for your loss."

"Thank you." Her determined, elegant pose smacked of class.

Queen Nimcha held her head high and straight, while her movements smoothly flowed from one into another. Her eyes filled with interest, but their spark was gone.

"What is it?" She took my hand. "Don't be shy."

Up close, her make-up wasn't as precise as I remembered. Her typically perfect manicure had suffered, with rims showing under her nails. Neither detracted from her elegance.

Dad once said that, like all beauty, Queen Nimcha's came from inside. The lift of her chin was fueled by pride in the face of a poverty-ridden childhood. Her expressive eyes were down to great genes, not the mascara she used. And her graceful smile came from a deep sense of empathy.

All that personality inside one woman had been intimidating to a teenaged me.

I dropped my gaze. "This competition wasn't just about the crown. It was about me earning Scimitar's recognition and his respect, the way he'd won mine many times. He was a champion. Someone you could rely on. Above all, he was my friend."

"Thank you for your kind words." She let go of my hand. "It's of great comfort that he will be remembered fondly."

Not sure whether I'd said what I wanted, or if I'd done any good at all, I shuffled toward Clay's corner of the room. For the briefest moment, it seemed he was going to smile, but the flicker of light on his face died too quickly.

All his emotions were there, on his face, especially in his eyes, but none were showing in the way he stood. Like me, he'd been trained in the art of appearing to not give a damn.

"Have they figured out what happened?" I whispered as I positioned myself next to him, shoulder-to-shoulder.

"He fell and hit his head on a rock."

"Scimitar?" I twisted my head up. "The guy who ran faster than a professional athlete, innovated forest freestyle running, and won at least three limbo trophies? *That* Scimitar?"

"Doesn't seem possible, does it?" Clay's quiet voice shook, but to any onlooker, he'd appear indifferent.

Being strong was what was expected of him. One day soon, he'd become the official heir to the crown, but his pack's eyes had been on him since he was a child.

Walk slowly. Straighten your back. Don't cry.

No one understood the confines of the golden cage in which he grew up more than those of us sitting trapped inside our own. At some point, the wall you built became a second skin.

Only Dad and Drake, and maybe Jonah, had glimpsed behind my barriers. Did Clay have a special someone in his life?

I tucked my fingers under my arm so I could touch his shoulder unobserved. "Has your dad been informed?"

"He's coming. At least as soon as he can find the time." He gave a jolt of his chin. "I hope things won't be awkward between him and your father. Scimitar claiming the throne did ruffle feathers, huh?"

"Don't worry about that. My father loved him like family. Nothing's more important."

The door opened, and Glendale approached. He'd been in and out for the past few hours, and each time, his strides seemed heavier. Had he considered Scimitar his friend? They'd clashed occasionally but had also taken fencing, swimming and riding lessons together.

"Your Ma—." Glen cleared his throat. "Your Majesties."

"What is it?" my father bellowed.

"Your Majesties." Glen bowed twice before throwing half a

nod at Clay and me. "The initial autopsy results are in. It appears, Prince Scimitar died of a traumatic brain injury."

Stuff etiquette. No one was watching us, so I arranged my hand on Clay's arm. He needed to feel a friend's touch.

"There are tests that still need to be performed, but the nature of the injury was what the examiner described as coup-contrecoup, meaning the blow was hard enough to cause an injury on both sides of the brain. From the location of the injuries and the blood evidence, Prince Scimitar's death is unlikely to have been an accident."

For a second, the Earth stopped spinning.

Glen wrung his fingers. "He was murdered."

Sixteen

CLAY REACHED OUT, HIS SILENT cry shaping his lips into a circle. His body sagged into my arms.

No idea where I found the strength to support a man twice my size. It was probably the position of my hands on his arm that kept both of us upright. Despite my effort, Clay wobbled as the moment came crashing down on him, rewriting his future into one touched by darkness.

"No. No." Queen Nimcha laid her hand over her forehead as her eyes lost their sheen. "I won't accept this. No."

Dad stood at a distance from her, his mouth distorted by terrible thoughts I couldn't guess.

If I could have thought of a way to offer comfort, to soothe the hurt, I would have, but my body felt frozen. My grip on Clay's body tightened, my lips trembled, and yet every part of me was numb.

Queen Nimcha buried her head in her hands, a display of emotion that startled my father straight. Alphas did not show weakness. Kingdoms stood and fell with their leaders.

I, too, lifted my chin and nudged Clay. By the time Dad's

scrutiny swept over our faces, we were the exemplifications of fortitude and perseverance, at least on the outside.

His look encouraged Clay to aid Queen Nimcha, who clung to her grief as only mothers did. Her open despair unnerved me, and for the first time, my admiration for her wavered. Like any alpha, she was meant to represent her pack; a living, breathing specimen of their values and status. And the Warrior Pack had a fearsome reputation.

On the other hand, she'd lost a son in a cruel upending of the natural order of things. I'd watched my father mourn my mother for the past twenty years, and the loss of a child had to be equally as painful.

Clay lurched to his mother's side and tenderly touched her arm, keeping his lips pressed together. This one gesture of comfort was enough to make her straighten her shoulders and tighten her features. She wouldn't share her grief again until her husband arrived and they could steal a few minutes for themselves.

Drake, my rock, sat on his chair, watching me. Lines were etched on his face, yet his eyes communicated the warmth and presence I'd come to rely on.

This was how I expected an alpha to behave in the face of adversity, uttering neither a whimper nor a flurry of assurances. Later, he'd hear my heartache and tend to my sadness, but here, in this room full of alphas, he'd quietly given me strength and offered compassion without making a spectacle.

My reward for his support was a smile dredged from the depths of my heart.

"Kensi, Drake, will you leave us, please?" Dad asked in his usual baritone.

"Of course." I shot Clay a buck-up smile before I exited with Drake by my side.

The hallway was at peace. Downstairs, however, the kitchen staff had begun breakfast service. Many of our guests who had been invited to our confirmation had selected to stay. The outcome of the Black Forest Cup mattered to them, too. Would have mattered.

The door to my living room fell into the latch and I stood, helpless, before the dining table.

Drake came up behind me and wrapped his arms around my waist, clasping his hand in front of my stomach. He blew warmth onto my neck with his breath. A few days ago, we'd stood like this at Jonah's place, surrounded by friends and joy. It felt like a lifetime ago.

"I'm tired," I announced. "This has been the longest day of my life."

"Let's go to bed." He kissed my cheek and marched into the bedroom.

I followed and sat on the edge of the bed. "No sex, though. Because honestly, I don't think I'd be able to stay awake for it."

"No sex."

"Mhmm."

He understood my lazy response and helped me get my shoes off, then my pants and shirt, and finally the running bra and shorts I still wore underneath.

"I could use a shower." I fell back onto the bed, naked as a newborn, not caring whether he saw me or not.

"Me too." He lifted my blanket and arranged my legs and then the rest of my body underneath. "We'll take care of it tomorrow."

"'kay." I rolled to the side to watch him undress. "How are you holding up, Hasi?"

"You're worried about me?" He pulled down his pants. "You're unbelievable. How are *you*?"

"I have no idea. What I want is to forget about the Cup and the throne and everything, and just cuddle with my husband. Think that'll be okay?"

A shadow fell over his expression, if only for a second.

"Of course." He closed the blinds and climbed into bed before lifting his arm to grant me access to my favorite spot, his chest.

"Thank you." I rested my ear near his heart and let its steady beat guide me to sleep.

~ ~ ~

By the time we woke up, it was early afternoon. My phone showed no missed calls. While I went into the bathroom for a marathon shower session, Drake called Jonah to update him. Once my hair was dry, I joined him for a late breakfast.

"I gotta tell you, German food's growing on me." Drake spread margarine on both sides of his bread roll and surveyed the different types of deli meats.

"I'm glad. I miss it. Not that cereal isn't nice, but nothing beats bread rolls and ham to start the day."

His short hair had almost dried. The delicious scent of his lemon shower gel infused the room, mingling with the promise of a bucketful of caffeine. Once again, he'd followed the dress code: dress pants, ironed shirt, polished black shoes. Suit and tie wouldn't become mandatory until he began royal bootcamp.

When he was full, he collected crumbs off the table and sprinkled them on his plate. "Let's go for a walk. Being cooped up's gonna make us stir crazy."

"I'm in."

We put on our shoes and headed toward the back stairs, where we were unlikely to run into anyone.

The outside temperature was typical of summer, although a moderate breeze added a crispness to the air.

"Feeling better?" he asked as we headed left, toward the tourist end of the castle.

"Physically, yes. As for the rest, it's going to take me a while. Too many questions buzzing, you know."

"Like, who'd want Scimitar dead?"

"Like that one, yes."

"When was the last time you saw him?" He stepped aside to let two kids run past, who were clearly less interested in the castle's architecture than their parents.

I swept my hair over my shoulder. "Ten years ago, give or take. No one would hold a grudge that long. If he was murdered, it wasn't anyone he knew from back then. It could have been random after all."

"I don't know about that. He was a fit and strong werewolf, you said it yourself. A random attacker against superhuman hearing and eyesight? A strong sense of smell? Fast reaction times, with alpha genes to boot? Doesn't sound like your average tourist could have taken him down."

We entered the well-kept visitors' park, where metal benches, ornamental trees, and water fountains in clear lakes dazzled tourists, who took in the scenery mostly on their cell phones.

Drake stepped onto a bridge that spanned the narrow middle of the lake and watched the fish swimming in the water. "It's even possible his killer came from the local pack."

"Oh great. Are you serious?" I glared. "Is this payback for when I accused your pack of harboring a killer?"

"For fuck's sake." He flared his nostrils. "Can we not get through one day without you picking a fight?"

He was the one who kept correcting me and listing my flaws, and now he'd taken aim at *my* pack. My dominance roiled and roared, and it took focus to keep it suppressed.

I closed my eyes to collect myself. "How did they find him in the woods? It's a large place. So, all I'm saying is we don't know anything at this point."

Another group of tourists got off a bus. With the Black Forest Cup in full swing, business was booming. The hotels in town would have been booked out for months, and the castle also did well this time of year.

"We should go back." Drake took a long look at the swans at the far end of the lake before turning around. "Your father might have news by now."

A few minutes later, I gestured to the area behind us. "So? What's the verdict? Do you like it here?"

"The castle's amazing. And the food…" He patted his stomach. "Love that apple seltzer, too. I wonder if the plane will cope with my weight on the way back."

"With hills and nature trails, you'll work it off in no time, don't worry. There's plenty to do."

"What did you do around here, growing up?" His tone was back to pleasant. Drake didn't hold grudges.

I encircled his waist with one arm. "When I didn't have to do homework or attend fencing lessons, I explored the castle's secret passageways, so I could *borrow* cookies and other goodies from the kitchen before they made it to the king."

He stopped in front of the castle's side entrance and regarded it with hesitation. "I don't want to be in your dad's skin right now. All eyes are going to be on him. He might need our support."

"If he needs it, he'll have it, but he's not likely to ask for it. Dad's a proud man." I kissed his cheek. "We might have to twist his arm for his own good."

"Agreed."

We climbed the stairs when a door slammed shut to our left.

Drake's head whipped around, and he stepped toward the source of the noise. "Are these where the ambassadorial suites are?"

"Yes. Most of our guests will be staying in one or several of these rooms. Turn left down there, and you'll get to the Warrior Pack's quarters."

"There are no guards."

"It's safe, don't worry. Any intruder would first have to pass the castle guards downstairs. While you may not see them, they're there, armed and ready. Also, all these rooms are secure."

He stooped for a better look. "I don't see any locks."

"See the ordinary slots under the door handles? The occupants insert disks that are keyed to their rooms. Anyone trying to enter without permission will wish they hadn't. I'm talking security bars dropping from the ceiling, a deafening alarm, and so on."

"How do these disks work?"

"Good question." I pursed my lips, uhm-ed once or twice, and confidently said, "It's a form of werewolf ritual magic thing."

He bumped my waist with his hip. "Is that the trade name they're selling it under?"

I bumped him back. "Once you're prince consort, you can look it up in the library."

He cupped my right butt cheek and squeezed. "The sexy, forbidden one?"

"Dork."

We left the ambassadorial accommodation behind and headed up to the top floor.

Glendale loitered outside our room, his arms crossed.

"Hi, Glen." Maybe my smile would be understood as the conciliatory gesture it was. "How are you holding up?"

"His majesty is waiting in his private quarters for your arrival. Dinner will be served at six." With those heartfelt words, the weasel turned on his heels and walked off.

I raised my chin in his direction. "And that's why he'll be the first one to go once I take the throne."

Drake raised his eyebrows. "Harsh."

"Oh no, was that insensitive?" I asked. "I didn't mean to imply that, now that Scim's dead, the throne is mine again. Not at all. I'm not even thinking that far ahead."

My flaws were glaring and many, but I'd cared about Scim. I couldn't bear it if Drake thought of me as an ice queen.

"It's okay. I understood what you meant." He made a calming

gesture. "And it's fair to assume your confirmation will go ahead, unless Clay's thinking of staking his claim, too."

"That's not funny." I pursed my lips briefly and then let out a sigh.

"We'll know our future soon enough." He snaked his arm around my waist and led me toward Dad's living room. "Let's not keep your father waiting."

SEVENTEEN

AT SIX, WE ENTERED MY father's living room and sat at the table. Food was served by three women who bowed so much, it was a miracle they didn't drop any of their bread baskets. Next, they brought in a selection of cheeses, lunch meat, and several salads. The only thing missing was my dad.

"No cheese pasta today?" Drake whispered.

"Typically, warm food is eaten for lunch, or 'noon food,' as Germans call it. This here is what the traditional dinner you'd find in most homes looks like."

"Didn't know that."

"Yes, it's shocking how little attention your history books pay to Germany's food-related customs." I shook my head. "Anyway, you have white bread, black bread, and gray bread."

"That's a lot of bread."

"We call this meal 'evening bread.' I know, we're masters of stating the obvious."

Dad entered through the door connecting to his private study. "You shouldn't have waited."

He wore the same suit as he had earlier. I'd have been surprised if he'd seen the insides of his eyelids in the past thirty-six hours.

"Of course we waited." That said, my stomach wasn't merely ready but pointblank giddy to accept sustenance.

"Has Kensi shown you the sights?" Dad spread margarine across a slice of gray bread and laid a thick slice of cheese and then a thin layer of strawberry jam on top. "You should get to know your future home. Which reminds me, as soon as the dust has settled, your confirmation will go ahead."

"May I ask about the elephant in the room?" Drake opted for ham on black rye bread, which he seemed to relish despite his initial reluctance.

If the landscape couldn't convince him to move to Germany, the food would seal the deal.

"Scimitar, you mean?" Dad helped himself to a large gulp of apple seltzer. "The humans have closed the case, which means we open ours. Delta will be heading the investigation."

"Delta?" I crinkled my nose.

Dad propped himself up with his elbows on the table. "Grieving will have to wait. Pack life continues."

"Can we help?" I exchanged a crafty look with Drake.

"I appreciate that, Schatz, but don't worry about me."

Drake subtly jolted his chin in encouragement. He had no concept of how stubborn my father could be.

"Why don't you let Drake shadow you for a while?" I perked up my voice. "What better way to learn the ropes?"

Dad's chin sagged slightly. "Now?"

"Wasn't Drake's royal bootcamp on the schedule anyway?" I fluttered my eyelashes. "As you said, life continues."

Dad bobbed his head from left to right as if debating the pros and cons in his head. "Yes, sure. We'll give it a try and see how it goes."

"I appreciate that." Drake sounded pleased, and yet he afforded me a nasty look.

I returned the glare. Why the attitude? Supporting my dad in this difficult time had been his idea.

"No time like the present." Dad let out a hard breath of air. "Pack loans are waiting to be dispensed and payments collected, which means I'll be reading documents and dictating letters tonight. Drake can learn our filing system."

"A bit of a demotion," I mumbled, disappointed. "He deals with loans and stuff every day as Jonah's protector."

"This isn't Jonah's pack." Dad's tone sharpened. "If he doesn't want to learn—"

"I will learn everything you have to teach." Drake, the suck-up, dialed up the charm.

As Dad steered his stern gaze in my direction, a suspiciously bright glint crawled into his eyes. "That will leave you unsupervised, which is rarely a good thing. Don't even think of interfering in Delta's investigation."

"Wouldn't dream of it. Although I want it on record that I've solved my share of murders, while Delta has been dealing with the theft of paper clips."

"I'm not kidding around, Kensington. You're a princess, and I expect you to behave accordingly. Have I made myself clear?"

Heat rose to my cheeks and my ears. Way to embarrass me in front of my husband.

"Fine." I worked a mighty frown onto my face, the sulky mouth's bigger sister.

"I'm sorry." Dad sounded resigned. "I'm worried. According to my advisers, and a very persuasive Delta, the person with the strongest incentive to kill Scimitar is you. You and Drake, to be precise."

I sat back, my spine straight as a pole. Me, a killer? Was this a fucking joke?

"That's ridiculous." Drake threw me an incredulous look. "Did you know about this?"

I gestured in a circular motion at my face. "Do I look like I knew?"

"If Scimitar had won the Black Forest Cup, your crown would have been his," Dad said. "Now, he won't get the chance. That's a strong motive."

"That's a stupid motive." I dropped my shoulders. "Tell Delta to take a closer look at Glendale. He seemed to have known about Scim's challenge before any of us."

"Kensington." Dad slapped the table, making the silverware clang. "For the last time. Until the real killer has been apprehended, we will give Delta our support."

"Yeah, okay." I lowered my gaze, even though the alpha in me was spoiling for a fight. "Jeez."

Dad formed a pyramid with his hands as if to center himself. "Good. This is important."

"You've gone quiet." I fixated Drake with a scowl. "They suspect you, too. Aren't you angry?"

"Angry? I'm not angry. What I am is tired." He picked up his glass, his grip strong enough to turn his knuckles white. "Tired of being accused of murders I didn't commit."

EIGHTEEN

I KEPT MY POISE UNTIL WE'D reached our living room, and even then I didn't explode. Instead, I sat in a chair at the dining table and fumed.

Delta might play a small role in the day-to-day running of the pack, but a full-blown murder was a step up from checking property boundaries and investigating mismanaged funds.

Taking interviews, reading boring reports, sitting through endless stakeouts, consulting with experts—he had no idea of the hard work a major case involved.

Drake stalked awkwardly in circles like a hunter wading through marshy undergrowth.

"This sucks." I spat out the words, feeling they deserved to be heard. "Having to watch Delta stumble his way through the investigation is bad enough, but his failure could ruin my future. How can I lead a pack when this suspicion hangs over me like a comic-strip rain cloud?"

"Delta has a job to do, so let him do it, and let him do it without looking over his shoulder. Christ, he hasn't even started, and already you're complaining about him." Drake fell into his chair and instantly crossed his arms. "That's all you do. I know you've been hurt, but negativity isn't going to change anything."

Negativity? What did he expect? My life had been good before I'd met him and his charmed small-town existence. I'd had a good job, a great new condo, and plenty of friends. Cue the Moon Promise. Its magic had offered love with one hand while stealing just about everything else with the other. Now even my crown was moving further out of reach.

"You don't know anything." My tone flattened. "I don't *want* to doubt Delta. I don't want to hate him or any of my pack members, and I'm so goddamn tired of feeling on edge when I'm near them."

"Then give him a chance and stay out of it. You're not kids anymore." His eyes dipped into dark grays I hadn't seen before.

"If I lose my throne—"

"For fuck's sake. If this doesn't work out, we'll go back to Marlontown and still have a good life."

His explosion sent my mind into a tailspin. My airways folded into loops and knots, creating a crushing pressure inside my chest.

Going back to Colorado sounded so easy, and for Drake, it would be. He'd comfortably slip back into his role as a protector, beloved by his pack. Me? I'd be his wife. Period. Ten years from now, I'd still be his wife. A small town had little use for a private eye.

I held on to the table with both hands. "Is that what you want? Go back?"

"Don't put words into my mouth." He did something screwy with his lips I couldn't figure out, although his words made his frustration clear enough.

A woman dressed in a discreet black jacket and skirt arrived, pushing a cart with our evening coffee, cupcakes, and two cups into the living room. Her buttoned-up uniform and subdued demeanor epitomized the future waiting for me in Marlontown.

"Jeez." I got up and put on my shoes, disgusted at throwing a pity party for myself.

This woman may not be a doctor or a CEO, but she was earning money, working for a king, no less. Who was I to look down on her?

"Where are you going?" Drake spun around, keeping his tone level, probably so as not to spook the help.

"I can't help it if they consider me a murderer." I gave an arms-only shrug. "But if that's the lie they told Clay, I need to speak to him."

"You're going to visit him now?"

"It's only seven o'clock." I directed my finger to the wall clock, which consisted of a white disk with Roman numerals and had probably cost a fortune. "Clay might need me."

"He's not a child. He's a grown man." He moved to the side to allow the woman to pour his coffee.

"What are you so upset about anyway?" I gave him a piercing look. "Aren't you helping my father tonight?"

He stared at me, or rather through me, as if I was made of glass. "Right."

Without a goodbye kiss, I stormed out.

Drake had a way of understanding me when I least expected it. Trouble was, he often didn't seem to like what he found inside my head. On some levels, we were peas in a pod and birds of a flock. More and more often, though, he wanted to fix me.

But I wasn't broken. Sure, I couldn't deny my childhood had wounded me; but I was walking, scrapping, fighting. That had to be good enough.

In the hallway leading to Clay's rooms, I ran a finger along the wall, feeling the bumpy stone under the paint. Our castle had witnessed its share of conflicts and yet it had patiently endured. Maybe patience was the key to success.

"Where are you sneaking off to?" Glen's voice stopped me in my tracks.

Thick, brown hair framed faint creases around his eyes. The full lips he'd inherited from his mother used to be a total chick magnet. The most marked change in my childhood bully, however, was that his skeletal cheekbones had filled out. He may not have been born with dominant genes, but he'd nevertheless grown into a commanding figure of a man.

I straightened to a more impressive height. "I'm going to visit Clay, not that it's any of your business."

"Oh, Kensi, Kensi, Kensi." He stepped around me to block my path. "I thought you'd have changed over the years, but you're still the same snob, aren't you? Thinks the sun shines out of her ass."

The initial stabbing pain in my heart quickly stopped. Now as before, it was "Your Royal Highness" and "Princess Kensington" when Dad was within earshot. The minute we were alone, out came the "asses" and the "what the hells."

"Strange." I scoffed. "I thought you'd acquired at least the maturity of a jellyfish by now."

Dad had drilled into me not to play by Glen's rules. True alphas did not insult or mock. They put their foot down and commanded.

How disappointed my father would be.

"Why would our precious princess leave her mate behind to visit another man?" Glen crossed his arms but remained obstinately rooted on the spot. "Trouble in paradise?"

"I want to see if Clay's okay. He's a friend. If you don't know the meaning of the word, look it up." I switched my facial expression to neutral. "While I have you here, let me ask you. The idea to challenge my claim to the throne. Did you put it into Scimitar's head?"

"Of course not." He stood so close, the hairs on his chin zoomed into focus.

I raised my eyebrows. "You checked out a book dealing with exactly that situation."

The rims of his ears turned an angry red. "Scimitar called *me*. He asked what would happen if more than one person had a claim to be named the royal heir. I thought it was, I don't know, hypothetical. He was quite a character."

"His questions about the rules of succession didn't strike you at all as oddly specific?"

"In hindsight, sure. Maybe they did at the time. But I wouldn't have thought in a million years he'd do what he did. Would you?"

"No." My vision lost focus, blurring Glen's face into a ball of fog. "Not in a million years."

"I'm not even sure it was his idea to begin with." He undid his shirt's top button and leaned against the wall, with one leg crossed over the other. "When he quizzed me about our laws, he made his contempt for them clear."

"How do you mean?"

"It's a feeling I got. Like, he was complaining how we weren't that different from free packs, and why didn't we all go bashing in each other's brains the way they did instead of pretending we were civilized."

"You're saying he hated the fact that he could challenge me, yet challenge me he did. Go figure. One more mystery for Delta to solve."

"You don't have faith in Delta?" Glen lowered his voice.

"It's not that. Dad says some people think Drake or I had a motive to kill Scimitar. Do you agree?" I watched for a reaction.

"Maybe you had a motive, but I don't think you're a killer." He worked up a smile that almost seemed friendly. "Your mate, on the other hand…"

"If you believe I didn't kill Scim, please believe I wouldn't have picked a killer for a husband."

"Women don't always make smart choices when it comes to husbands." He gave me a thorough look that itself gave nothing away. "Not for nothing, but they do even worse when it comes to mates."

Was he yanking my chain or being seriously misogynistic?

"Your turn." He scratched his nose. "Did you honestly believe I'd invite a foreign prince to challenge you for the throne?"

Ah. That.

I flaunted a smile I hoped was enigmatic and pushed past him. "Make sure Delta doesn't screw this up. If he does, it'll be your ass I kick."

"Tell me something I don't know," he mumbled with an unexpected lightness of tone.

Weirdly, I walked away with a bounce in my step. Never before had we had a conversation that could pass for amicable. Maybe there was hope for him yet.

I marched up to Clay's door, stoked by this upturn of events. If my former enemy didn't consider me guilty of Scim's murder, Clay wouldn't believe the accusation either.

I knocked forcefully. Three seconds later, Clay opened the door. His eyes widened.

I raised a hand. "Before you say anything, you know I wouldn't hurt Scimitar, right?"

He stepped back and crossed his arms. Once again, he stood rigidly, discouraging any inquiry as to his wellbeing.

"Clay?"

His gaze drifted to the hall behind me and then back to my face. "Yeah, I know."

Before meeting Drake's Wild Pack, I hadn't been a touchy-feely person, but I'd since discovered the benefits of everyday physical contact.

So I spread my arms and slung them around Clay's neck. "I'm so, so sorry."

"I know that, too." He abandoned his resistance and rested his hands on my back, completing the embrace. Slowly, his breaths became deeper, his shoulders relaxed.

"Does any of it seem real to you?" I untangled us. "Because it doesn't to me."

He let me in and trudged to his sofa, where he sat like a sack of potatoes. "Who'd kill him? Everyone loved him."

"Of course, we loved him." I sat next to him and grabbed his forearm with both hands. "The few who held no great affection still respected him."

"This is so messed up." He rubbed his hands across his face as if trying to wake up. "Okay. Come on, Kens. You're a detective. Detect."

"If only."

"I'm serious."

"So am I." I cut his objection off with a swipe of my hand. "I'm too close to this. Besides, my father specifically forbade it."

"Your father also said not to sneak out at night."

"Touché." I crossed my right leg over my left. "But we're no longer children. We're the children of kings, and disobeying our alpha's command isn't a healthy option."

"Hypothetically, where would you start your investigation?"

"Hypothetically?" I dragged the word and stared at the ceiling's recessed lights. "I usually start with the victim. But we shouldn't—"

"You knew Scimitar pretty well." Clay wiggled down into his seat until his shoulder came to rest against mine. "So that takes care of that."

"Assuming he was still the same guy. Next, I'd make a list of possible motives."

"That's obvious. Hate. Someone smashed his head in. Hardly a matter of self-defense. Only, who'd have hated him that much?"

"I have no idea." I puffed up my cheeks and then let out a long stream of air. "In truth, brutal murders can be motivated by a slew of different emotions. Hate's only one of them."

"What else is there?"

"Like, did Scimitar get in the way of anybody's convictions?" I fumbled with my fingers, lost inside a bad memory for a second. "This motive is rare, but since I once nearly died because of the convictions of an unhinged person, I thought I'd mention it."

"You nearly died?" His jaw seemed to relax before tensing up. "What happened?"

"A wolf who didn't like mixing with humans happened. He

took his narrow-mindedness deadly seriously. Anyway, as I said, that's a rare one. Next, there's money or power. Was anyone hurt financially by Scimitar, or did he threaten anyone's power?"

"Yours, I guess."

I shot him a thorough glare. "It wasn't me."

"Sorry. A bad joke, that's all." He mhmm-ed for a while. "No, I'm certain my brother didn't owe a cent or blackmail anyone."

"Speaking of blackmail, stopping Scimitar from blabbing could be a motive, too. Maybe he saw something during the Black Forest Cup he wasn't supposed to see."

"Like what?" Clay laid his arm next to mine, his palm up and fingers wiggling.

Unable to deny him a connection with a more warm-blooded creature than his mother, I laid my hand in his. "Maybe a couple of competitors used the Cup for shady deals, or Scimitar overheard them conspire to commit a crime."

"Now we're talking."

"Love's also a popular motive for murder."

"Scimitar was loved by many people, but he hasn't had a girlfriend for months." Clay lifted our intertwined hands. "He did once have a crush on you."

I swung my head around. "On me? What? When?"

"Last time we were all together. Remember how he nearly broke his leg jumping across the stream?"

"You mean when he fell ass-first into the water? Yeah. I was what, sixteen, seventeen? He was showing off. Although he did find that pretty flower he gave me, so I didn't rib him too hard."

"He only jumped across to get you that flower, dummy."

"No way." I nudged him.

Clay shoved me back. "Yes way."

"Crazy." I let go of his hand and found a throw-pillow to cover my face with. "I swear I didn't know."

"Now you do."

"Hang on." I lowered the throw-pillow and pivoted my butt

until I sat facing him. "You're screwing with me. You jumped the stream, too. You two were constantly competing against each other. I remember, because that year, the doctor announced you were done with your surgeries."

"I jumped for the competition. He jumped to impress a girl."

I play-punched his arm. "Are you saying you didn't have a crush on me, too? How disappointing."

"Oww." He rubbed his bicep. "Anyway. I'd say love as a motive is out."

"I like the 'Scim knew something he wasn't supposed to know' theory best."

"Then we should go to the Cup's camp tomorrow and ask around. Someone could have seen something."

"I'm sorry." I stretched out my legs and studied the toes of my shoes. "This isn't the time to disobey my alpha's orders."

"I'm going anyway." Clay took a few thoughtful breaths. "If you happen to be free, I'll be needing a translator."

He'd caught me in a vulnerable moment. Things between Drake and me were shaky. I couldn't face my husband's disappointment in me. Worse, I had no idea how to repair the damage to our relationship. A distraction would be perfect.

Except, my marriage wasn't the only thing under pressure. Between Scimitar's death, the crown's guests, and everyday pack business, Dad's dance card was full. A princess on her way toward becoming a queen wouldn't add to his worries. This was my chance to prove I was his worthy heir.

Clay's stare softened and he lowered his head. "It's okay. I shouldn't have asked."

Some things, like friendships, were important enough to take a risk. My friend's determination to chase ghosts to avenge the senseless loss of his brother cracked my heart. What broke it into pieces was the idea of him doing so alone.

I set my jaw and met his gaze. "It's okay. I'll be your interpreter."

Nineteen

Drake spent the morning brooding. The living room was large, huge in fact, but he was a big man, so watching him pace in circles was like being trapped with an elephant inside a caravan.

Even though I was no longer angry at him, keeping quiet about my plans with Clay felt like an anchor around my shoulder. But he wouldn't approve. In fact, I had trouble meeting his eyes.

Today's lunch was roast chicken with potato salad, but neither he nor I showed much of an appetite.

"Are you really considering returning to Marlontown?" I pulled some meat off the bones but didn't eat it. My throat had become too narrow to force food down it.

"Unless things change, what choice is there? Your father hates me, I'm standing accused of being a murderer—again—and you're carrying on behind my back, doing your own thing and to hell with the rest of us."

"I don't know about my dad, but you're making too big a deal out of last night. I visited a friend. That's all." I crinkled my nose as I put my fork down. "Would you, I mean, would you leave me behind?"

Drake pushed his plate to the side. "Would you want to come with me? Doing so would ruin your chances of becoming alpha queen."

Those chances were already low. Without him by my side, they were zero. Finding the strength to continue my fight for the throne? I wouldn't even know where to look. Besides, we'd spent every day together since our Moon Promise, and a life without him was unimaginable.

Drake arranged his interlocked fingers on the table. "Your silence wasn't what I expected."

"As always, my brain's trying to beat down my heart," I whispered. "In truth, I'd follow you anywhere, the way you followed me to Germany. But please understand: as excited as I am about my life with you, whatever its form, I'm every bit as terrified of giving up the only future I've ever known."

"I'm not ready to capitulate either, but we need a plan in case this situation gets worse. A plan we both agree on." He blew out a short breath. "I'm sorry. I was frustrated and let my anger out on you. It felt like you'd pimped me out to your father, so you could spend time with Clay."

"I wasn't pimping you out. I genuinely took on board what you said about Dad being stressed and figured you could support him. You're a protector and familiar with the work he does. I would probably just get in the way."

"You wouldn't be in the way." He smiled, and the sight of it filled my heart. "In all fairness, last night wasn't entirely lousy. Stirling's had to travel, leaving your father to do the work of two. I managed to take some admin off his hands. That was pretty awesome."

We were moving back into sync. Underneath the quarreling and the barbed comments beat the heart of our love. Maybe it was unbreakable.

Not that I was willing to put it to the test.

"I keep telling you, you're adorable." I rounded the table and sauntered toward him. "If Dad lets you do his paperwork, he likes you. Trust me."

"Maybe he's warming up to me. We'll see."

I lowered my gaze to the comfort of the solid ground. "This whole relationship thing, you know. It's a learning curve, I guess."

He pulled me into his lap. "We can keep the training wheels on for a while. There's no rush."

"Good." I gestured at his chest. "You're looking awfully snazzy again, by the way. Any plans I don't know about, or did you pretty yourself up for me?"

He lifted the collar of his gray shirt as if he felt uncomfortable, but his nervous ticks couldn't take away his edgy confidence. This modern version of him was no less attractive than the small-town boy I married.

He gave a tentative smile, wide enough to push dimples into his cheeks. "I'll wear whatever you want me to as long as we're together. And I don't mean as long as we're in the same room. I want a real relationship, Kensi. A beautiful, ugly, complicated, messy relationship with the woman I love."

My ribcage expanded, allowing my breath to circulate again.

"That's all I want, too," I whispered. "Everything has gone so wrong."

"We'll figure it out."

"Until then, maybe we could…" I gave a suggestive whistle and eyed the bedroom door.

"Here I was hoping for an honest conversation, and you can't wait to get me into bed." He kissed my neck. "I don't want you to lose your respect for me."

"I'll respect you when you're naked." I slid off his lap and pulled him up.

Drake didn't need much encouragement. His lips were on me

by the time we'd reached the door. His tongue was inside me a second later. Minutes after that, we were on the bed, where we playfully fought for control, rolling this way and that, until he stopped moving.

"Here we go again," he said. "I don't want to make love only to your body. I want to make love to your mind. Be one with you."

"Okay. Sounds good." I undid the first three buttons on his shirt. "Any idea how we do that?"

"None." He brushed aside my hand and flopped onto his back. "I have this love for you. It's not just huge, it's all-consuming. Sometimes its power threatens to swallow me whole, maybe even to rip the sanity from my mind."

"Oh." Guess he wasn't into a quickie after all. I felt myself still, letting the passion in his words wash over me.

"Like the souls of our ancestors, I want ours to fuse." He swung his head to the side. "Damn. Listen to me. Think my sanity's already a lost cause?"

"No, I don't." I trembled and closed my eyes. "This is how I feel, too. When I say I love you, those aren't just words. When I search for approval in your eyes, I'm not simply being insecure. I can't say if the Moon Promise ritual put a curse on us or if it gave us a gift. What I do know is you've become the air I breathe and the wind on my skin, and yet it's not enough. Jeez. Sometimes it's like I can barely feel you."

"I'm right here." He took my hand and pressed it against his chest. "All you have to do is talk to me."

Drake had proven his commitment to our relationship over and over. He'd told me he'd see to it that his pack would welcome me, and he hadn't let me down. He'd promised to follow me to Germany, which he'd done without complaint. If he thought communication was the way to saving our relationship, what was there to do but take him by his word?

"It's going to be messy," I warned.

"Messy's good." He propped himself up on his elbow and brushed a strand of my hair aside. "Just tell me what's on your mind."

With my brain empty, I'd have to rely on my heart to find the right words. "When Scimitar turned up, the idea I could lose the throne scared me only a little. It didn't seem like it could happen, you know, because you gave me strength. I'm not talking about your words or your actions, although they helped. No, your presence was everything I needed to keep on going. Then…"

My gaze darted around the room. What, if I told him what was on my mind, and he'd think it was silly? What if he didn't understand?

"It's okay," he coaxed.

"Earlier, when you said you might return to Marlontown, for the first time, it felt like I could really lose my crown, because of course I'd go with you. There's no doubt about that. But that certainty took me by surprise. I've always prided myself on being independent."

"The two of us being together doesn't change that."

"Yes, it does. Every action I take affects you. You can tell me a thousand times you'll be okay, but I still worry about what my decision will mean for you. So, I guess what I'm saying is, yes, the crown is something I want, but wants and dreams are just that. They're things that aren't real yet. You are real *now*. My love for you goes deeper than wants and dreams. It just is. No matter how much you protest and no matter how much I complain about it, our love is."

He lightly brushed a finger over my hand. "That frightens you."

"It terrifies me. And it's also wonderful."

He lightly kissed my mouth. "Yes, it is. But you should know I will do whatever it takes to give you what you want. Not because I owe you, but because I want you to be happy."

"That's why I want you to have everything you want, too." I brushed his already short hair aside. "Only, I don't know what that is."

He trailed his finger down my cheek and let it circle my lips.

"I want you" He tapped the tip of my nose. "I love my pack, every one of them, but I want you to become the queen you deserve to be. I believe in you. Don't look at me like that. I'm not your cheerleader. You have the drive and the strength to lead a pack, and watching you do exactly that, that's what will make me happy. It's going to be awesome."

"But what about you? Where do you want to fit in?"

"Being an alpha has never been in the cards for me. While I'll happily give my life to defend my pack, the idea of killing another to seize power repulses me. I'm not talking about some bastard alpha who has it coming, but killing someone like Jonah? Never. Maybe that makes me weak." He looked at me with the trust of a puppy. "But I cannot be irrelevant either. I want my life to have meaning."

Not long ago, I'd been worried about being stuck in Marlontown without a role in life. What made me think he wasn't having the same concerns about his future in Germany?

"There has to be a compromise." I smacked the mattress. "You know how to relate to people and understand our kind better than I ever will. You spot history's mistakes in today's patterns. In many ways, you're better equipped for royal life than me. So I promise, when the time comes, you will not be a token partner. You are, and always will be, my real partner. Okay?"

"Okay." He kissed me without hurry.

The words we'd spoken were many, and unsophisticated, and would make poor love letters in written form, but they'd been the words straight from the heart.

Even while our tongues connected, the real contact between us took place further down, where his hand held onto my waist. The feel of it was exquisite in its tenderness. For many men, this would be a gesture of control, but not for Drake. His fingers would leave no mark on my skin. Their influence took root further down, in my stomach and between my legs.

He shifted his hand onto my hip as his breathing intensified. His grip tightened, maybe because there was less soft flesh here. He pushed himself closer while pulling my body toward him.

On their tips, his fingers tapped toward my ass. Around to the front, and up, where they undid my button and zipper. One digit at a time slipped inside my pants to my panties. He lifted the elastic to—

He sucked in air so suddenly, I opened my eyes mid-kiss and pulled away. Something in his face had changed. Not the strong, rounded jaw. Nor his high cheekbones, or his expressive eyebrows. The *otherness* came from his eyes. They seemed to glow, and not from a reflection of light either, but from within.

His finger plunged into me, forcing a moan from my lips. He'd met no resistance on his way in nor on his way out. Physically, I'd been ready.

He smiled smiled. "I love you," he said.

"I love—"

His finger entered me again, drawing another sharp intake of air from me.

This wasn't how we made love. We got naked first. There was a process. I gave a disapproving look, hoping for remorse. Instead, the expression on his face became predatory with a hard, unyielding edge.

"Are you okay, Hasi?" I asked.

His features softened, and he nodded.

I held my hand against his cheek and resumed our kiss, mingling my warmth with his. His tongue nudged gently here, coaxed with more urgency there.

He removed his finger from my pants.

I stilled. This wasn't what I'd wanted to happen either. What was he doing?

The kiss continued, both of us probing, letting our passion grow.

But where was his hand? It should be somewhere on my body.

Squeezing my ass. Teasing between my legs. Doing *something*, for crying out loud.

I opened my eyes and nudged him away. "What's going on?"

"What do you mean?" His innocent tone didn't sound true.

"Your eyes glowed. That's number one."

"My eyes glowed. Seriously?" He chuckled. "A trick of the light, I'm sure."

I felt myself blink quickly. "Okay then. But why have you stopped touching me?"

"Touching you how?"

"Drake, I don't know what it is you're doing."

"Neither do I. In fact, it's time you told me what it is you want me to do in bed. I want to make love to you, but I'm done guessing."

"You've been doing fine so far. No complaints."

"Not long ago you accused me of favoring one breast over the other. What you didn't tell me was whether that was good, or if you'd prefer the other one, or if you want me to spend time on both equally. We're communicating. Remember?"

"Oh." I pursed my lips.

"Hell, Kensi, if you don't want to—"

"No, I want. I mean, our usual way of having sex has always worked for me. Although, well, earlier, with your fingers, you surprised me." My core wiggled from the memory. "I liked that very much."

"Yeah?"

"Yes. I like my life to be organized, but maybe a surprise here or there would be nice. And for your information, I have no favorite breast. I was merely noting the fact that *you* seemed to have one, and I don't like that you pick it for expediency."

"There's no expediency involved with you. Ever." His raspy intensity made my pelvic muscles contract as if he were already inside me.

I lifted my knee and slipped my foot up his leg to his ass. "What is it that *you* want?"

"I love what you're doing right now. On top or under me makes no difference in terms of my level of enjoyment. I do like noise, especially when you shout out my name. And maybe..."

He had no way of knowing what this conversation was already doing to my composure, but hell, this kind of foreplay was as good as any we'd had before.

Forcing my breathing to slow, I casually lifted my chin. "Out with it. What else?"

"I love it when your knees are all the way up, like this." He arranged himself between my legs and pulled them up, pushing the bulge in his pants against the seam of mine. "And then, rather than squeezing my waist, you could open wide."

He pried apart my knees to leave me with a sense of utter vulnerability.

"Really?" Heat rushed into my head, and I was beginning to crave the feeling of him inside me.

We hadn't even undressed yet.

"Think you can do that for me?" His words dripped into me like honey.

"Yeah." I cleared my throat. "I can do that."

My breathing was all over the place now. This hadn't been how I'd expected this to go. But his madness was working, because I was lying under him in my shirt and pants, and I'd never been wetter in anticipation.

He dug into the back of my slacks and pulled them and my panties past my ass all the way down. His dress pants took him even less time, and he was already inside me while we were still ridding ourselves of our shirts.

By the time my bra came off, my body was trembling as my walls closed tight around his shaft. He kneeled before me, his thighs supporting my ass, and moved back and forth without apparent rhythm.

My ears were humming. My breath hitched here and there, before coming out in one long exhalation, followed by a couple of short intakes. This wasn't the most effective way to get air into my lungs, but I was barely hanging on.

He raised his eyebrows, his upper body stiff while his length pushed into me in regular strokes.

Oh hell. Okay. I could do this. As my knees rose up and widened, my lips opened, too. My mouth felt dry, and no words found their way out. This was how he wanted it, and I was going to make sure he'd get his wish.

He leaned forward, and I spread my knees even further. He closed his eyes and sank into me with a deep groan, almost wolfish in its nature.

A shudder ran down my spine. If this was doing it for him, it was definitely working for me.

His lips clamped around my breast, and the overload of sensation caused my head to lift off the pillow.

He pushed his hand against the inside of my knee to open my legs wider still.

I let out a moan, and my wolf stirred inside me. *She* sat up, intrigued, waiting to see where this experiment was going.

His sweat became my sweat, his shaft became a part of me. Every time he withdrew, he tore a chunk out of me. Every time he returned, the reunion was all the sweeter.

He kept my legs apart, his full length buried in me for longer with each push.

"Yes," I mumbled as I fell into the rush of endorphins.

He switched between my breasts.

"No." I nudged his head back to the other one. "You were right. The left one's better."

He did as I'd asked, and the pressure inside my head amplified. How much could my brain take before it disintegrated?

He moved a hand to my clit and began manipulating it.

My eyes fell shut as more sensations arrived from every corner of my body.

He growled again, and her head, my wolf's head, lifted. I moaned, wanted to cling to him with my knees, but forced myself to stay open. This was what he wanted. And just as he'd taken my direction a minute ago, it was my turn to give him what he needed.

He ran his teeth over my nipple.

"Yes." I nearly laughed, if only to release the tension in my brain, but a new wave was already building between my legs.

He deserted my breast to kiss my mouth, deep and hard, denying me oxygen. I became disoriented, gripped his shoulder hard, made a wheezing sound, when he pulled back to play with my breast again. My desperate gasps for air became groans as he thrust into me with his full weight.

"Yes," I shouted. "God, Drake, yes."

As my senses tunneled in on sensations alone, things got fuzzy. I remembered signals arriving from across my body—the hardness of his mouth on mine, the skilled tickling of my clitoris, his powerful pushes inside me, the soft, wet plucks of my nipples. Never before had I had so little control over my body, and never before had I relished it so much.

"Drake," I whispered.

His wolf replied.

I felt it underneath his chest.

"Drake," I called.

He growled in a way no human throat was capable of.

I opened my eyes, and there it was. Two gray irises that swirled and glinted, and inside, a pacing wolf. A powerful focused animal with a voracious appetite, but not lusting for food. It looked at me, at her, bared its teeth, just as his tip slid in for another push.

Caught between Drake the Man and Drake the Wolf, neither I nor *she* dared move.

"Drake," I pleaded.

I didn't know if he was still capable of speaking. He grunted with his motions, moved faster, and then let out a long growl that tore into my flesh. *She* trotted forward, cautiously. Again, I struggled to keep sane, to keep breathing, to keep still.

He readjusted my legs, landed so far inside he struck a wall, just as my wolf pounced.

"Drake," I wanted to shout, but *she* was in charge now.

She growled. He growled.

Drake teased my clit. *She* purred.

He thrust hard. The heat inside my head pushed against my eardrums, my throat, as more pressure rushed up from below.

My body rocked, trembled, shook as if I was on fire. My mind exploded in a howl, in a freaking howl I couldn't voice, but *she* could. His wolf joined in.

And then we lay, intertwined, breathing hard.

Whatever it was that had just happened, our relationship would never be the same. He'd met my wolf. *She'd* met his. And *she* approved of him very, very much.

No argument, no murder allegation, no crown could split those two apart. *She* lay coiled up inside me now, satisfied, feeling loved, and though her face would never show it, inside, *she* smiled.

<h1 style="text-align:center">TWENTY</h1>

IN THE EARLY EVENING, DRAKE and I went up Solstice Hill, which offered the highest local peak. The sun was out, and, even though the castle was in deep mourning, I was just so damn happy. No one watched us slip out the side entrance, and no one was there to watch us get naked in front of each other and shift into our animal forms.

After ten minutes of running, as the trees grew thinner and less dense, we reached a clearing set up as a picnic area, with wooden tables and benches. There, we sat on our haunches and chilled. A wisp of stratus clouds in the blue sky guided our sight all the way to the Swiss Alps. In the valley at our feet, a wildly undulating sea of trees shimmered in a hundred shades of pale green, interrupted sporadically by small villages and towns.

I nudged Drake's neck with my nose. *Look. All ours.*

It wasn't easily possible to compare this view to the Rocky Mountains, and the color impact of our surroundings would have been greater when viewed through human eyes, but hopefully, he'd see the beauty I saw. I licked his fur and his snout, drinking in his silver gaze. What had linked us earlier was at once ancient and brand new, and I carried that connection inside, heavy with warmth and comfort.

Since Drake's wolf didn't have hug-enabled arms, I snuggled up against his soft fur and listened to the rhythm of our breaths. With the heat of his body flowing into me, we lay below the sun until its strength was waning.

When we headed back, in human form, down the hill, a lightning strike couldn't have wiped the happy grin off my face.

"Next time, let's bring a picnic and a bottle of wine," he said. "Local wine. Your dad promised me a taste, remember?"

"That reminds me. I have a surprise for you." I almost skipped with excitement. "I've booked you into a private wine tasting later."

"As in, just me?" He grounded me with a look. "What about you?"

"I love showing you around, but I also want you to experience this place on your own. Meet people. Have fun."

The softness of the earth had withstood another day of sunshine, with the ground springing back as soon as my feet lifted for the next stride.

"What will you be doing while I'm gone?" He positioned his arm across my shoulders. "Pining for me?"

"Um, of course." I smiled so hard it hurt because it was no longer fueled by honesty.

He would not approve of my plans with Clay.

"Okay then," he said. "Wine tasting sounds like it could be fun. Do I smell and spit, or will I be allowed to swallow?" He laughed so hard the movement rocked back his head.

"You make wine tasting sound dirty." I shoulder-checked him as we stepped through the castle's side door. "Anyway, do whatever gets you off. No one will find out except you and Croydon, the man in charge. He's been around forever, and he knows the area really well. He's excited to meet a fellow history buff."

We had dinner together with the candles lit, and then I sent him on his way, waving him off like a good wife before slipping out of my room for my meeting with Clay.

Tomorrow, I'd come clean. Drake had been dead set against my meddling in the investigation, and I fully agreed with him. Meddling wasn't what I was doing, though.

To be honest, I wasn't sure what I was doing. Drake and I were finally on the right track, and I wasn't going to risk our relationship for anything. And if I'd been thinking clearly, I'd have canceled tonight's excursion. In fact, I'd had my hand poised, ready to dial Clay's number, several times. Then I remembered Clay's face when he learned about his brother's violent death. I remembered his determination to question witnesses, to do something, anything, as long as he didn't have to sit at home alone, brooding over the many things his brother would never get to do. Like, marry. Have kids. Find his calling.

When I knocked on his door, Clay didn't invite me in. Dressed in black, he was buzzing to go.

"We don't know where tonight's camp has been set up, and I don't have a lot of time to search," I whispered and checked over my shoulder. "If my dad finds out—"

"He won't."

He'd better not.

"Besides," he said as we sneaked out of the castle's side entrance. "Your father gave Delta a copy of the official Black Forest Cup map to assist with the investigation. I caught a glimpse earlier and know exactly where the new campsite is."

"Oh. Good then."

In reality, my father wasn't my main worry. Drake would be returning home at around eleven, so an efficient and speedy fact-finding mission was essential.

The sun set over the trees, spreading its bounty over a grateful sky. Rich hues of red blended with oranges and purples, soon blocked by the leaves above as we headed into the woods.

As soon as we had enough cover, he and I disappeared behind different trees. Getting naked in front of Drake had never been easy, so I certainly wasn't going to strip for Clay.

Once I was in my birthday suit, I stuffed my clothes into my clothes-tube, clipped it around my neck, and initiated my shift into wolf form. Immediately, my muscles and joints twisted around and around, wringing waves of pain into my flesh. I set my jaw until it, too, broke and rearranged itself and I tasted the bitter twang of coppery blood in my mouth.

At once, the agony eased. I padded cautiously out from my hideout, my head held high.

Clay's wolf was an almost entirely black specimen, with a couple of white patches around the nose and neck. Even though I'd seen his wolf in the past, this was the first time he'd seen mine. He traipsed around me on light paws, studying me from all angles. When he came too close to my hindquarters, I expelled a shot of dominance, which forced him back.

After my first-ever shift, I'd asked Drake what my wolf looked like. He'd described me as tall, with gray-white fur across my back and brownish patches near my tail. More importantly, he'd assured me I looked like any other wolf—only prettier.

Clay took a couple more sniffs and eventually nodded.

Dad and Drake's behavior had been easy to interpret, but Clay's apparent seal of approval puzzled me. Was this a rite we were expected to pass when meeting others as wolves? Or was this an alpha thing—in which case I'd better play my part, too.

So, I circled him, sniffed demonstratively without being sure what markers to check for, and finally gave a firm nod.

Whatever the meaning of this ritual, my performance had the desired effect. He took off and led the run toward the campsite.

Our journey took about thirty minutes through dense trees at first, then across a clearing and past a tarn, whose gentle waves reflected slices of the moon.

To avoid upsetting unsuspecting humans wandering around, we shifted a good distance away from the noise. Then, with our clothes-tubes slung over our backs, we walked into camp in our dress pants and neat shirts, looking not in the least like we belonged.

The scent of barbequed meat and BBQ sauce reeled us toward the far end. Several tents had been erected, their arrangement describing a crescent around the picnic tables and benches that were once more overflowing with people.

Maybe it was the sad reason for coming here, but my perception of the Cup's competitors had shifted. Gone was the happy atmosphere we'd bathed in that night. Instead, tired faces and the stink of sweat greeted us.

Like the people in the camp, I was feeling the fatigue, either because of Scimitar's death or because of jet lag.

"Snake," Clay shrieked and pointed at the ground.

I leaped into the air and threw my body five feet to the right, my heart drumming like crazy in my throat. Snakes were fast. I had to be faster.

The second I landed, I checked the ground. Had I evaded certain death?

"Where?" I pivoted in tight circles. "Where is it?"

"Oh, man." Clay hadn't moved except to double over laughing. "Your face!"

Air rushed back into my lungs as realization dawned.

"You bastard," I pressed out between my teeth and then kicked a rock, which sped away but sadly not in his direction.

"Sorry. Not sorry." He wiped away what might have been a tear yet didn't dial down his grin. "I've been wanting to do that all night."

The camp lay close to the *grinden*, a type of boggy heath found at the highest parts of the forest. Its moist, tall grass provided the perfect habitat for the common viper, a poisonous snake that lived here.

Which he knew too well. We'd never actually seen one, but tonight could have been the night.

"That wasn't funny." I pushed my knuckles into my waist. "I could have had a heart attack."

"No, it was definitely funny." His maniacal chuckles died down. "Besides, the snakes here aren't exactly killers. You should come to South Africa."

"Even if I had a death wish, I wouldn't want to die by lion, hyena or rhino, and definitely not by whatever snakes you have running around."

"Snakes don't run."

"Shut up."

Drake's sense of humor was equally twisted. He kept making fun of me when I trampled like an elephant through the woods back in Marlontown. It was only common sense to scare away anything that could bite or maul. How was it my fault his survival instinct had become blunted from living near snakes, bears, and possibly crocodiles for too long?

Good thing one of us had the awareness to keep us safe.

"I'll pay you back," I said grimly.

"Ooh." He waved his hands about. "I'm scared."

I shot him an evil look, and then he and I each picked up a cup of water from a long side table. To blend in further, we also heaped potato salad and hamburgers onto paper plates before joining a group of people I remembered seeing on the first day.

Once Clay was locked in conversation with a couple of Australians, I left to join a small group of Germans. They came from places as far away as Berlin and Hamburg, and I made sure my accent didn't immediately give me away as a local.

"Do you know what happened to that runner, number 177?" I asked wide-eyed between bites from my burger. "He was leading the race at one point, wasn't he?"

"You didn't hear?" One tall guy with blond straight hair and a mustache shook his head. "He was taken ill."

"Like, food poisoning?" I demonstratively stared at my salad.

"No, he fell."

"I heard he's not doing well," a brunette in a super-clingy top and bike shorts said. "It's touch-and-go."

Her polar opposite, a blond woman in casual wear, cocked her chin toward the woods. "You know Simone, the one who made such a fuss about someone taking her water bottle last night? She said 177 was taken away on a stretcher with a sheet covering his face."

"You mean he's dead?" I hated talking about Scimitar like this, hated that they were gossiping about him as if he hadn't been a person with feelings and a bright future, but gossip was why we'd come, after all.

"Yes." She nodded excitedly, which caused her bangs to fall in front of her eyes. "Apparently he was found by a walker."

"Is Simone here?" I looked around.

"No, she went home after her tantrum. Wasn't feeling well. She didn't stand a chance anyway."

"As I said, something's clearly going around." The brunette let her gaze drift over the crowd. "Probably what that guy got as well. I don't believe for a second he died. They wouldn't let the Cup carry on if he had."

I stood with them for a few more minutes before lifting my plate to indicate my need for a second helping. Then I slipped away and picked up Clay on my way.

"Did you find out anything?" I asked.

"Yeah, Scim was found near a mine." He squinted into the woods. "You know the place better than me. Any idea where?"

"I think so. The police told Drake and me it was about two miles from here, which narrows the options. The weird thing is the mine I'm thinking of is nowhere near the trail we ran on Monday. Scim had a map. No way did he get lost around that area."

"Can we go to the mine?" He moved his left foot forward as if trying to get a head start. "Then we'd know for sure."

"Do you really want to?" I glanced into the night.

Wild boars would be particularly active at this hour, and although they usually avoided wolves, accidental encounters could lead to confrontations.

He pushed his hands into his pant pockets and lifted his shoulders. "Oh, you want to go home, right?"

I softened my voice. "I meant because it might be where your brother died."

"I don't care." He let out a harsh breath. "I can't sit around and do nothing. If we don't find anything, fine. At least I've tried, you know."

"Okay. Sure. I guess we can have a quick look." I gave him the signal to leave, and we slipped out of camp.

Soon, we glided as wolves through the trees, making our path across the overgrown roots, the wildflowers and the fallen branches crunching beneath our paws. Each breath flowed like water into my chest, cleansing and energizing my body, if not my mind.

I didn't slow until we were near the mine, and then we used our wolf noses to find the spot.

Soon, Scim's scent took shape, a masculine smell mixed with metal, which could come from the copper mine or from the blood he'd lost here.

Clay and I converged onto the same space, a dip in the ground, roughly twenty feet from the blocked entrance to the mine.

I didn't want to be here, and not just because Dad and Drake had urged me not to interfere in the investigation. A visit to the camp was easy enough to explain, but a trip to the crime scene? Worse, not once had I considered how being in this location would make me feel. This was where Scimitar had taken his last breath. Had he stared into his killer's eyes? Had he known he was about to die?

I darted behind a couple of trees to shift into my human form, taking a moment to regain my composure. The deed was done. Scimitar's death was in the past.

The dark obscured all visible evidence, but Clay had thought to bring his cell phone and lit the area.

"This is it." He used his finger to single out a patch in front of him, where the ground had been disturbed.

Under leaves with dried stains, Scim's blood had sunk into the moist soil. The scent was unmistakable now.

"Yeah," I croaked.

Clay crouched and stared at the ground, but not as if searching for clues. His hand hovered inches from the blood residues, and he let out a breath that could have been a sob. This would be the last time he'd get to smell his brother's scent.

"Are you okay?" I rested my hand on his shoulder. "Maybe coming here wasn't a good idea."

Delta should have locked down the site and manned it with guards until his investigation was over, but as I'd feared, he had no idea what he was doing. Either that, or he honestly thought he'd found the killers in me and Drake.

"I was his big brother and should have protected him," Clay whispered. "Yet I can't even solve his murder. It's like I'm still the kid that can't run."

"You haven't been that kid in a long time. You're a grown man. Besides, I watched you earlier both run as a wolf and walk as a man. Your leg's working just fine."

"No, it doesn't." He stood straight without turning his gaze away from the spot. "I can't shake the weakness in my foot any more than I can make it magically grow to the same size as the other."

Neither of his shoes showed much of a polish. Rather, dead leaves and dust covered the formerly shiny leather. But by all appearances, they were ordinary loafers, betraying no hint of his former deformity.

I puffed out a breath. "Hey, you listen to me. You're not in a cast, you're wearing normal shoes, and even though I looked for a limp, I didn't notice one. I promise. You're fine. There's nothing you can't do."

"Thanks." He finally met my eyes. "I shouldn't have asked you to come. There's nothing here."

"It's dark." I glanced around.

"Can we come back tomorrow?" He gave me the full puppy eyes, even while his jaw was clenched. "Just to make sure nothing was missed. No one will know."

"We can't contaminate the crime scene."

"Contaminate what?" He pointed in a circle around us. "Delta and his guys are done here. I'm not saying they didn't do their job. I just want to make sure. Please?"

Maybe there was a way I could convince Drake we had something to be gained from this, too. He was Delta's prime suspect. Worst case scenario, I'd make sure Clay wasn't interfering in the official investigation. Best case, we'd find something that would exonerate Drake. And if nothing else, I'd be by my friend's side to offer comfort.

Drake would understand that.

We shifted and ran home. Clay might not have limped, but the pain from shifting, the ache caused by Scim's death, and my fear for Drake's future weighed on my bones. What should have been a twenty-minute sprint turned into a forty-minute stumble. If Clay hadn't kept circling me, nudging me along, I might have curled up under a bush and gone to sleep right there.

When I got home, Drake was already in bed. No doubt I'd have to find answers to questions I didn't want to hear in the morning, but for now, I got naked and curled up by his side, telling myself I'd done nothing wrong.

T̶wenty-One

Propped up on his elbow, Drake brushed my hair behind my ear and ran his thumb across my cheek. There was warmth in his gray eyes, but the smile I so desperately wanted to see didn't show.

"Good morning." I sat up and shook my head until hair fell over my eyes.

"Morning." He rolled onto his back and clasped his hands behind his head.

His blanket ran up to his waist, leaving his chest exposed. The perfect way for me to wake up if it weren't for his closed-off face.

He was right to be upset with me. I'd sneaked out without so much as a word. If he'd pulled that crap on me, I'd be furious.

I lowered my voice. "I should have called. I'm sorry."

"Where were you?" he asked.

I knew the question was coming, but I hadn't prepared an answer. He'd asked for honesty and communication, and it was no less than he deserved.

"Clay wanted to go to the Cup's camp to interview the

competitors and asked me to translate." I smoothed the blanket around my legs. "He needs closure."

Drake pushed his breath through his nose. "It's heart-warming to see the effort you make to accommodate another man while ignoring your mate's advice."

I spun my head in his direction. "Jealousy doesn't become you."

He sat up and swung his legs over the edge before reaching for the clothes lying folded on a chair three feet from him.

"Oh, jealousy becomes me great." He stuffed his feet into his pant legs and got up off the bed. "It'll be all I have on those lonely nights when you're out with Clay."

"Clay's my friend, not some guy I'm having an affair with." My dominance wanted out, but I kept it in check. Unleashing it would complicate things.

As his head appeared through his buttoned-up shirt's collar, he threw me an icy look. "No, he *was* your friend, many, many years ago. For someone who turns into a nag every time I run into an ex, you're surprisingly oblivious when the roles are reversed."

"Don't make this about Clay." I rolled my eyes toward the ceiling. "For crying out loud. I love you. I thought I'd made that clear."

He threw his hands up. "Then what? What was so important that you felt the need to sneak out without a word? Help me understand."

His chest was shifting quickly, and the fragile heart underneath pumped loud enough to have me wincing at every aching beat.

"I don't know why I went with him. It sounds crazy, but I don't." I slumped my shoulders. "I can't explain it."

"You know what?" His head had turned red, and he kept his hands balled into fists. "Fine. Go, have a shower. We'll talk about this when you're done, okay?"

Grateful for the reprieve, I trotted into the bathroom. The shower's hot jet massaged not only my tired bones but also my head, kickstarting my brain. From Drake's point of view, my behavior had to look awful. Sometimes we were so in sync, I forgot he couldn't read my mind.

When I was done, fresh clothes had magically appeared on the toilet seat. Drake, my fairy godmother, had struck again. He constantly put me first, even in the middle of a fight.

I dried myself off and quickly changed into the formal pant-and-shirt combo. Then I stepped into the bedroom, where Drake had parked his butt on the bed, waiting.

"I'm sorry," I said. "What's worse is that I promised I'd go to the crime scene with Clay today. How stupid am I, huh?"

"You're not stupid." He raked his hand through his hair. "You let your heart guide you, that's all."

"You're so good at this, you know. Being married, I mean. Or bonded. You never mess up." I wrapped a small towel around my head and attempted a smile. "If I didn't love you, I'd be pissed."

"Guess I'm lucky, then." He watched me through narrowed eyes.

"Do *you* still love me?" I smiled cautiously.

His expression darkened.

"I'm not doubting you." I sat by his side and calmly massaged his shoulders. "But I messed up and could do with reassurance."

He turned, and my hands fell into my lap. Unable to avert my eyes, I awaited his judgment.

After an eternity, he leaned forward to kiss my head. "Yes, I love you. Always will."

His answer was what I'd expected—and more than I deserved.

"Then we're good?"

"That depends. Will you be going to the crime scene with Clay? It sounds like an odd thing to do considering your dad will freak if he catches you, but clearly that alone won't stop you."

"Yes, I want to go." I took his hand in mine. "And I need you to be okay with this."

"Hell, I can't tell you what you can and can't do. That's not my job." He bumped me with his shoulder. "I'm glad you're telling me, though."

That fleeting contact brought a smile to my heart. Why hadn't I told him the truth yesterday? What did I think was going to happen?

"What are you hoping to find at the crime scene?" he asked.

"I honestly hope we'll find nothing. But for my own peace of mind, I must be sure Delta has collected all the available evidence and left nothing behind."

"You don't trust him to get this done, do you?"

"This is nothing to do with his abilities. He's never had to work on this level, with so much riding on it, and although he can ask for support from the Lord High Constable's army, he's basically a one-man show."

"Okay then. If this is so important to you, we'll make it work." He laughed. "How about I'll try to keep your father busy? I could ask him questions about the budget or the distribution of land."

"You're amazing. Thank you."

"I really am." Drake fell onto his back, pulling me along, and patted the mattress suggestively. "I expect you will repay me for my sacrifice right here, in this hallowed room."

"Anything you want, I promise." I buried my head in the hollow of his neck and draped my leg over his. "How you keep your sense of humor is beyond me. You treat being in a foreign country as if it's no big deal, even though my pack has already pegged you as a murderer."

"Pegged us, you mean."

"Yeah, more you." I peered up from under my eyelids. "Glen doesn't believe I was involved in Scimitar's death, but you…"

"Wow." Drake's nostrils flared, but just as quickly his inner zen returned.

His self-control around me was out of this world. I'd watched him tear into members of his own pack for a lot less trouble than what I'd put him through.

"Wish I could give myself a pat on the back, too," I said. "My pack's pointing fingers at you, and I don't know how to make them stop."

He leveraged my leg to drag my body closer. "You don't have to protect me."

I gave a deep laugh. "The same way you'd abandon me if the roles were reversed?"

"Sure." He ran his hand down my ass, triggering all kinds of shivers inside me. "I'd let you rot in prison, that's how sure I am you don't need my help."

"Uh-huh." I ran my thumb over his lips.

"We have a few hours to kill until you have to leave." He lifted my hand to his mouth and kissed my wrist.

"We should use the time to make a list of all the things you want to learn from Dad." I licked my lips. It was clear where this was going, and even though he'd rocked my world not long ago, I was sure ready for the next round.

"You read my mind once again." He kissed me.

His eyes wrinkling with a smile was the last thing I saw before I relaxed into his caresses.

TWENTY-TWO

MOSS AND LICHEN COVERED BOULDERS in the rocky ground. If this earthy smell could be bottled and sold, I'd perfume every space I entered with it. Feeling my lungs bursting with forest air, I smiled at the afternoon sunlight cascading down the gaps between the trees.

"You look happy," Clay said.

"Sorry. The woods have always been a happy place, but looking happy at a time like this isn't very tactful of me, I know."

"Don't let Scim's death spoil the outdoors for you. He loved it here, too. So many opportunities to lie in wait and scare the crap out of you."

We both gave a solemn laugh.

After lunch with Dad, Drake had kept his promise and volunteered to spend his afternoon learning the trade. My father had no reason to refuse his wish, not when Drake was so eager. The truth was, he'd probably enjoy the lessons Dad had to teach.

Clay and I hiked to the crime scene on four feet between us. Running as a wolf was freeing, but I needed a break from shifting. The nice weather was my official excuse, which Clay had accepted at face value. Why wouldn't he? The sun was up high, with thick, white clouds dotting the sky as if making a statement. Around us, the vegetation was lush with dew and resembled a lake, glistening in the breeze. It could have been the perfect day for a walk. Except, neither of us had come here for the exercise.

Like the night before, the area around the mine was unguarded. Scim's scent hovered over only a small patch of ground, where leaves rested over earth that was moist with his blood even days after he'd been killed.

Occasionally I caught a whiff of another person. Drake's nose was more discerning than mine, and he could probably distinguish the individual notes and assign them to names in a heartbeat. It took my fullest concentration to make out three distinct human signatures with a hint of wolf about them. One of those signatures had to have been Delta's, who led the investigation, and the other two most likely belonged to his helpers. If my nose was to be believed, they'd focused their search on a fifteen-foot radius around the scene of the murder.

Fifteen feet struck me as limited given the nature of the crime.

"Why was Scimitar here?" I used my foot to carefully nudge leaves and other debris aside to check for tracks. "The mine isn't located on the trail to camp he was supposed to follow that night. Scim would have known this, especially considering he had a freaking map."

Clay bent over to disturb a rock with a stick he'd picked up. "That he had a map bugs you, doesn't it?"

"Don't get me wrong. I don't care about the cheating, but I can't help thinking about who gave him the map, and why he wasn't using it that day to get to camp." I stepped away from the blood and examined the area outside of Delta's arbitrary crime scene radius. "The answer could tell us if his death was about him getting my crown or about me *not* getting it. Or if there's an entirely different explanation."

A scent that wasn't human drifted up from my left. It was different from the three I'd caught closer to the mine but wasn't gamey enough to originate from a wild boar or a hare.

Could another wolf be standing nearby right now, watching us? I raised my hand to stop him from talking but caught no suspicious sounds, other than the chirping of birds and the gentle play of the leaves above.

I dropped my arm and shrugged. Maybe it was an old smell.

An old smell.

Had I caught my first whiff of the killer?

Clay directed his glance to where I'd been looking. "Assuming someone helped him in order to kick you out of the line of succession, why would they then kill him?"

I tried to hone in on the source of this new scent. "I know, it doesn't make sense, and to be honest, the only person who might be able to answer this is Delta if he does his job right. He's the one holding the puzzle pieces."

Taking a deep breath, I gauged the direction of the wolf's scent. The odor molecules streaming into my nostrils dissolved and rang the jackpot bell. At some point in the near past, a wolf had sat right here on the ground, next to a tree with a trunk wider than my arm span.

If this wolf had been the killer, he could have used the trunk's girth to shift undetected into his human shape and might even have left behind a footprint or a fiber of clothing. I brushed aside leaves and twigs to study the earth underneath but couldn't say whether it had been disturbed.

There.

Tufts of fur clung to the tree bark.

"I found something," I shouted out. "I got fur."

Clay came running. "Scimitar's?"

"I don't think so. It's brown and white."

He kicked a branch by his feet. "Great, so it could belong to anyone."

He was right. My own fur included patches of brown, while Drake's wolf was almost entirely brown. If Delta had gotten a hold of the hairs, he'd have considered it further proof of our guilt and locked us in jail.

I glanced up. "The fur proves another wolf was here, and recently at that. The scent is quite weak, yet the fact that I can smell it means it must have been within the last week."

"Could the smell belong to one of the investigators?"

"I don't think so. Their smell is limited to the crime scene. Besides, they'd have had no reason to shift into their wolves." I wiggled my fingers. "Tough to collect evidence without opposable thumbs. And whoever was here undoubtedly came or left as a wolf. "

"Because of the fur. I get it. Can we run DNA on the hairs?"

I shielded my vision against the rays from the sun that stood behind his head, wrapping him in a halo.

"Me personally?" I laid my palm on my chest. "No. I could send it to a friend of mine who runs a lab back in the States, but getting results is going to take a while."

"Could we give it to Delta?"

To give him more ammunition against Drake? That seemed counter-productive. On the other hand, we all wanted the truth, and Drake was innocent after all. If this could help Delta get on the right track...

"Here, I brought these." Clay held out two plastic sandwich bags.

"Good thinking. I've left my P.I. gear at home. After all, I'm not here to investigate, remember? In fact, I'm not supposed to be here at all."

"Naughty Kens." He wagged his finger and showed me an extra-sparkling, superior grin. "Don't worry. I'll say I found it. No one's going to get angry at me for wanting to see the place where my brother died."

I scraped half the fur off the tree into my bag. "Thank you."

"Better yet, I'll send it to Delta anonymously." He squinted. "I'll slip it into the mail with a letter explaining where I found it. They have to investigate it, don't they?"

"Not sure anonymous evidence alone will convince Delta." I rocked back onto my heels and stared at the evidence in my hand. "But he'll probably come and check it out for himself, yes."

He glared defiantly. "Does this mean we've made a difference?"

"Maybe." I pushed up to my full height and held the bag out so he could pocket it. "Even if Delta believes this fur belongs to the killer, there may not be any DNA left to run tests on."

"Oh." He stared at the bag in his hand. "Then, what else can we do?"

"Let Delta run with this new evidence."

"No, you said it may not be enough. What about the map? Is it even possible to find out where Scim got it?"

I rolled my eyes. Clay was full of great questions today. Unfortunately, I'd run out of answers.

Twenty-Three

When I returned to my room in the afternoon, Drake lay on the couch with his feet up, reading a book. The last strong rays of the sun caressed his hair, giving it a golden glow. A tingle ran through my stomach, instantly putting me in a good mood.

"That looks exciting." I kissed his forehead and then lifted the cover so I could read it. "Military Spending Since the 1990s. You really are a nerd, aren't you?"

He grinned without taking his eyes off the handwritten columns inside. "You're investigating the wrong crime, princess. Whoever decided against using a computer to keep the books deserves to be thrown into the dungeons."

I lifted his legs so I could sit by his side before laying them on my lap. "We'll call this number one on our agenda once I take the throne, okay?"

"Deal." He snapped the book shut and looked up. "I got interrogated today."

My body stilled. "You what?"

"They called it an informal interview, but there wasn't anything informal about it." His casual air didn't fool me, because the slight rasp in his voice told its own story.

"What kind of questions did they ask?"

He pressed his book close to his chest. "Delta had the same questions the human police asked, plus he kept straying into politically charged territory. About the Wild Pack and our attitude to violence."

"You mean the way free packs handle the issue of who gets to be alpha?" Incensed, I pushed my bottom lip out. "That's not violence, that's letting strength determine who's best equipped to protect the pack."

"These challenges are usually fought to the death." He shrugged. "I mean, I get it. It must look vicious to civil society."

"It might, to civil society." I felt the heat rise into my head. "Which we're not."

Delta hadn't lived among the Wild Pack. Hadn't come to benefit from their generosity of spirit and unflinching loyalty. Our own Boroughs Pack could learn many lessons from the wolves of Marlontown.

Drake's weak smile cut deep. "In any case, the gist was that if anyone were to kill, especially kill a genuine prince, it would be a member of a free pack who has no regard for court rules and royal laws."

For Delta, a member of my pack, to treat Drake in this way wasn't just hurtful—it was embarrassing.

"I'm so sorry." I stared at my hands, which had gone cold, while my face was burning. "That sounds more like an indictment than an interrogation."

"That's what your father said when he put a stop to it." Drake gave a satisfied rumble. "He told Delta he was overstepping the boundaries of the inquiry. After all, and I quote, 'one way or another, Drake is my daughter's mate, and you will show him respect.'"

"Dad said that?" I looked up. That quote wasn't exactly a

ringing endorsement from Dad for the man I loved, but at least it had saved Drake from further interrogation.

"Yeah, and exactly in that tone." Drake reached out to briefly squeeze my fingers. "Tell me you discovered something that'll put an end to this."

"We found fur that might belong to the killer."

"The killer's definitely a wolf, then?"

"It's likely, yes, but the color of the fur alone doesn't rule anyone out. If anything, it might rule you and me in. Clay's going to send it to Delta anonymously, together with the location of where we found it. Maybe they'll get DNA off it."

"Really? Who are they going to compare it to?" He leaned over to set the book on the table, exchanging it for a cup of what I assumed to be coffee.

"One problem after another. I mean, my dad could order the pack to get tested, although I doubt he would."

"No person should be forced to bear witness against himself."

"Something like that, yeah, but less American-sounding."

"Of course. How stupid of me." He took a sip from his cup. "But could DNA keep me out of the dungeon?"

"It would never get that far." I pushed my hand into his pant leg and rubbed his shin, all soft and hairy. "Even if it did, I'd break you out and we'd go on the lam. We'd live off the land and work odd jobs until we could buy our way out of here and back to the US. It'll be romantic, you'll see."

"You've put thought into this." He squinted. "Should I be worried?"

"Not yet."

"Of course not. Giving up's not in your nature." He let his head drop back onto his throw-pillow. "What are you going to do next?"

I banged my head against the back of the sofa. "Clay asked the same question, but I don't have an answer."

"Clay, huh?"

I rolled my eyes to the side. "That again?"

"No, I'm over it." He lifted a finger and wagged it in mock-warning. "For now."

"We'll have to be careful. I'm already putting myself at risk, but as long as you keep Dad occupied and I only 'accompany' Clay, I should be fine."

"Or, how about I tag along with you for once?" He held out his hand again until I'd put mine inside. "We can make it look like you're showing me the sights. A mated couple walking through town almost sounds like something people might believe as a cover story."

"I wish it were that simple." I pursed my lips and blew air out of my nose, every bit as frustrated as him. "As you've come to witness today, you're an outsider. If you get into trouble, they will throw the book at you. Until we've been confirmed, you must be careful."

His dominance tiptoed forward, though still under his control. "I told you. You don't have to protect me."

"Yes, I do. Every fiber inside me tells me I must protect you because if you're caught, they could expel you. Maybe throw you in prison. Or worse. Please..." I tightened my grip on his hand. "Lie low."

"Okay, fine. At least tell me what you're planning."

"Not sure yet. I want to find out where Scim got his map. Glen said he didn't give it to him, and I don't imagine King Lance slipped it to him either."

"Where would you start a search as part of a case?" He lowered his voice. "Where did you start when you were looking for Raven?"

Raven was the reason we'd met. She'd also been Drake's friend. About two months ago, I was sent to Marlontown to track her whereabouts. What I found was her body and a whole lot of trouble for Drake and me.

"With Raven, I started at the beginning," I said. "With who she was, what she was into. Her social media, that kind of thing."

"Maybe the beginning is a good place to find the map, too. Find its birthplace. Who drew it? Who decided on the racecourse? Who knows where the printed copies are being sent? Do kings get the same version as the stewards running the race? That kind of thing."

"Nicely done, Watson." I patted his legs. "The Black Forest Cup Committee has an office in town."

"There you go. As promised, I'll keep your dad busy, but do me a favor." His voice sharpened.

I raised my eyebrows. "Anything. What?"

"Please take Clay with you. It wouldn't feel right to send you out without him."

I stuck out my tongue. "You can be a real jerk, you know?"

"Good thing you love me." He reached for his book again.

TWENTY-FOUR

FIRST THING IN THE MORNING, Drake encouraged me to pick up Clay and track down the elusive map. Ironically, I was reluctant to leave this time. Drake was vulnerable now that the Master of the Hunt had his eye on him. Sure, he was strong, broad-shouldered, and had access to killer pheromones that could bitch-slap Delta from here to Moscow, but against the crown's might and Dad's unshakable belief that justice must prevail, he was helpless.

Besides, Delta might be looking to interview me next. In fact, I was spoiling for a face-to-face meeting, because I had a few choice words to say to him. Questioning Drake was one thing—a good thing. This was a murder investigation after all. But those questions should have been about what he might have witnessed in the run-up to the Black Forest Cup or during the race. Delta's personal gripes had colored his judgment.

Eventually, Drake said to stop worrying and told me to go already. Considering how jealously I safeguarded my independence, I could hardly blame him for kicking me out. Both of us carried the alpha gene, and alphas didn't look to anyone for protection.

Clay opened the door at 9:30 a.m. He wore tailored pants with a mauve shirt today. On me, mauve looked pretty good, but on him, it brought out a red-purple tone in his skin that I knew wasn't real. Like a hyper-beautified yet hyper-masculine prince in an animated movie.

"What?" He flashed his pearly whites. "Why are you looking at me like that?"

For all the growing up he'd done, the boy I once knew was right here in this smile.

"I was thinking about when we were kids. Back then, you wore tracksuits twenty-four seven and had breakfast crumbs on your face until lunchtime. Now look at you."

"Shush. You're making me blush." He stood aside. "Come in."

"Thanks." I made my way through his stylish yet generic room toward the sofa.

Once upon a time, Clay would unpack his rock collection with its polisher and microscope the minute he arrived. Bits of limestone and mineral nuggets would cover the table and desk. Even though I'd have rather played video games myself, I'd help catalog his treasures, writing out measurements and geological data as he dictated them.

Seeing the place without a breath of his personality sucked.

I took a seat on the sofa. "I have a plan."

"Me too." He arranged his chair opposite me and sat, his legs spread-eagled. "Let's break into Delta's office."

"Huh." So not what I'd expected him to say. "Come again?"

"You heard me. Scim's map has to be part of the evidence Delta collected, and maybe looking at it will help us figure out who gave it to him. Right?"

Good thing my voice recorder was safely stowed away in my laptop bag, or there'd now be hard evidence of his plans to commit a serious felony.

"I applaud your enthusiasm." I gave him a thumbs-up. "But

what happens if we get caught? Tampering with evidence will be the least of our charges."

"I can go and do it myself if you're afraid." He put a tease in his voice. "But you're a princess, and I'm a prince. What could they possibly do to us?"

"Plenty."

"Chicken." He laid his elbows onto the chair's back.

Jeez, he was serious. Had I been wrong to encourage him? There were rules to successful sleuthing, and he was breaking them left, right and center. Of course, he'd always been impulsive.

"I don't know." I grabbed a mustard-yellow throw-pillow and patted it flat on my lap to give myself time to come up with an excuse. "I don't mind coloring outside the lines, but what you're suggesting is going a step too far."

"We're not going to get caught. Promise." He stared at the wooden floor and gently bobbed his head. "Delta's going to be out most of the day. I overheard him telling my mother he'd have to pop into town to check with a lab, maybe about the fur we found, so this is the ideal time."

Clearly, our investigation had blown new vigor into Clay. Potentially too much vigor.

Resigned, I fluffed the pillow and laid it back in its place. "Fine. Any idea how we're going to get into his office?"

He got up and pushed his chair back under the table. "I know it has a simple lock." He grinned. "I assume you can do something about that?"

"My kit's back in my room." I frowned. "But I can't imagine Delta would be leaving the evidence out in the open."

"One problem at a time. Go and get your equipment." He checked the wall clock. "Say, meet you in five minutes outside Delta's office?"

I pushed myself up from the sofa. This was an idiotic plan, and the punishment, if we got caught, would not be proportional to what we could learn from Scim's map—if there was anything to be learned at all. Yet once again, I didn't have the heart to piss in his cheerios. A loss like the one Clay had had to endure needed a response.

But I wasn't only doing this for Clay.

For all his faults, Scim had never made me feel inferior for being a girl. He hadn't whispered behind my back or told lies about me. At his worst, he'd stood head and shoulders above the bullies of my youth, and more than once had taken pleasure in humiliating them on my behalf. I never got a chance to thank him for it.

Showing gratitude didn't come any easier to me than apologies, but this, helping his brother find peace, this was how I'd say thanks.

My living room was empty. Drake and his book had gone. Dad would keep him safe from Delta, while Drake kept me safe from Dad. Besides, who knew what other fascinating tasks my father had in store for poor Drake? Could it get more exciting than our military spending over the last few decades?

As I rushed toward the Master of the Hunt's office, I kept checking over my shoulder, but today, like most days, the corridors remained empty.

"There you are," Clay whispered when he saw me coming.

He was pressed flat against the wall outside Delta's office.

"Why are you whispering?" I unzipped my lock-picking set. "If you think we might be overheard, maybe we shouldn't be breaking in in the first place."

"I'm getting into the character of a traditional private dick."

The lock-pick in my hand, I stilled. "Not sure about the private part of that statement. But since you can be a bit of a dick sometimes, getting into character shouldn't be all that difficult."

His mouth opened for a second, then he nudged me. "Bitch."

I chuckled and made short work of Delta's door.

The office we entered was painted white—exactly the dull, by-the-book, nothing-to-see-here color I'd expected from Delta. There was a single floor-to-ceiling window facing the private parking area in front of the main entrance. As before, most spaces were taken, which meant our guests hadn't abandoned their vacation at my father's expense yet.

On Delta's desk sat a computer and a notebook without any notes, and a stack of papers had been shoved into the corner. Incident reports on missing garden gnomes and three stolen dogs. I understood the need to steal, and presumably destroy, gnomes, but what was up with the dog thieves? That was wrong on so many levels.

Behind the desk stood a swivel chair, and another one in front of it. At the far end of the room, the air conditioner was blowing on a medium setting.

"I don't see any evidence." He picked up the three pens lying in front of the keyboard and stuffed them into the pen holder.

I pulled them back out and replaced them on the desk. "And we don't want to leave any evidence for Delta to find either, so try not to alter anything."

"Oh yeah. Sorry." He twirled around. "There's no other door. Where does he keep the stuff from the crime scene?"

"One of those cabinets, I'd say." I pointed at the wall to my left, which was taken up by what looked like custom-made cupboards consisting of doors of varying sizes. Each door came with a lock, and each lock came with its own silver key. "That's how Delta 'secures' evidence?" I used air quotes.

Clay pulled on a door, then rotated the key to open it.

"What do you mean?" He scoffed. "He locked the doors. That's kind of secure, right?"

"Guess I shouldn't complain." I started searching the cubby holes on the other side of him. "Let's hurry up, though."

"Already found it." He bowed over a long slide-out tray at the bottom of the first cabinet he'd inspected. "These are Scim's things."

His breathy words were the only warning I got before he stepped back, clasping his chest. While his skin tone didn't let him go pale, his eyes had become so large they were bulging.

I ran across to steady him and made him sit on the visitor's chair. "Are you okay?"

He sat still for a long moment. "I don't..." Then for another moment. "His death suddenly felt so real."

His eyes darted without focus, his right hand opened and closed as if reaching for something that was no longer there.

My only frame of reference for what he was feeling was the loss of my mother when I was a kid. Luckily, I'd never had to face any uncertainty as to how she'd died. A wolf in our pack had become obsessed with her and couldn't handle her rejection.

My father's justice had been swift, yet his grief never-ending. His Moon Promise to love her forever had trapped him inside a prison of his own making.

I cleared my throat. "Sit here. You found the evidence. Least I can do is go through it."

He didn't object.

I returned to the large, flat drawer. On it lay evidence bags containing a pair of sunglasses, a ring, and lip balm. Scim's clothes filled another plastic bag, while his clothes-tube lay opened and empty. With shaking fingers, I lifted a stack of printed photos.

On the first, Scim lay dead on the forest floor. His head had been smashed in on one side, with blood covering the rest of his face. His eyes—

I wobbled on my feet.

His eyes were half-lidded, his lips slightly parted. His bare arms and legs had carried so much power in life, and his shoulders should have blocked any attack. Yet there he lay, amid leaves, branches, bark, and stems, never to walk again.

The photographer had been thorough. Aside from close-ups on the wound in his skull and a scratch on his calf, there were also pictures of footprints. Even though I was by no means an expert, their size suggested they were Scim's. If memory served, the need for large footwear had been a source of juvenile pride for him.

As expected, Delta and his colleagues had only sifted through the immediate area surrounding the body. They hadn't searched as far as the tree where Clay and I had found the fur.

"I don't see the map." I frowned. "I don't see the fur we found either. Are you sure you sent it?"

He straightened. "Yes. Yes, I put it in an envelope and slipped it in among my mother's correspondence as soon as I got home yesterday. That way, no one can trace it back to me."

"The internal mail would have been distributed last night or first thing this morning."

"Maybe it's in the lab to be analyzed."

"Let's hope so. Because there's nothing here that's going to help."

He let out a long breath. "Kensi?"

"Hmm?"

"Be honest. What are the chances my brother's killer will ever be caught?"

I slid the drawer back into the cabinet and locked the door. "On this evidence, they're slim to none. But we have the fur. Plus, the investigation is young. There's still a lot that can be done."

"Right."

"Hey. Look at me." I sharpened my tone.

Clay's eyes regained focus.

"It's going to work out." My confidence held, even though I didn't feel it. "Trust me."

"Okay." He nodded. "I trust you."

A triple beep sounded, and he retrieved his phone from his pants pockets. "Whatever we do, we'd better do it soon. Guess who's arrived?"

He held the display up.

A swell of cold air from the air conditioner caught my arms. "Your father?"

He got up and headed to the door without giving me another glance. "Time to face the music."

TWENTY-FIVE

MY DAD'S OFFICE TODAY REMINDED me of St. Peter's Basilica in Vatican City, with its great dome, which soared high above the altar, embellished with mosaics and stucco. The same respectful silence that was observed back then on our first and only visit greeted Clay and me now.

King Lance and my father stood opposite one another, with the desk between them. Drake completed the uncomfortable triangle.

The South African alpha was intimidating without ever uttering a word. The years had taken away his hair on top of his head and added inches to his waist, but like my father, he appeared to be as strong as a young man. A tangle of black beard and his thick tattoo around his right eye hid much of his face, but I knew he wasn't smiling.

Clay walked past me and bowed. "Your Majesty."

Dad shot me a warning look, and, belatedly, I gave a curtsy.

"Claymore." King Lance's gaze quickly scanned across Clay's forced pose. A lot of white showed around his deep-set eyes, which were significantly lighter than the color of his skin.

I didn't even warrant a cool glance. The man in front of me wasn't just feeling grief—his heart seemed to be frozen by it.

Drake's face was pale. The morning might have started out for him as a protégé learning the ropes of kingship, but the arrival of Scimitar's father had clearly sharpened the atmosphere.

I sidled up to him and furtively touched his hand.

The desk phone rang.

Dad pressed a button. "What?"

"Delta has returned. He's on his way up." Desha, the Quartermaster General, spoke in an even, business-like tone.

Dad cut off the call without further acknowledgment and gave King Lance a meaningful look. "Any minute now. Are you sure you don't want a cup of coffee, Lance?"

"What I want is the killer's head on a platter." King Lance connected one word to the next in his typical sing-song way.

"We're working on it." My father sounded tired. "Delta is going to brief you in a minute."

Scimitar's death had hit my father, too. Although he wasn't a guy to play favorites, it was an open secret he used to prefer Scimitar's company to Clay's. He valued strength, especially strength of character, and Clay's countless hospital visits and limited mobility made Dad lose interest.

That was one more reason why I'd hoped my choice of life partner would have pleased him. Drake might be a fish out of water, but at first, second, and third glance, he projected confidence. Even now, his face was a mask of attentiveness, his posture straight and bold.

But I knew better. The pale gray in Drake's eyes only made an appearance when he stood under pressure.

The five of us waited silently around the desk for Delta to hurry up the stairs and ease our minds. I wouldn't have minded if he'd burst into the office announcing the killer's name. I might even congratulate him on a well-run investigation.

Anything to cut the tension in this room.

Drake moved just enough to nudge me and remind me I wasn't alone. Even though his gesture wasn't enough to relax me, it did help lessen the pain in my knotted shoulders.

Finally, the knock came.

"Come," Dad shouted.

But the door was already opening. Delta rushed in and to his credit immediately figured out the atmosphere—and the role he would have to play in improving it.

"Lance, you may remember Delta, my Master of the Hunt." Dad gestured vaguely at the man who'd hopefully have answers.

King Lance clasped his hands behind his back and gave a nod. "What have you found?"

Delta, who'd come clutching a brown drawstring bag, set the bag on the ground before bowing. "Your Majesty, we're making excellent progress. The facts we have established so far are as follows. Prince Scimitar suffered a coup-contrecoup blunt force injury to his head, caused by a heavy rock. Death would have been instantaneous."

My breath caught hold on a knot in my throat. His factual tone didn't make his words easier to bear.

"The fact that the murderer used a weapon of convenience rather than bringing his own tells us the death wasn't planned."

I cleared my throat.

"You have something to add?" Dad asked, not thrilled by my interruption.

"Yes." I shot Delta an apologetic glance. "It wouldn't be totally unreasonable to assume you could find a rock or a heavy branch in a forest, would it? Just something to bear in mind before we rule out premeditation."

Dad's nod meant everything to me. "Duly noted," he added. "Please continue, Delta."

"Upon examination of the crime scene, we found a number of shoe prints that, although of the same size, did not appear to belong to Prince Scimitar." Delta seemed proud of this discovery, and rightly so.

I'd seen the photos, visited the crime scene, but I hadn't spotted any difference.

"The second set consisted of a different tread pattern. Interestingly, however, the footwear impressions we collected showed an uneven weight distribution." Delta spoke with confidence. My earlier correction hadn't knocked him out of rhythm. Good for him.

"What does that mean?" King Lance asked.

Delta shot a cautious look at my father, who nodded for him to continue.

Delta squared his shoulders. "We suspect the shoes did not belong to the killer, whose real shoe size—and possibly stature— would have been smaller. Yet the tread was worn, indicating the killer hadn't purchased the shoes new. We're currently investigating who they belonged to and whether the real owner is in league with the killer."

Damn, if Delta carried on like this, I'd have to eat my words. He was undoubtedly more on the ball than I'd thought. Unfortunately, his discovery didn't rule out Drake or me. His shoe size could be smaller than Scim's or not, but mine definitely was. Damn.

"Do you have suspects?" King Lance sounded less impressed. He'd probably hoped for a quick resolution, so he could return home and bury his son.

"We've interviewed witnesses and are narrowing our focus." Delta's glance darted to me and then to Drake.

I gripped Drake's hand to stop him from displaying dominance, but no one stopped my dad. The spikes of his power whipped forth and struck Delta straight in his smug face.

Delta's head snapped to the side as if he'd been smacked.

Dad immediately retracted his dominance, but King Lance couldn't have missed the static it left behind.

"What's going on?" He arched his brows. "I demand to be told the truth."

"You are being told the truth." My father used his calm voice, the one he'd use when accidentally running into a bunch of human children taking a school trip to his castle. "But there are parts of the investigation we cannot share. Not even with you."

"It is *my* son who died." King Lance brought his large fist down on the desk. "I believed he'd be safe here, or I wouldn't have approved his journey."

"Did you merely approve his journey or did you instigate it?" My father's harsh words hit a nerve.

King Lance abandoned his fury for a moment and slumped his shoulders. "Scimitar's challenge wasn't my idea. In fact, I told him it was foolish, but that doesn't mean his death was warranted. I deserve answers."

"And you're getting them." Dad looked expectantly at Delta. "Do you have any further leads?"

"Not at the moment." Delta, who'd remained silent throughout the alphas' exchange, gave a regretful shrug.

Why hadn't he brought up the fur? Testing it would take a while, as would verifying that it actually came from the tree near the crime scene, but it was a lead worthy of mention nevertheless.

"Have you given any thoughts as to who may have wished my son dead?" King Lance turned around to look at me. "I assume his surprise visit created quite a stir?"

"Don't go there." Dad's voice was dangerously low, and his dominance returned as a gradually building wave.

"I do not believe in playing games, so let me ask you directly, Kensington." What King Lance no doubt considered bravery could so quickly turn into an act of stupidity that might spark a war.

Drake's dominance pushed at King Lance from the other side, no less powerful than my Dad's. Yet the king wasn't backing down.

I could have added my own alpha powers to the mix, but I was beginning to see the wisdom in Dad's words when he reminded me, over and over, that dominance should be a last resort.

"To save you further embarrassment, sir, can I ask you something instead?" My stiff smile clarified I wasn't asking for permission. "Do you honestly believe I could hurt Scimitar, let alone kill him?"

"I did not accuse you. However, you and your..." His lip curled in disgust. "...friend—"

"Mate," Drake said.

"You and your mate had a reason to want Scimitar dead. Do you deny that?"

Despite my best intentions, my dominance was itching to come out and play, but with the two powerhouses by my side hissing and fizzing like live power lines, one of us needed to keep a cool head.

"Oh, I definitely deny that." I straightened, using every ounce of teaching my dad had pounded into me.

King Lance's pheromones didn't leave me waiting, even though they were merely nipping at me for now.

"I was upset with Scimitar, that's true. This throne is important to me." I pressed my hand against my heart. "One day, I will lead my pack, hopefully with as much wisdom and as much love as my dad has for all these years. And while these things weren't on my mind when I chose my mate, I know Drake will do the same." I took a deep breath. "But I won't kill to get my chance, and I certainly wouldn't kill a friend. In fact, if I had a choice, I wouldn't have to take on a queen's responsibility at all because my father would outlive me."

I let my gaze drift to the window, where the high sun cast no shadows. At this point, I didn't care if King Lance believed me. Even though this hadn't been my intention, my speech had become a declaration to my dad.

I was born an alpha. I didn't rely on anyone's death to become one.

Dad cleared his throat. "There you have it. And Lance?"

The king lifted his head just as his shoulders slumped again.

Dad gripped the edge of the desk. "The next time someone accuses my daughter of murder or insinuates it, they will die."

King Lance gave a curt nod.

"What about the fur?" Clay asked. As a kid, he rarely opened his mouth in his father's presence, but luckily, he seemed to have outgrown his shyness.

"What fur?" King Lance snapped his head around.

Clay startled at his father's barked question.

"The fur I found at the crime scene, on a tree about thirty feet away." He kept his gaze low, but at least he didn't retreat into his shell. "I wasn't supposed to go there, but I did and found wolf's fur. I sent it to Delta's office yesterday. So, when Delta says he has no other leads, that's not entirely true."

Delta lifted his nose. "All this is news to me. I received no fur."

"Claymore?" My father encouraged him with a nod.

"I sent it yesterday. Stuffed it in an envelope and slipped it inside my mother's mail, which was definitely picked up last night."

Delta crossed his arms. "Maybe it's on its way, but this is the first I'm hearing about it."

Clay shot me a confused look.

"That's the story you're sticking to?" I asked Delta. "Our footmen distribute internal mail five times a day without a hitch, but this vital piece of evidence happens to have been mislaid?"

"Why didn't Clay hand it to me?" Delta nearly shouted. "If this so-called evidence even exists."

"Delta." His name exploded from my dad's mouth. "Remember who you're talking to."

Delta scrunched up his face and bowed to Clay, which must have hurt him more than he'd ever admit. "I apologize, Your Royal Highness. I shall track down your evidence at once."

"One last question before you do that." I stepped next to Clay. "Scimitar had a map of the entire route with him."

I looked at King Lance, but his expression didn't change. Maybe he was that good of a poker player, or this was the first he'd heard about it.

"Where would he have got that?" I felt calm inside.

Guess putting Delta on the spot brought out the zen in me. Clay and I were putting on a united front, and I didn't have to check to know Drake had my back.

Delta lifted his bag and pulled on the drawstring. "The details of the Cup are kept secret. Only alpha kings are handed copies. I thought this was common knowledge. More to the point, we found no map on Scim, I mean, on Prince Scimitar."

"Really?" I raised my eyebrows. "Drake and I both saw it."

"Look for yourself." Delta opened the bag. "I've brought Prince Scimitar's effects to return to King Lance, but there was no map."

I didn't bother checking. The map had been absent from his office drawer, too. If he hadn't found it on Scim, where was it?

Damn.

"Kensi, Drake." My father angled his hand toward the door. "Leave us now, please."

I turned and joined Drake but stopped at the door. "King Lance?"

"What is it?" He sounded tired.

I kept my glance fixed at the door. "Whether you believe it or not, I'm truly sorry for your loss. I miss him too."

With that, I stepped out into the hall.

TWENTY-SIX

DRAKE AND I LEFT MY father's office in silence. I was glad I no longer had to bear King Lance's probing looks, but his behavior was understandable. He was looking for blame.

"Why was Delta lying?" I glanced at the door behind me. "I refuse to believe vital evidence just happened to get lost."

"Why didn't Clay hand the fur you found to Delta in person?" Drake rested against the wall on the opposite side of the door, plucking imaginary lint off his shirt.

"Clay didn't want to get in trouble." I draped Drake's arms around my shoulders and sank into his body as far as the hard planes of his chest allowed. "Come to think of it, no one told him off. If I'd announced I've been checking Delta's work, I'd be exiled, no doubt."

"Claymore's mourning his brother, so they'll go easy on him." Drake rubbed his hands over my back. "Listen. Your father has been keeping the heat off me and you until now, but at what point will he have to give in to outside pressure?"

"Dad's not going to sell us out."

"He might not have a choice. We're caught between two impossible situations. No one can think we're interfering in Delta's investigation, but we must do something. I mean, *I* must do something, to clear our name."

"I still haven't visited the Black Forest Cup Committee."

"Okay. It's noon, but we can go now, if you want, and have a late lunch."

"That's quite a sacrifice coming from you." I patted his stomach. "But actually, I'm waiting for Clay. He deserves to be a part of this. Besides, if they go easy on him, they have to go easy on me. After all, I'm just offering my company."

"What about me?" Drake drew in a stuttered breath. "I need to get my hands dirty. Do something useful."

"We have to be smart about this."

"Kensi."

Damn. He had as much skin in the game as me. As much as it pained me, excluding him was unfair.

"Okay." I forced a breath from my lungs. "You're right."

His eyes flew open and he pushed me at arm's length. "I'm right? Shit, why isn't anyone here to witness this? Don't you have a court reporter who could take notes?"

"Klugscheißer." I blew a raspberry. "Do you want to know how you can help or not?"

"When I'm done." He flared his nostrils. "Wow, being right smells good."

I raised my eyebrows and waited, suppressing a grin.

"Hang on." He closed his eyes for a second. When his lids opened, he gave me a nod. "Okay. I'm done."

"Chrissakes." I pinched the bridge of my nose. "Anyway. The map's important because Delta didn't find it on Scimitar's body. To me, this suggests he might have been killed because he'd changed his mind about claiming the throne."

"But if he changed his mind, what's the big whoop? Why kill him?"

"Because maybe the person helping him didn't want anyone to know his identity, and he was worried Scimitar might talk. Imagine the scandal if it's discovered that, say, the alpha king of Belgium conspired to interfere in the German line of succession."

"Okay. That makes sense."

"On the other hand, the helper and killer could be different people. To pin down a motive, we need way more information than we currently have. I'd send you to go knocking on doors, but I'm not sure how helpful my pack members would be. However, here's something royal packs and free packs have in common when it comes to intelligence."

He jerked up his head. "Both use spies."

"Yes. Can you call around? The alphas of most free packs have probably already heard what's going on, and I'd sure like to know their take."

"That I can do. I'll get Jonah on it, too."

"You don't think he'll tell Dad? If my father finds out we're using spies from free packs to nose around royal business, he'll lose his shit."

"Jonah knows what's at stake." He gripped my upper arms tight, almost shaking me. "You can trust him as you trust me."

"Okay then." I gave a smile that, in my mind at least, was filled with fluttering hearts and candy.

He studied my lips for a second before leaning in for a kiss.

I hadn't invited his kiss, in truth his mouth and tongue surprised me, but I welcomed both as soon as my mind caught up. We'd picked a public place for our display of affection, but who cared? A delicious heat rose up my body, leaving me a love-struck puddle in his arms.

Voices sounded behind the door, and slowly, Drake and I became unglued. Yet our gazes stayed coupled for a few seconds longer.

The door opened, and I swung around.

Clay had a confused look on his face and stared at his ring, which carried his pack's emblem. No doubt his father had reminded him that king and pack came before personal grief.

Belatedly, he lifted his head. "Oh. Hi."

"Hey." I approached him, dragging Drake behind. "You two haven't been introduced yet, at least not without the etiquette, so, Clay, this is Drake."

The two shook hands, yet Clay's eyes remained unfocused.

"Are you okay?" I patted his shoulder.

"What?" His gaze cleared. "Yes. Although I can't figure out why Delta lied about the fur."

"That's what I said, right?" I gestured to Drake, although my question was rhetorical. "But let's not worry about that now. He said he'll be looking into it, which I assume means he'll visit the crime scene again. As for me, I'm more interested than ever in how Scim got the map."

"My idea was a flop, so got any better ones?" Clay scratched his nose.

"Yeah. Let's go ask the people who made the maps." I wiggled my eyebrows. "Are you in?"

"Absolutely." He shot an almost fearful glance at the door. "Let's do it now, though, while they're occupied."

"Okay." I pivoted to Drake. "Are you good?"

Drake stared at Clay, who rotated his ring around his finger again. His responsibilities clearly pushed hard on his shoulders. Did King Lance hold his oldest son responsible for his brother's death?

"Is Drake not coming?" Clay asked without great enthusiasm.

Drake gave him a prolonged glance. "No. I have to call a friend about something. Just make sure no one sees you."

As if I needed a reminder of the metaphorical knife dangling over our heads.

TWENTY-SEVEN

CLAY AND I HEADED OUT of the castle and into town, where a few passers-by nodded at me with a glint of recognition. My friend didn't attract much curiosity. Not during Cup week. All nationalities, religions, and ethnicities were made to feel at home, and if there was one thing Wildbach knew how to do, it was rolling out the metaphorical welcome mat.

The town consisted of a grid of lanes and sidewalks. Traffic was heavier than usual as tourists rushed to pick up last-minute souvenirs. Tonight, the Cup's winner would be crowned, and tomorrow the mad rush out of town would begin.

"Wildbach is its own universe, isn't it?" Clay rolled up the sleeves of his blue-striped shirt. "Do you wonder what would happen if its human inhabitants discovered who or what we truly are?"

"Sometimes." I returned a wave from an elderly lady with a flowing dress, who stood waiting outside a coffee shop. "This woman used to own a magazine stand not far from here. She knows everyone's name. Going by the gossip she used to hear, nothing would surprise her, believe me."

"I like the intimacy of small towns, even if everyone ends up knowing my business."

"This is it." I stopped outside what in the 1980s used to be the copying place and now served as HQ for the Black Forest Cup Committee. A handwritten poster in the large display window announced it to anyone who didn't already know.

The original sign high up on the storefront was old, most letters illegible in peeling black paint. But the window was clean and showed desks and swivel chairs, computers and desk lamps, and printers and everything else that had turned this store into an office.

We opened the jingling door and entered.

The smell of ink clung to the air, being more noticeable to us than to the humans. A man at the back held his hand in front of his nostrils, which led me to believe he was a pack member. One day, I'd make it a point to meet every werewolf in town.

"Our detective has returned." The man stood up and clapped.

Six other people got to their feet and applauded.

"Well done," one young woman said. And another, "I read all the articles."

I smiled politely. In the States, a few people had recognized me after I'd helped the police solve the Society Strangler case, but no one had told me news had traveled all the way to my home town.

I made my way across the worn carpet, shook hands and exchanged pleasantries, doing my best to appear like "one of the people." Clay lapped up the attention he was paid vicariously. His back received almost as many pats as mine, even though I didn't remember him staking out a house for two days in a row, eating nothing but goldfish and peeing in a bottle.

We were finally rescued by a woman, who I guessed was one of the main organizers.

"It's so nice to meet you." After a firm handshake, she ushered me and Clay into a separate office in the back. A thick stack of books teetered at the edge of her desk, and a dozen newspapers lay strewn behind her chair. This was a woman who thrived on chaos.

Once the door was closed, she curtsied. "Your Royal Highness, I'm honored to finally meet you."

I raised my eyebrows. "You're one of us?"

"Women in charge aren't a common sight in our world, are they?" Her short burst of laughter died quickly. "I'm confident this is going to change as soon as you are confirmed."

She was also well informed. Clearly, my feminist leanings had filtered through the ranks.

"Yes, it will." I caught a hint of her sweet perfume.

Her eyes were the color of toffee, and so were the freckles that covered her nose and upper cheeks. Something about her said 'competent,' which meant we'd come to the right person.

"I must confess, I didn't expect you'd visit our humble office." Despite her noticeable accent, her English grammar couldn't be faulted. "But of course we're honored."

"Let me introduce you." I made a sweeping gesture that encompassed Clay. "This is Prince Claymore of the Warrior Pack."

She curtsied, her blonde straight pony-tail bobbing as she did so. "My deepest condolences, Your Royal Highness."

"I appreciate it." Clay pointed toward her chair. "Please, sit. And call me Clay. What's your name?"

"Oh, I'm sorry." She smoothed down the back of her business skirt before she took her seat. "I'm Hollywood."

We sat in the two chairs opposite her, and Clay immediately rolled his one closer to the desk.

"Hollywood. What a lovely name. Isn't it unusual?" He halfheartedly included me in his flirtation, which made me feel quite uncomfortable.

Drake was right. Clay had grown into a man, and going by the beam on his face, he was a man with an ulterior motive.

I couldn't fault him for his interest in this woman, of course.

She wore light make-up and didn't need more, with her naturally pink lips and her large, expressive eyes.

"A very unusual name," I confirmed so as not to leave Clay hanging. I'd be his wing-woman any day, except we'd come here for a reason. "What have you heard of Prince Scimitar?"

Hollywood's gaze became guarded. "A lot of speculation, that's all."

I liked her. Her movements, her attentive gaze, the way she spoke with caution, I liked all of it. She felt like the best friend I'd longed for as a child, someone to confide in without holding back. Someone who, unlike Clay, would have been in town all year round.

Back in America, I wouldn't have hesitated to confide in her now, tell her what we were after and why. But here, I wasn't Kensi, the private investigator, or Kensi, the friendly neighbor. To this woman, I was Princess Freaking Kensington.

"Now, the reason we came is this." I opted for a detached smile, even if my insides froze from my cool mannerisms. "It's my understanding all information relating to the organization that goes into the Black Forest Cup is need-to-know."

"Oh, it is." She frowned before aiming a cautious smile at Clay. "We keep the route secret from all participants and humans."

That much we already knew.

"Can you talk us through the planning?" Clay placed his forearms on her desk, a charming smile brightening his face. "I'm sure a great deal of effort goes into such an important event."

Hollywood kept eye contact with him as if I weren't in the room. "The first thing we do is we walk the route and mark it on our map."

"Is this the kind of map you buy in the shops?" I asked.

"No. Those would contain information our competitors don't need to finish the course. Instead, we create our own. We only include the landmarks that will be most useful in any given year."

I crossed my legs. "Landmarks like boulders, particular trails, tall trees, that kind of thing?"

"Yeah. I mean, yes. We create this map on the computer. Next, we add the checkpoints and camps. Only five people on the committee, including myself, and six stewards are privy to the locations."

"The volunteers are not?" I placed my hands on the armrests, careful not to advertise the reason for my questions.

"No. Every morning, the volunteers are shown to their stations by one of the stewards."

"You take your job seriously." Still glued to her eyes, Clay tilted his head.

"Yes, I do."

"Can you give an example of a typical day?" he asked.

"Sure. Before the first competitors leave camp in the morning, one steward leads two volunteers along the trail to their checkpoints, while another steward guides another ten to that night's camp, where tents and tables await them for set-up. Another group of volunteers takes the tents in the old camp down after the last competitor has left. Our volunteers work in shifts, as do our stewards."

"Sounds like an excellent routine." Clay's smile showed no sign of waning.

Not that I minded. His gentlemanly side helped put Hollywood at ease and kept her talking.

"Let's go back a bit." I twirled my two index fingers in a rewind circle. "When do you decide on the obstacles and mental tasks and pick the checkpoint locations?"

"Our original map inspires us to create the physical tasks. Say, a clearing allows us to set up obstacle courses, whereas denser areas lend themselves to riddles. Speaking of which, the riddles and questions are the brainchild of three of our brightest student helpers and were devised over the past twelve months. These students are not involved in the remaining planning stages and do not know the route either."

I rocked my foot up and down, dissatisfied with my lack of progress. "You're saying if there was a leak, it didn't come from you."

"Not a chance. These people have been working on the Cup for years or decades. After we crown tonight's winner, we'll be back in the office on Monday to plan the next one." Hollywood gave a measured breath. "Maybe if I knew what exactly you're looking for?"

Her tone of voice told me she was eager to help, but Clay and I were skating on thin ice with our investigation. If she came forward with our questions, it could leave us open to accusations of tampering.

Clay shuffled in his seat. "Do you send maps to anyone other than the royal houses?"

Nice to know he remembered why we were here.

Hollywood reached for her blond hair, twisting one strand around her finger. "No. And if the royal packs didn't foot part of our bill, we'd only send the invitation and nothing else."

"The privilege of power." Clay yanked his chair forward so his knees rested flat against the desk's backboard. "Who are the maps addressed to?"

"To the alphas directly. Who they pass their copy on to is up to them." She pressed her lips together before leaning forward conspiratorially. "To be clear, they receive the map, but not the riddles competitors must overcome as part of a task or in order to find their way. In addition, the maps we send out do not indicate the elevations, the condition of the trails, and so on. Plus, no one can predict the weather."

"I feel like I can trust you, Hollywood." Clay beamed as if he'd just invented sliced toast.

And book us a place in my father's dungeon? Fantastic.

"Call me Holly. Please." A hush of pink covered her cheeks.

"Okay. Holly." Clay let her name melt on his tongue as if it were the most exquisite meal he'd tasted all week. "Scimitar had one of your maps, and we are trying to find out who gave it to him."

He made for a surprising Mr. Darcy with his suddenly sexy smile and dulcet voice. Annoyingly, though, Mr. Darcy wasn't disturbed in the least by my frown and had probably failed to notice it.

Holly returned his soft gaze, her pink blush now a deep red. "I can't imagine how this could have happened. I want to help. But… Oh, hang on." She opened a drawer next to her and retrieved a folder. "Give me a second, please." She rifled through her papers and finally pulled out two sheets.

She laid two maps on the desk, with the writing facing toward us. "This is the stewards' map." She directed our attention to a white sheet with simple black symbols, lines, and blue crosses and triangles. "The blue shapes are the checkpoints and the camps. Everything in black is the original map of the area."

"And this is the one you sent to the kings?" Clay tapped the other one.

I rolled the chair up for a better look. The royal map was almost the same as the other one but included color pictures of obstacles, maybe not large enough to make out in detail, but sufficient to communicate what awaited the competitors.

This map looked like the one Scim had carried. Well, almost. His pictures had been in black and white. A copy, then.

Holly set her arms on the desk, her perfectly manicured fingers pressing down on the maps. "Our human stewards would be disappointed to find out we shared these copies with outsiders, and worse, that one of our competitors carried a map."

"This isn't your fault." Clay reached for her hand and patted it before chastely withdrawing it. "Besides, you said yourself many stations require skills a map alone cannot provide."

"Yes. Of course, you're right."

Jeez. I felt dirty just watching these two.

"Can I have a copy?" I asked as coolly as I could.

Clay pivoted toward me. "Does this look like the map Scimitar had?"

"Yes. I will show it to Drake, though, to be sure. He has an eye for maps."

"Because he uses technical terminology like *South* and *West* instead of *up* and *left*, like you?"

"No, because he has an eye for maps." I kicked the side of his leg.

He winced but held in the cuss word that had probably slipped to the front of his tongue.

Holly gave me a photocopy of both maps.

Then I got to my feet. "Thank you very much, Hollywood. You're a credit to the committee."

"Thank you." She rose. "If there's anything else I can do, please let me know. I hope you catch whoever…"

"…killed my brother?" Clay lowered his head for only a second before glancing back up with a coy smile. "Maybe when this is over, you might wish to hear the whole story?"

The pink returned to Holly's cheeks. "I would like that."

We left the office, and finally, I was able to let out my inner teenager. "Clay and Holly, sitting in a tree. K—I—S—"

"Shut up." He nudged me. "I thought, seeing how she's helped us, she'd like to find out how this all ends."

"That's mighty professional of you." I glanced down at the level sidewalk. "I tell you what. Once you know who did it, please tell me too, because I don't have a clue."

"We know Scim didn't act alone."

"Glen says stealing my crown wasn't Scim's idea." I let the breeze brush my hair into my face, smiling at the tickle on my nose. "Which leaves us with so many questions. Is Scimitar's death connected to my confirmation? The timing would seem to suggest so. On the other hand, what if his killer couldn't give a crap about my confirmation and only needed Scimitar in town?"

"Why?"

"Someone he knew as a kid had a score to settle, or maybe he's made enemies in other packs. We have so many tourists in town, anyone could be the killer."

"Mhmm. True."

The town's church bell rang four times and then gave another three rings in a different note. Three o'clock. No wonder I was starving.

"Maybe your father can pull Scim's phone log," I suggested. "And what about his emails?"

"Don't think my father's going to help. He can't wait to get out of here."

"You're leaving?" I grabbed his shoulder. "When?"

"This Sunday." Clay pulled away and forged ahead, his mind probably as confused as mine.

Damn. Sunday. That didn't leave us much time.

"Let's assume the killer, hired by his king, did use the confirmation ceremony to lure Scim to Wildbach." I pursed my lips as I picked my way through my new theory. "What better way than by sending Scim a map that would guarantee his win? How tempting for him. Imagine, you'd be on the South African throne and Scimitar on the German one. That would be one hell of a win for your pack."

"Maybe. But what if my brother threw the damn map away and it's entirely irrelevant?" Clay's breath came faster now, while his gaze didn't leave the sidewalk. "Wouldn't that be annoying?"

Way to throw water on my ideas. "Don't worry. If this lead fizzles out, I'll find new ones. I promise I won't give up."

Clay puffed as if he didn't have the stamina for the steep up, up, up over the final stretch to the castle grounds.

"Maybe I *should* start investigating *me*." I clenched my hands into fists. "Everyone keeps saying I had the best motive."

"It's more likely we'll never find out the truth." Clay didn't even give a polite chuckle to reward my attempt at humor in the face of adversity.

Was he pissed at me for failing? My meager results weren't for lack of trying.

Once we reached the castle, we said our goodbyes; mine apologetic, his, brisk. Something had happened between us. Something I missed. He made a sharp turn and walked off, leaving me to my thoughts.

TWENTY-EIGHT

EFORE RETURNING TO UPDATE DRAKE, I needed to talk common sense with my dad. If King Lance and his family were to leave this weekend, we needed to speed up this investigation. Because once they were gone, so was my access to Clay's information about his brother. Having to rely on cell reception or the Internet would slow communication.

I knocked on Dad's door and slipped into his private study. "Hey, Dad."

"What's up, Schatz?" he asked, distracted. With reading glasses on his nose, he sat behind his gray desk, perusing colorful brochures.

Jonah was a workhorse, too, but he didn't have to deal with what my dad called 'the drag,' like countersigning contracts, approving loan requests, or mediating land disputes. That was what Jonah had Drake for.

Royal alphas, by contrast, didn't have protectors. Rather, they had Stirlings and Glendales and other protocol-eagles with fancy titles, who left the paperwork to the guy in charge.

"Admin?" I winced in a show of sympathy.

"Catching up." Dad leaned back and swiveled his chair. "For

the past two years, we've been supporting two wildlife trusts for the protection of wolves in the wild. I want to understand where our money's going."

I took a seat in the chair standing on the other side of the desk. "Sounds like a good cause."

After all, the wolves' survival related to our own. If they disappeared from our landscape, how would we explain our existence to curious human eyes?

"Were you aware we lost three members of our pack over the last twelve months? Two women, one man. All three were in their twenties, not much younger than you, and all of them vocal about integrating with humans and possibly revealing our existence."

"You didn't tell me." I kept my hands tight in my lap, half-hidden by the sleeves of my crisp green shirt. "You sent the hunters after them?"

"Once wolves leave our pack to become drifters, I no longer have a choice. I'm sorry."

"No." I waved him off. "I get it. You'd love to protect every one of your pack members, but the pack as a whole comes first."

"Exactly." Dad's raised eyebrows stayed up for a few seconds. "Moving away from Wildbach has done you good. You've grown up."

Growing up seemed to have become the theme of this trip. Not that I was a fan of growing up. What with being married to a man I loved but was still getting to know, and Clay, the boy I once knew so well, becoming a stranger, things had been easier before this adulting craze took off.

"Drake worked as a hunter before he became a protector." I stared at my intertwined fingers. "I used to distrust hunters, but now that I know Drake was one, I don't mind them anymore. Weird, huh?"

Dad's shoulders gently fell. "Not at all."

The overhead lights hummed, and the blinds were drawn,

showing neither the trees outside the castle nor the stunning blue sky.

Elbow on the desk, I cradled my chin between my fingers. "Okay then. What do you hope to learn about the wildlife trusts you're sponsoring?"

"Everything. I'm no longer content to leave conservation in the hands of humans. We need wild wolves and their habitat so we may run safely, too, especially since pack-owned territory keeps shrinking."

"And how do the three members who left figure into this?"

"Werewolves are half human and half wolf. The two sides are in constant struggle with each other." He held up a brochure showing a wolf's face on its cover. "Eager to establish their identity, young people are seeking a connection to their human cousins. If we can divert this desire to connect to our wolf relatives instead, get kids involved in conservation issues from an early age, and make them understand how we're different from humans, maybe we can strike a balance."

"That might work."

Sometimes, Dad was this flawless, distant alpha hovering above the pack. Today, the real him shone through the cracks. His love for his subjects was absolute. Protecting and guiding them was a duty he'd accepted despite the cost in terms of his happiness.

Yet in his words I also found admonishment. My inability to shift or show dominance had often seduced me into believing I *was* human. Here I was, with my human detective skills and my human values, coming to rescue the pack from itself.

But what good was a human queen to a pack of werewolves? What right had I to demand their respect? What our people needed were werewolf solutions to werewolf problems.

Maybe they would have been better off with Scimitar in charge.

I squeezed my lips shut for fear they'd tremble. "It's a great plan."

"I'd say so." Dad made a satisfied gurgling sound. "It's your mate's."

I breathed through my mouth, but no words popped out. Why was I even surprised? Drake had been trying to open my eyes since I'd met him. How quick I'd been to brush aside his cautions about embracing my human side and how quick I'd been to dismiss his gentle corrections when I called him my husband. All along, I'd thought he was trying to wind me up. Maybe it wasn't Drake who needed to take lessons from my father but me.

Dad, who'd been watching my moment of realization, cocked his head. "But you didn't come here to talk about pack problems, did you? What is it?"

"Okay. So, I need you to hear me out." I gave a loud sigh and straightened my shoulders, chin up, expression blank—the perfect alpha pose. "Everyone here has a role to play, and we play to our strengths, right? For better or worse, my particular strength is detective work. For this reason, I'm asking your permission to investigate Scimitar's death, before King Lance leaves. I would work in parallel with Delta, of course, since I have no intention of interfering with his efforts."

A perfectly reasonable request, given the situation.

Dad peered over the rim of his thinly framed reading glasses. "What in the world is wrong with you? Do you not see how inappropriate that would be?"

"Yes. Normally it would be." I pressed the balls of my hands into my eyes. "But this is torture for Claymore and his parents, and it's torture for Drake and me. We must find the killer, or I'll never win our pack's trust."

"You and Drake are no more suspects than anyone else." Dad threw his reading material onto his desk and interlocked his hands. "And if Delta can't find the killer, the murder will be filed away as an unsolved case. Ten years from now, no one will remember."

"I will."

"Kensington, I will not repeat myself." His dominance shot from his body like a tornado of knitting needles. "Leave. The investigation. Alone. That's an order."

The sudden pain robbed me of my sight for a second, and I doubled over. "Dad!"

A forceful triple-knock rattled the door, while I sat shaking, rallying, fumbling to pick myself up. It had been years since my father had unleashed his dominance on me, and I hadn't expected this attack over a mere request.

But even while his pheromones struck my skin like little bullets, my breathing was coming back under control, my face relaxed, and I sat upright in my chair, with most of my dignity intact.

Much more difficult was keeping my own dominance in check. My wolf itched to pay him back, to hammer him with her power until he lay whimpering before her. But I loved my father. For all his obstinacy, I still loved him.

"Your Majesty." Delta's excited voice sounded as he knocked a second time.

Dad extinguished his power. He wasn't smiling or giving any indication he'd enjoyed going alpha on my ass, but it would take me a while to forget his attack. Forgiving it would take longer.

"In a minute," my father shouted in reply to Delta's knock. "Have I made myself clear, Kensington?"

"Oh, crystal clear." Keeping my eyes down, I got up on wobbly knees. "May I slip out the back, sir?"

"Yes." Dad blew out a puff of air. "You understand that, when you are queen, you will have to deal with people like Delta occasionally?"

I headed to the door leading to my father's private library, mumbling, "When I'm queen, the first thing I'll do is fire Delta's ass."

Dad pretended he hadn't heard me, but I knew better. I stepped through into the library and left the door ajar so as not to tip Delta off to my presence. The time when Dad was willing to overlook my transgressions was over. The daughter that had returned to him was grown up, and like all wolves, I had to learn my place in our hierarchy.

My dad's library backed directly onto the rest of his quarters, with multiple doors leading into many rooms, most of which he no longer used. His favorite armchair, a monstrosity that smelled of leather and years of wisdom, stood just off-center. Its back rose at ninety degrees to the firm seat, and the arms were like rudders of a boat. Dad used to sit in it in the evenings, legs crossed, studying reports under the floor lamp's spotty light.

I opened the door into his living room.

"He's in the Royal Library?" Dad shouted. "Why haven't you arrested him?"

We had an intruder? Maybe a break-in would take the heat off me for a while. I retraced my steps on tiptoes and listened.

"Why would Drake even be there?" Dad asked. "I gave him reading material for a month."

My shoulders stiffened.

Why would Drake take such a risk?

Jeez, he'd found a clue. He'd found a clue and probably headed straight to the Royal library. Maybe one of his contacts had come through. Whatever the lead was, it wasn't worth the repercussions if he was caught. Damn.

I dashed through the far door into my dad's living room and from there into his bedroom. The stalker-like photo wall dedicated to my mom adjoined a wall of old shelves, which hadn't changed since I'd last seen them. I tilted the fake encyclopedia metal book toward me, and a click sounded. A straight crack ran up the length of a shelving unit, and a slight breath of cold air wafted through it. With a push, a false wall slid to the side and opened an entrance into a narrow staircase.

If Drake had gone into the forbidden library, he'd be trapped. As with our ambassadorial suites, unauthorized entry caused shutters to come down, effectively transforming the room into a cage without any possibility of escape.

Unless you knew a back way.

Guided by my cell phone's flashlight, I sprinted down the stairs, taking two at a time. How long did I have?

Dad couldn't stand people who disobeyed his orders, and that was on a good day. As his reaction to my request had proved, today was a bad one.

Why would Drake do something so stupid? If he'd uncovered a lead, we could have followed up on it in a hundred different ways. Damn it. He'd been the one telling me to be careful, and on he went, putting his freedom and my future on the line for a fucking book? Under pack law, there'd be no trial, no mitigating circumstances. He'd be incarcerated or exiled.

The sole of my shoe slipped on a thick layer of dirt, but a protruding rock in the wall helped me catch my balance. More than once my face got caught in a spider's web, but I kept my gaze on the cone of light, swallowing my phobias one by one, driven by one overarching fear: that Drake might be discovered before I got him out.

As I propelled myself along the craggy walls, dust and grime coated my hands. The tunnel-like passageways smelled like a stagnant pond. I came upon a T-junction.

Which way? Think, Kensi. Think!

The sense I was too late swelled up inside me. My frantic gaze stumbled through the darkness, as I relied on a memory nearly as old as I was.

I was seven when Andalusia, my nanny, had chased me into an almost empty drawing-room. I'd unlocked the hidden door in the wall and slipped unobserved into the darkness. My veins were laced with fear as I sprinted past a mural depicting a famous werewolf battle.

That painting should be here. I shone my light up to my left. Then to my right.

The edge of its beam lit a wolf's canines clamping down on an arm.

Thank God. I knew where to go now.

I headed East before descending another staircase at full speed. Bingo.

A golden ring sparkled as the cone of light struck it. Quietly, I rotated the metal loop until the wall creaked open into the brightly lit library.

The stale smell of the hidden passage gave way to the odor of yellowed books and dry dust.

"Drake?" I shout-whispered as I tiptoed past books no one had read in decades, toward the empty middle of the room, dominated by a tiled chessboard floor. Thirty-or-so shelves fanned out from this central area, without a chair or table in sight.

A scrape less than a hundred feet from me raised the hairs on the back of my neck. Dad and Delta had arrived, and the sound of a good number of boots on the ground proved my father meant business.

"Drake," I shouted again, louder now. The time to be discreet was over.

"Kensi?" Drake crashed forth from between two rows of shelves. "I think I'm in trouble."

"You think?" I grabbed his hand and dragged him through an aisle back into the hidden passage.

The door slid into place, and I didn't exhale until the lock engaged.

"I messed up, didn't I?" Drake spoke quietly.

"What were you thinking?" I tossed my head, dislodging dust particles from the walls on either side of us, doing my best to keep the tremble in my voice under control. "If Dad had found you, we'd be exiled. Do you understand that? Exiled."

"It's okay." He slung his arms around my neck and soaked in my scent.

Voices approached, accompanied by the shuffle of many pairs of feet.

"Let's go," I whispered, even though I hadn't yet fully said my piece.

"There's no one here," my dad shouted. He was beyond pissed.

How long before he remembered the secret panel in the wall?

I turned my flashlight back onto the stairs and extended my arm behind me.

Drake took my hand. "Where are we?"

"These passages run between the castle's interior and exterior walls. In the past, kings used them to satisfy their base desires with mistresses and those aspiring to be mistresses."

"Kinky."

We headed up two sets of steps, squeezed through a corridor so narrow it made Drake swear off candy bars and cheesy pasta forever, then down a different staircase, until we reached a cellar door.

The green wood panels opened amid bunches of shrubs with large, waxy leaves.

We stepped out into the light and carefully replaced the panels, which had handles only on the inside. The afternoon sun showed no sign of powering down, and I turned off my cell's flashlight. A breeze brushed across my face and back, making me shudder.

"I didn't think my excursion would spark World War Three." Drake repeatedly shook his head. "I'd hoped to slip in and out without anyone knowing."

"I told you, the castle's security is tight, even though it might not look it." I dusted myself and Drake off as best as I could. "Dad will know what you did, and that I got you out. You thought he didn't like you until now? Wait to see how he'll treat you from now on."

"I'd hate for your father to think I disrespected him. When

you called it a forbidden library, I thought it was a nickname or something."

"The records of our origins, the earliest material relating to our rituals, that's where they're kept. Believe me, someone breaking in is a big deal. One that could cause a rift between the Boroughs Pack and Wild Pack. Don't forget, you're Jonah's pack brother now."

"Oh, man. I knew the Boroughs Pack owned our most sacred texts. I didn't expect them to be kept here." The blood drained from his face. "I figured, maybe a vault with, like, laser-based alarms and pressure plates."

Okay, what was done was done. Now we'd have to enter damage-control mode.

"If anyone asks, we've been strolling through the garden with the fish pond." I turned my back to him. "Am I still dusty?"

"Hang on." He brushed his hand across my back and ass and then turned for me to do the same to him.

Once we were halfway clean, I turned my mind toward establishing our alibi. Dad might know what Drake had done, but proving it was another matter.

I slung my arm around Drake's waist as we strode toward the castle's main entrance. "What were you doing in the library in the first place?"

"I spotted something that had me confused. There's a lot at stake here, so I needed to make sure I was on the right track."

"You have a lead?" The tension inside my chest unraveled on his nod. "Careful. The guards are out today."

Drake grabbed my arm and lowered his face, letting me feel the warmth of his breath on my cheek. Then he kissed me.

It was good to feel his mouth on my lips, to get the delightful jolt in my stomach when his tongue met mine. My body went into a state of frenzied calm, where every tingle and spark pulled me closer, wound me tighter, until I was happily lost in his arms.

To think only a few days ago, I'd worried we'd reached the end of our journey together. A real werewolf would have trusted the Moon Promise. A real werewolf would have trusted her mate.

Whatever pack law had in store, I couldn't change it. My path was no longer defined by my father, but by the man kissing me.

When we separated, he laughed. "Do me a favor? Let's not mention the library incident to Jonah, 'kay?"

"I don't know, Hasi. That's quite an ask. I assume you have a way of making it worth my while?"

He nibbled my earlobe. "I'll think of something."

My only reply was a contented sigh.

He pirouetted me out of his embrace and gently nudged me toward the castle. "The guards certainly got an eyeful. Let's hope we look like a couple in love, enjoying an awesome day out in the sun."

TWENTY-NINE

WE AMBLED HAND-IN-HAND TOWARD THE main entrance, which was blocked by five guards. They stood stiffly in their starched and pressed uniforms the color of ash. These guys were boss. They pushed their muscles in the gym every day of the week, including weekends. Our last war was one for the history books, and with luck, they'd never see combat, yet they could run far, march farther, and assemble rifles in the dark within twenty seconds.

"Coming through." My face hopefully reflected innocence as I opened a gap with my one free arm.

They parted to allow us to pass and, as protocol demanded, bowed their heads before me. Drake received a halfhearted nod.

"You don't often come out of your rooms." My mouth was bone-dry with worry, but my voice was locked up tight. "Are you in the middle of a drill?"

"The Royal Library's alarm went off." The tallest of them fixated on Drake.

"Is there a problem, Desha?" Delta shouted from the stairs.

My dad, who'd been following him, collided with his Master of the Hunt.

Delta winced as he lifted his right foot, but knew better than to tell off his king.

"Hey, Dad." I waved. "Everything okay?"

"Not for me." Dad speared Drake with a look.

"Desha?" Delta asked again, lengthening the second, stronger syllable of his name—de-SHAY—into a form of rebuke.

"Nothing to report," Desha replied.

I hadn't recognized Desha in the half-light of the castle's entrance. He and Delta were brothers, although the only things they had in common were their height and the fact that both had been bullies.

As I exchanged looks with my father, he gave me a grim nod. "False alarm. We got lucky this time."

What he meant was that Drake and I got lucky. Maybe it was his love for me or the guilt over his earlier attack, but it appeared he wasn't going to pursue this matter. Still, he'd put us on notice, and I knew not to push him for another favor any time soon.

I lifted my nose and fixated on Delta. "Any news on the fur?"

"I've dispatched my men to scrape up the fur that Prince Claymore left behind." Delta had at least enough intelligence to stare at his shoes rather than throw another accusation at me or Drake.

"Clay will be pleased to hear it." I offered up a saccharine smile. "I'm sure you'll have the case cracked soon."

My dad circled around Delta to disappear up the stairs. "Come on, Delta. We have a report to fill in."

His Master of the Hunt hung his head and followed his king.

Drake and I stayed behind. I wanted to put at least five minutes' worth of distance between them and us.

"Princess Kensington has told me much about the famous castle guards." Drake turned to the five uniformed men by the entrance. "Can I ask what your jobs entail?"

Desha straightened his neat side parting of hair and pushed out his chest. "We guard the entrance to the castle."

My eyelids squeezed like trigger fingers, shooting out one hell of a nasty look. About the same time, dominance spilled from Drake's body, a brutal hit that made Desha wince. Sometimes, I forgot Drake was every bit the alpha my dad was. Every bit the alpha I *should* be. My mother's genes had blessed me with power, but being a novice, I lacked precision. And being the stubborn type, I lacked wisdom.

Drake lacked nothing. He aimed, fired, and never missed.

Within a second, the warning shot was over.

Judging by Desha's expression, though, one shot had been enough.

He bent his head, his chin trembling. "I meant no offense, sir."

The four other men also bowed, a sign of respect that Drake, as a member of a free pack, wasn't owed, yet one he'd now earned.

"I believe I asked about your work." Drake's voice made no effort to tell Desha off nor to forgive.

Why should he? He was going to be our prince consort, and if there'd been doubts in the guards' minds as to his alpha credentials, Drake had obliterated them.

"We only stand guard outside the castle in emergencies." Desha angled his finger toward various locations on the ceiling. "These cameras allow trained staff to monitor the corridors from our control room. While we're on duty, we reside in rooms near the various entrances around the castle, to be deployed when needed. Tonight, the library's intruder alert drove us to our posts, where we will remain until we're ordered to stand down."

"What's your response time?" Drake glanced at a door Desha had also pointed at a second earlier.

"It currently runs at twenty-four seconds, sir."

"Impressive." Drake's comment caused more chests to puff. "What kind of threats do you typically encounter?"

"It varies, but we mostly deal with nuisance visits by subjects wishing to seek an audience with the king, yet without prior appointment." Desha stood even straighter.

"What's your SOP for these situations?" Drake moved his head to include the other guards in the question without addressing them directly.

"Our standing operating procedure is to stop visitors and refer them to Montparnasse, Glendale's secretary."

"His majesty mentioned he no longer receives as many off-the-book requests for mediation." Drake's tone sharpened. "Would you say that's true?"

Desha's eyes darted to the side, but his hesitation was brief. "No, sir. The number of requests remains high."

Accusing Montparnasse or Glendale of screening my father's visitors? Definitely an answer that could land him in trouble with Duval, the Lord High Constable, who was in charge of our army. On the other hand, Drake was about to become a member of the royal family. Not an easy choice, but Desha had picked Drake.

"Thank you, Desha." I smiled at my former bully, whose eyes flew open.

He bowed before me, and as he came up, he winked.

I winked back.

Our silent conversation had taken less than three seconds, and in those three seconds, our history had changed and the record between us had been wiped clean.

"Yes. Thank you." Drake dismissed them. "Carry on."

All the guards stood to attention as Drake casually wrapped my hand around his arm and led me toward the stairs.

"You're smiling." His voice was quiet, even though we'd put enough distance between us and the guards to be sure he wouldn't be overheard.

"I wasn't aware." I tightened my hand around his arm. "You were awesome."

"Doing what?"

"Handling the guards. If you were planning a coup, they'd be following you to their deaths."

"Whoa. My plans are way less bloody." He laughed, but the lightness in his voice quickly vanished. "Let's hope your father's plans are, too."

Thirty

Drake and I had dodged a bullet. No guards were waiting upstairs to take Drake into custody, nor had Stirling arranged for our suitcases to be packed, ready for our flight home.

Drake might never know how close we'd come to absolute disaster. As Jonah's protector, it was his job to enforce the law. Why had he chosen to break it now?

I waited for the lock to our living room to catch before I whirled around. "Okay. What were you doing in the library, risking your life and my future?"

"I honestly didn't think it would be such a big deal." He folded his arms over his chest. "I'm surprised you waited this long to ask me, though. This must have been killing you."

"I wasn't going to ask you with other ears around." I wrinkled my nose. "What is it? You said you noticed something?"

He rocked on his heels. "It's about Clay."

"That old spiel again? I can't keep having the same argument with you." I gripped his face between my hands. "I love you. Only you. You must stop torturing yourself over this."

"That's not what this is about." He removed my hands from his cheeks and held them. "Remember how Scimitar showed us his ring with the Warrior Pack's official coat of arms?"

"Sure."

"And did you see Clay had one like it after we left your father's office?"

"Yes."

"I think they're the same ring. Delta gave King Lance Scimitar's personal effects, right? Including the ring, I assume. And then King Lance passed it on to Clay."

"And that's important?" My skin tingled, possibly because I feared his conclusion.

"Royal rings are presented only to the presumptive heir to the throne." He stared hard as if to ensure my undivided attention. "That's why you were given one for your confirmation."

"You're saying Scimitar was going to be the South African crown prince?" I pulled away from Drake, but he tightened his grip. "Claymore's the elder son, not Scim."

"The book I found in the forbidden library confirmed my suspicions." Drake's voice gentled. "The day King Lance acknowledged the illegitimate Scimitar as his son, the two brothers became equals, with an equal claim to the throne. Even though tradition makes it appear like the alpha crown always passes to the oldest brother, there is, in fact, no law that requires it."

"Scimitar wouldn't do this to Clay." I swayed on my feet, trying to keep my thoughts from running too fast. "I don't believe it."

And yet, I wouldn't have thought Scim capable of trying to deny me the throne either. Had I been so focused on the past, I'd forgotten to open my eyes to the present? We'd grown up and changed. If the passing of time could turn Glen civil and Desha into a decent person, could it have turned Scimitar's character inside out as well?

"Neither son would have had a say in their father's decision,"

Drake explained. "And if I'm right, I have to wonder why Claymore failed to mention this."

"Oh." My lips trembled, and I took a cleansing breath.

"The South African throne is now his—unless you pull a Scimitar and stake a claim." Drake deflected my glare with a grim smile. "Bad time for a joke, I know. Seriously though, is there a reason why Clay would have kept this hidden from you?"

My eyes burned, but I wouldn't cry. I was Princess Kensington, the future alpha queen of the Boroughs Pack.

And the alpha queen was no crybaby.

"No." I lifted my chin. "I can't think of one."

"What if there's more Clay hasn't told you? What if, to spare himself embarrassment or to protect his crown's interest, he held back vital information on purpose? Maybe even something that could have helped us?"

Clay's silence had made me and Drake the only suspects in Scimitar's murder.

I tore myself away from Drake and charged across the room. Stomping. Punching the back of my sofa. Once I even kicked my old stereo. Why hadn't Clay told me he wasn't going to be the crown prince? It wasn't like the topic hadn't come up.

"Kensi." Drake's voice reeled me in. He was sitting in a dining chair, swiveling back and forth to follow my dashes from one corner into the other. "There's no need to destroy the room."

"It's so stupid. Clay knows I would have been there for him if he'd told me about his father's crazy decision." I raised my arms. "It makes no sense."

"Look at what *you'd* be willing to do to become an alpha. You were ready to camp out in the woods, home to snakes and wild boar." He laid an open palm on the table. "Makes you wonder what Clay would have been prepared to do, doesn't it?"

"I know what you're getting at. No way." I gave a suppressed scream. "But hey. Say, Clay did want the South African crown really badly. So what? Scimitar clearly had no intention of taking it away from him. Maybe this is why Scim went after my crown in the first place. So he wasn't competing with Clay for his."

I peered at Drake triumphantly. He was the guy with all the answers, but surely he couldn't fault my logic.

Drake jerked his foot, wagging his head from one side to the other. "Okay, but my point stands. If Claymore had told you all of this in the beginning, you wouldn't have wasted your time trying to figure out why Scimitar came here."

"Yeah." I stared at the wall, the blinds, the sofa, looking for inspiration.

This was a case that, from the start, had lacked any substantial motive. I didn't buy that some kid from back then had held a grudge against Scimitar all these years. And that Scimitar had stumbled onto some evil plot was also far-fetched.

Would this case become my greatest professional failure?

When Drake had suggested steering young werewolves' interests from humans toward wolf conservation projects, he'd drawn from his experience as Jonah's protector. When he'd talked to Desha, he'd proven his leadership skills through strength and kindness.

I definitely hadn't covered myself in alpha glory since I got here, but solving mysteries, well, that was supposed to be my thing. So, why was I as clueless today as I had been in the beginning?

Maybe it was a lack of detachment that had prevented me from seeing connections. Where was my objectivity? Not once had I regarded this case as murder with a victim, a motive, and suspects. Rather, I'd fixated on getting closure for Clay and shielding Drake and myself from suspicion.

This kind of half-ass snooping was no way to conduct an investigation.

"Okay. Hang on." I darted to the corner of my room where my laptop bag had sat unused since my arrival.

Drake watched my actions with open curiosity.

Once my notebook and my recorder were by my side, I wrote a big, fat number one onto the first blank page.

"Let's start with what we know." I kept my pen poised. "Scimitar died away from the course he should have been on. Go."

"You want me to go?" Drake's lips turned down.

"No, I mean, go brainstorm. Scim was ahead of us and should have reached camp before us. Why had he gone off course?"

"To meet someone. Someone he knew. Someone with smaller feet than his own."

"Seems like a logical conclusion." I wrote 'knew killer, boot size' and underlined it.' "This is supported by the fact that he wouldn't have allowed anyone to sneak up on him. As we've already noted, he was fast and strong, and if he'd seen it coming, there would have been defensive marks. I believe he let his guard down, which you only do around a person you trust."

"Good. Did they pre-arrange to meet by the mine?" Drake asked, proving he was quite good at snooping himself.

"Either that, or he had his phone on him. It wasn't among his personal effects, but the killer could have discarded it later." I added 'where's his phone' to my list. "We should check his room and see if it's there."

"Okay. You also found fur at the crime scene, which Clay said he'd mailed to Delta. Delta, however, claims he hasn't received it." He aimed his index finger at my notebook. "Write that down as well. But assuming Delta retrieved the remaining hairs from the original murder scene, will they help us? Brown and white fur's kind of everywhere."

"And if Delta's guys retrieve DNA, we have no one to compare it to until we have a suspect."

Drake bit his bottom lip. "Next, the map. Who gave it to Scimitar, and what happened to it?"

My man was definitely getting into the flow.

"That reminds me." I handed over the copies of the maps

Holly had given me. "The one with the photos of the obstacles is the one the kings received. Do you agree this looks like the map Scimitar had?"

Drake studied the sheet. "Yeah. Definitely. That doesn't necessarily mean his helper was a king, though. Maybe a king's member of staff?"

I stretched out my legs, seeking and finding comforting contact with him under the table. "Which pack, though?"

Drake waved as if to shoo an offending thought away. "Not yours. Agreed?"

I believed Glendale's assurances he'd had no hand in this, and Stirling or my father certainly wouldn't have helped a foreign prince. And Delta wouldn't have been allowed within five feet of the safe, where Dad kept his copy.

"Agreed." I punctuated my statement with a firm nod. "But don't you think another king could have wanted to install Scimitar on the German throne?"

"Don't bite my head off." Drake raised a hand. "But it's unlikely. People who don't like seeing a female alpha on the throne generally don't have a high opinion of women, period. If I were a scheming misogynist, I'd throw my whole support behind you and thereby buy my way into your good graces."

"Because as a woman, I'd be incapable of seeing through your flattery."

He cocked his finger. "Exactly. That, or I'd try to con my way onto your throne at a later point. The last thing I'd want is a strong guy like Scimitar to be in charge, making decisions that impact the future of all royal packs, including my own."

"That reminds me. Glen suggested Scimitar wasn't excited about coming here. Rather, he considered it a burden."

"Whoever gave him the map may have put the idea of this coup into his head to begin with." Drake tapped the table, shooting demonstrative glances at my notepad.

"Challenge not Scim's idea," I said while simultaneously writing the words down. "Let me get this straight. Having received the keys to his kingdom from his father, which he didn't want because of Clay, he took a shot at mine because someone pushed him into it?"

"It seems we've drilled down to the heart of the matter." Drake peered up cautiously from under his eyelashes. "I know of one person who might be able to speculate on Scimitar's train of thought and maybe even on who this mysterious instigator might be."

"Clay." I summoned a deep breath and stared at my list.

1. Knew killer. Small feet.

2. Where's the phone?

3. Delta didn't receive fur.

4. Where's the map now?

5. Challenge not Scim's idea.

6. Who benefits from Scim going after German crown when SA crown was already his?

7. Why didn't Clay tell me about Scim becoming crown prince?

Drake's suggestion to ask my friend probing questions was the rational next step, but he hadn't spent the past few days with Clay. Hadn't seen how his brother's death had affected him.

"Clay *was* acting weird earlier." I picked up my recorder and pressed a button to display its state of charge. Four out of six bars, enough for a few hours of recording. "On our way back from the Black Forest Cup Committee, we were talking about Scimitar's map. I got the feeling Clay was withholding something from me."

"We won't know if he did or not until we make him talk to us." Drake's face was open, without a hint of gloating.

Whether his jealousy was alive or not, this wasn't about getting one over on Clay, or about clearing his name. I'd bet my crown on Drake having caught the P.I. bug.

Hallelujah. If my investigative habits rubbed off on him, his alpha skills may yet rub off on me.

"Can you take this? My pants only have one pocket, and it's tiny." I pushed the recorder across the table. "Don't worry about turning it on or off. It'll keep recording by itself."

"Okay."

"So, the plan is, we'll get Clay to show us Scim's room to see if we can find his phone. Once Clay relaxes, we'll hit him with our questions." I tore the page with my notes from the pad and pushed it into my pocket. "Let's go."

Drake and I left the living room in silence. Our hands had found each other by the time we'd reached the back stairs. I hadn't held out my arm, nor could I remember Drake doing so, and yet within a minute, we'd locked onto one another.

"As soon as the plane landed, I was overwhelmed." My voice was low, even though the staircase was empty. "While I didn't doubt our feelings, I wasn't sure how bonded life would work out for us with all that pressure."

"Sure. We haven't known each other that long."

"Exactly. Then there was the confirmation ceremony and the faces from my past. I freaked. I'm truly sorry, you know, for starting fights with you and for making you stay with my dad while I met with Clay."

"You weren't the only one who was freaked." Drake laid his arm around my shoulders, and we went down the stairs. "Becoming a prince consort, let alone prince consort of the Boroughs Pack? The idea alone sent me into a tailspin."

We'd reached the floor that housed the castle's ambassadorial suites. Outside of Clay's door, Drake and I exchanged an encouraging look. Then I knocked.

THIRTY-ONE

LAY GREETED US WITH A subdued smile. Maybe Scimitar's death had begun taking its toll on him. I wanted to help him find closure, to end this limbo of not knowing, but I couldn't do it without his honesty.

"Can we come in?" I kept my voice casual.

"It's six o'clock." He blinked with heavy eyelids. "Dinner's on its way."

"You can have dinner later." I waved him off, not least because I smelled alcohol on his breath. "We want to have a look around Scimitar's room. Do you think you could swing that?"

"What for?" Clay's charcoal-gray pinstriped shirt sported a large red stain. On the table behind him stood an empty bottle of wine and the glass that held its remnants.

"Most likely, your brother was killed by someone he knew," I said while giving him an energetic yet sympathetic smile. "We need to know if Scim had his phone with him in the woods to arrange the meeting with his killer, or if it had been agreed in advance."

Clay's darting gaze revealed spidery red veins in the whites of his eyes. Finally, he grabbed a disk to unlock his brother's door and then trudged ahead of us. Either he was wasted from the wine, or all that running around the woods and the long stroll through town had stirred up his old foot pain.

Drake ambled after us, doing his protector thing, where he blended into the background yet nothing escaped his notice.

Scimitar's living room was a replica of Clay's, with a dining room/living room combo and a long cabinet with a coffee machine, which contained old coffee. The drapes made a ruffle as I swung them apart. Next, I opened the blinds to let in natural light. A plate of half-eaten pasta stood on the table by the door, with the tomato sauce forming an unsightly crust, and next to it, a half-eaten sandwich. His last dinner and breakfast. Maybe Queen Nimcha had been too distraught to return to Scim's rooms and tidy up.

I'd ask Dad to send up a housekeeper to take care of it.

"Our lead with the map didn't pan out. You really think the phone's going to help?" Clay asked.

"Either way, I'm not going to stop digging until our names have been cleared." I stared him down. "Besides, I thought you wanted to know who killed him, too."

"Of course." He ducked aside. "But my father's about ready to leave, with or without answers, Delta's investigation has stalled, and you're not allowed to do anything. We're done, Kens."

Clay looked small. Beaten.

"No, we're not." I singled out two opposite corners of the room. "Clay, you check over there. Drake, take the side by the door."

While the guys checked the surfaces, looked into the high-hanging cupboards, and swiped the green velvet throw-pillows off the sofa, I headed next-door.

The bedroom appeared spacious because only a few pieces of furniture had been arranged in it. The whiteness of the walls was broken up by an abstract painting, which I assumed had been created by a talented pack member.

Scimitar's bedsheets were crumpled, and the blanket and pillows were also messy. A choice of clothes lay on top of the bed—mainly shirts, ties, and black pants—and a row of shoes stood in front of a wooden wardrobe, which had been hand-made and decorated with loops and fleurs-de-lis.

It was impossible to say if anyone had stolen shoes from Scimitar's selection to fake the prints found at the crime scene. Only one pair showed a chalky residue on the surface. Possibly the pair he'd worn when he arrived in Wildbach. I crouched and picked up the left one to bend its flexible sole with my hands. Despite their size, they could have both fitted inside a clothes-tube.

"Anything?" Drake shouted from next-door.

I drew in a breath but wasn't ready to answer.

Clay had been born with a clubfoot. While operations, casts, and braces had returned normal or near-normal function to his foot, his left had always been smaller than the right by one or two shoe sizes.

Was it possible he'd left the shoeprints Delta had found?

"Kensi?" Drake's head popped in through the door. "Did you find the phone?"

The hairs below my cotton sleeves stood on end. "No. But I haven't checked over there yet."

"I'll do it." He strode in and slid open the night table's small drawer. "Got it."

Clay entered. "We'll need his fingerprint to unlock it."

I rounded the bed. Drake was already typing numbers into the lock screen.

"Do you know his passcode?" I cocked my head at Clay. "Six digits."

He shifted his gaze to his feet. "No idea. Sorry."

I didn't believe him. And if there was one thing that never failed, it was my built-in bullshit detector.

"Try his birthday." I leaned over Drake's shoulder and tapped in the digits myself. "Many people use a date for the code."

Drake gave a triumphant cry. "We're in. Let me check his messages."

Clay continued to study the pattern of the floor's wood grain. My suspicion about the shoes didn't amount to any evidence, and he lacked any apparent motive to kill his brother, but if he was innocent, why was he so reluctant to help us?

"Check Sunday, too," I said. "He could have talked to someone the day before the Black Forest Cup started."

Drake untucked the hem of his shirt from his trousers and used the fabric to clean the screen. "No messages or calls on Sunday or Monday."

"What about the trash folder?"

Drake shook his head. "Nothing. I assume he arranged the meet with his killer in person."

"Yeah, probably." I squinted at the device in his hand. "Why did you wipe the cell's screen earlier?"

"Just a spot of dirt."

I took the phone from him and held it under the light. The front and the metal backing showed tiny brown smudges.

"That's soil." I rotated it in my hand to the audio jack, which contained a dried leaf fragment. "You know, I think he had the phone with him on the trail. Where else would he have picked up clumps of dirt and dried leaves between South Africa and the castle?"

"Then why is it in his room?" Drake took seemingly casual steps toward the door and installed his large body inside the frame. "A room that's so secure, only Scimitar's immediate family have access to it?"

Clay jerked his head around, his eyes narrowed. "What are you saying, farmer?"

"What the hell?" My dominance shot out of me, off-target but with a spread so wide it caught enough of Clay to make him flinch.

Clay pushed forward as if to barrel past Drake, and I dialed up my pheromones. Even though my mixed loyalties had initially skewed my angle, *she* was loyal only to Drake's wolf, and her aim was true.

Before he made contact with Drake, Clay fell sideward, clutching his stomach and then his arms. The tone emerging from his throat was high-pitched, like the shriek of a donkey.

"When did royal standing ever matter to you?" Blood rushing into my ears, I frowned while Clay struggled to stay on his knees. "Who the fuck are you, and what have you done to the decent boy I once knew?"

Clay rolled up in the fetal position.

"Shh." Drake draped his arm around my shoulders. "Too much dominance, Kensi. Too much."

My breathing slowed—I hadn't noticed it speeding up—and my dominance ebbed away. The only sounds in the room were our heartbeats and Clay's pitiful whimper.

"Did I get you?" I ran my hand across Drake's cheek.

"It's okay." He quickly planted a kiss on my finger. "Let's say we have work to do when it comes to your alpha skills."

I slowly turned toward Clay, while Drake resumed his position by the door. Despite his protective instincts, he knew this would have to be my showdown.

I pulled the list I'd made earlier out of my pocket.

"Scimitar's phone's in his room, even though it looks like he'd taken it with him on the trail. Next, Scimitar was killed by someone he trusted. The killer was a werewolf with smaller feet than it appeared—or possibly one smaller foot. And finally, Scimitar was going to be confirmed as the South African crown prince instead of you, and only a small number of people knew."

Clay kneeled and stared at his ring. "You know about that?"

"What do all these things have in common?" I tagged him with my index finger. "You, my friend."

"You believe I killed Scimitar." Clay was done asking questions. Going by his posture, he was done with this entire situation.

"What am I supposed to think?" Nausea bubbled up from my stomach. "All the arrows point in your direction."

He shuffled to sit against the bed and stretched out his legs. "In that case, I have nothing to say."

"When did you find out you were no longer next in line to the throne?" I crouched, holding Scimitar's phone in my hand like some undeserved trophy.

"Two months ago. Dad said Scimitar was going to be confirmed early next year. My brother didn't want to, but Dad's word was final. I wasn't strong enough, he said."

"Your foot?"

"Of course. As if that's even my fault. I worked so hard, too hard, to see the throne disappear into the night."

King Lance had bowed to public pressure, as my father had suspected. If Dad's backbone had been as brittle as his pack brother's, I, too, would be in Clay's position.

But I wouldn't have killed. My father was also my king and my alpha, and the choice of his successor was his, and his alone.

Drake stood by the door, watching Clay with a fiery gaze. Ready to tear him apart if he made a wrong move toward me.

Only a few wolves were blessed with the urge to become an alpha, to lead a pack, and to protect it. Drake was prepared to fight his instincts and be content being my prince consort. That took a great deal of love.

He was twice the man I'd believed Clay to be.

"You're blaming your foot for this?" *She* snarled at his cheap excuse, causing me to bare my teeth. "Don't be such a cliché."

Clay sniffed. "I never cared about the throne. The rules, the power plays, all bullshit if you ask me. But even though the path to the crown hardly seems worth it, it's the only path I knew. Once my father handed my future to Scimitar, I was lost. What was going to happen to me?"

"Right. Poor little rich prince." I swished my hand through the air, disgusted by his pity party. "When did you decide to kill him?"

Clay turned his face away.

"Come on, then." I rose to my full height. "If you're not prepared to give us the whole story, my father will find a way to get the truth out of you."

Clay pushed himself into a standing position with the grace of an old man. "No. I want to speak to my father. Scim's death is a family matter and doesn't concern you."

Clay might be inebriated, but had he also imbibed stupid?

"Except we're the prime suspects." I exchanged a look with Drake.

His breath exploded from his mouth, while his hands had already clenched into tight fists in case our prisoner caused trouble.

He surged forward and grabbed Clay by his collar. "Come on."

Clay coiled out from under Drake's grip. His speed came out of the blue. As did his spray of dominance, which struck Drake square in the ribs.

Clay scurried toward the door leading into the living room, but Drake was faster. He seized Clay's arm.

"Let go." Clay kicked Drake's shin.

Drake's arm flung out and catapulted Clay across the room past the corner of the bed.

I ran toward Drake and touched his arm to see if he was okay.

"Come on, Clay." He shook me off, his glare telling me to stay away. "Be a man and accept responsibility."

"Shut up." Clay ducked down and disappeared from view.

"For fuck's sake." Drake thumped the door frame. "Are you hiding? What are you, eight?"

He approached the bed.

A flash of black fur exploded from behind it. The wolf's muzzle aimed for Drake's jugular as Clay's dominance scattered in all directions.

"No!" I threw myself in his path, and his jaw chomped down on my shoulder.

"Kensi," Drake shouted seconds too late.

A crack of fire tore through my flesh, and I let out a howl before poking my fingers into Clay's eyes.

He whirled away with a whine and retreated behind the bed.

My shoulder was burning, and warm blood trickled through my top, staining its pastel green a dark brown.

Something moved on my left. Drake's wolf pounced and landed, his tail high, in front of Clay.

The black wolf snarled and crawled out from his hideout. His pants draped comically across his hindquarters, and patches of his shirt hung off his back. In a flash, the two locked jaws. Their growls and dominance saturated the atmosphere.

The hot stabs in my shoulder caused my arm to dangle. As I edged forward, Drake's growl kept me back. I'd done my part. He wanted to finish it.

His clothes lay crumpled on the floor. I crawled over to the door frame and folded his shirt with my good arm, my vision blurred from pain.

What was I doing? I wasn't even the domestic type. Maybe he didn't need my assistance, but how about a nudge?

"Clay's left hind leg is the weak one," I shouted, suppressing the minor pang of guilt.

The images of a caring Clay and the monster slaying his brother continued to clash. Maybe Scim's death had been an accident, and Clay's remorse prevented him from telling the truth. Like, he wanted to be punished.

"Tell me if I'm right." I stared at Clay, who wasn't holding up well against Drake. "You called Scim and convinced him to meet you in a remote location. Maybe you argued about his plan to challenge me or about whatever you two had going on. You push him. Scim pushes back. You pick up a rock. Does that sound right?"

Clay angled an undecipherable glance in my direction. An interrogation where the suspect was in wolf form was new to me, too.

Drake snuck around Clay and snatched his hind leg between his canines. Clay howled and kicked, but every jolt of the foot earned him an extra squeeze.

"That's why you took the phone with you when you left your brother's body behind." I leaned my head to the side and regarded Clay, whose kicks and snarls had died down.

Blood was dripping from his fur into the cracks of the wood panels.

King Lance would definitely get billed for that.

I exhaled, tired. "If a phone had been found, even with the call deleted, we would have suspected Scimitar had been lured to his death. Without it, and with the murder weapon being a rock, Delta dismissed the idea that the killing could have been premeditated."

Clay lowered his head to signal his submission.

"How angry you must have been to strike down your brother." My voice held sympathy I didn't feel.

A dizzy spell swept over me, and I swayed, but I wasn't done yet. There were too many things I wasn't clear on yet.

Clay slipped back into human form. Drake's canines, however, remained embedded in his calf. A protector never took unnecessary risks.

"I think he's given up." I spoke softly.

Drake wagged his head to the left and right, drawing a scream of pain from Clay, and then shifted into his birthday suit.

My heart soared. Not only because he was naked, but mainly because he was uninjured.

"As promised, I didn't protect you." I beamed weakly.

"You look like you expect a thank-you for that." He sat back on his legs and wiped blood from his mouth.

I gestured down his body and licked my lips. "Consider this my reward."

He stayed within striking distance from Clay. "It's time we called your father."

"Yeah." Except my brain was still working through the story.

Everything pointed toward a cold-blooded murder rather than one borne out of anger. Jealous rages left their marks on the victims, and Scimitar's body hadn't looked like it had been bludgeoned by an angry person. Clay had many strengths, but planning wasn't one of them. Spontaneity had always been his most endearing feature, from his insistence to skip classes as a kid to his recent spur-of-the-moment decision to break into Delta's office.

His eyes downcast, he dragged one of Scimitar's shirts off the bed and pulled it over his head. Even with my P.I. hat on and in full objectivity mode, I had bought his entire tale hook, line and sinker.

I pushed myself off the ground, wincing against the throbbing in my shoulder, and fetched Drake's clothes. My glance drifted to where tufts of fur and small puddles of blood signposted the battle scene. Clay used to joke he was the only "truly black werewolf" in his family. But the fur I'd found near the crime scene hadn't been black.

"Earth to Kensi." Drake stood in front of me, in all his naked glory, beckoning for his clothes.

For a second, I indulged myself in the sight of his breath-taking smile, his powerful biceps, and his football-player thighs.

So I was shallow. Sue me.

I reluctantly handed him his shirt, pants, and underwear and returned to Clay, who was sitting on the ground, a right mess.

I touched his arm. "Scim challenged me for the German throne because he wanted you to take the South African throne. He was trying to undo your father's decision, wasn't he?"

Clay blinked with heavy eyelids. "Yes. I doubt he expected to win against you, but he wanted to try."

"He had help."

"Your father's people advised him on the protocol he'd have to follow."

"Glen?" I lifted my hand to my shoulder and pushed against the pain. "Yeah, advise him was all Glen did. I'm more convinced than ever he didn't give Scim the map."

Clay pressed his lips together.

"Your fur's black. What color is your father's?" I leaned my head to the side. "It's a light gray, isn't it?"

Clay's eyes widened, and he balled his hands into fists.

"Oh, man." I briefly closed my eyes. "I'm sorry, Clay."

THIRTY-TWO

THE SILENCE THAT FOLLOWED PRICKED the tense atmosphere. The hollow feeling that started in my stomach grew to envelop my heart.

"What's going on?" Uncertainty flickered across Drake's handsome face.

"We were wrong," I said, my mouth dry. "Clay didn't kill his brother."

"Yes, it was me." Clay, fully dressed now, leaped to his feet, wobbled, and fell back onto the bed. "I killed him."

"Clay, c'mon."

"It was me." He nursed his injured calf. "I confess."

"The fur we found will prove it wasn't you."

"Your investigators didn't receive it. Without it, you have nothing." Clay's pleading tone contradicted his defiance.

"Kensi?" Drake raised his hands. "What, am I invisible?"

I expelled a long breath. "Clay sent the fur to our investigators via internal mail, but I suspect his mother intercepted it."

"His mother?"

I gave a sad smile. "What better motive to kill a man than to safeguard your son's future?"

"His mother did this?" He blew out air. "Are you serious? She killed her own son?"

"Her husband's son. Her step-son."

"No one needs to know." Clay's tone fell to a desperate plea. "Take me in. I confess. Everyone already considers me a screw-up. No one's going to question it."

"You're not a screw-up." I rested my hand on his neck. "And you're not weak. Your father is an idiot for listening to the nay-sayers. I saw you run. I saw you fight. You deserve to lead your people."

"Scimitar was stronger."

"Scimitar wanted you to take the South African crown. He knew that running and fighting weren't the only qualities a leader needs. Everything he did was because he loved you. You owe it to him to become king one day."

Clay swallowed, yet his eyes wouldn't meet mine.

"How long have you known it was her?" I sat next to him, phone clutched in one hand, taking his hand in my other.

"When we found out Scimitar's map could only have come from an alpha. My father wouldn't have helped Scimitar, but then I started wondering about things. Why Mom hadn't tried to change my father's mind about the succession. She always said she couldn't wait to see me be confirmed. I also remembered how adamant she'd been to let my brother come to Germany. If she hadn't insisted, Dad wouldn't have allowed it. Then the two whispering behind closed doors. Suddenly, I knew. I just knew."

"I'm so sorry."

"What's going to happen to her?" Tears glistened in his eyes, but none of them rolled. He was an alpha through and through.

My face shuttered. "Your mother promised to love Scimitar as if he were her own. She broke that promise. For that, she'll have to pay."

Clay buried his face in his hands.

"Stay here." I pursed my lips and stood. "We'll take care of this. Okay?"

His heavy breaths had no fight left in them.

Drake and I returned to the corridor, and he slowly closed the door.

I fell against the wall and brushed both hands over my face. "What a mess. Now I have to confess to my dad that I meddled *and* tell him his pack brother's wife killed her son. Yay me."

"I had a better idea. While you were talking to Clay, I messaged your father and asked him to send Delta to Scimitar's room." He raised his head. "And there he is."

Steps sounded behind me. Glendale and Delta came running, their faces unreadable.

Delta's expression as he admitted his failure would be a moment I'd been waiting for, and yet I didn't feel like celebrating. Clay's life lay in ruins. Scimitar's was lost. And mine would move forward as I'd planned. How was this fair?

Drake pushed out his chest and let a veil of dominance fall over him. The absolute control that marked him as an alpha male took my breath away.

Delta's jaw hardened, but he and Delta bowed, once before me and, unnecessarily, once before Drake.

We gave them the low-down of what we'd uncovered.

"The shoe prints." Delta consulted his notes on his cell's display. "Queen Nimcha made them?"

I stood level with Drake and lifted my chin, forcing Delta's look toward me. "Initially I thought the 'small feet in large shoes' were due to Clay's practice of wearing matching sizes."

"But in the end, your initial assessment was correct." Drake's tone included more praise for Delta than was warranted. "Clay's mother most likely used Prince Scimitar's own shoes to create the impression the killer is a man. She had access to his room."

"I can't believe it." Glendale looked shaken. "Queen Nimcha?"

"It's a delicate situation," Drake said. "Did you collect the remaining fur from the tree near the crime scene?"

Delta nodded. "I did. It's being analyzed."

"If it includes DNA, you should be able to match it to Queen Nimcha's. That should give you all the evidence you need."

"And if you can't, lie to her." I pointed at Drake's groin area. "If it helps, we have Clay's testimony."

"Excuse me?" Drake stared at me as if I'd lost my mind.

"The recorder, Hasi. It's in your pocket."

Glen's lips formed a shaky smile that barely covered his chuckle. Delta lacked the confidence to laugh at Drake, although his eyes were definitely twitching.

A red glow enveloped Drake's head, and he stuffed his hand into his pocket. "You had to call me Hasi, did you?"

"Oh, sorry." I winced. "Not cool."

He handed the recorder to Delta. "You didn't hear that, understood?"

"Understood, sir." Delta grinned. As his brother's face had done earlier, his too transformed into that of a young man's, as kind and sweet as any I'd met.

Why had I never seen this smile before?

I softened my tone. "We can also assume, as the king's mate, Queen Nimcha was perfectly placed to make a copy of the course map. I'm sure she's the one who suggested Scimitar should go after the German crown in the first place."

"If she wanted him to win it, why kill him before he had the chance?" Delta asked.

My frown returned. "You'll have to ask her to be sure, but I suspect she wouldn't have been able to kill Scimitar at home, under her husband's nose. But here, I would be the obvious suspect, and yet my position would all but guarantee no one was ever going to dig too hard. This was never about the German crown."

"A miscalculation." Drake wrapped his arm around my shoulder, careful not to touch my injury.

"Are you okay?" Glen asked in an uncharacteristically gentle tone. "You're hurt."

I straightened my spine. "I'm good, thanks."

"This whole thing is, well, it's fucked up, is what it is." Glen's colloquial English would send Stirling into a rant, but he'd hit the nail on its ugly head.

I looked to the side, determined to keep my emotions in check. "Scimitar thought of her as his mother. To lure him away from South Africa, she'd have built him up, played on his love for her, maybe even told him how confident she was in his ability to win. He was going to make her proud. Why... He couldn't have suspected she was going to kill him."

Glendale moved uncomfortably on his feet before drawing my gaze with his raised hand.

"You did it." He showed a thumbs-up. "You solved it."

"The rest is up to you, Delta." Drake pulled me tight. "We're out."

With these words, he gave away the win I'd been hoping to lord over Delta. Yet a victory parade no longer seemed important. Delta had done a good job. He was the one who'd figured out the footprints, after all.

Besides, the less reason my dad had to suspect that I'd gone behind his back, the better.

Drake brushed something off his shirt. "If you agree that the case against Queen Nimcha is solid, you should tell King Aldwych and then charge her. But do it tonight, before King Lance takes his family home."

Glendale nodded. "We will. Thank you, Your Royal Highness."

He rushed away, signaling with a raised hand for Delta to follow. Delta bobbed his head toward me and Drake and ran after his friend.

Glen had prematurely referred to Drake as 'his royal highness.' A by-the-book guy like our Marshal of the Pack wouldn't have made that mistake unless he was trying to make a point.

He'd finally accepted Drake as the future king consort of the Boroughs Pack.

"You're a better person than I am." I smiled at Drake. "I would have humiliated Delta and bathed in his shame."

"No, you wouldn't." He laughed. "Do you remember what the Wild Pack's objective is?"

"To change hearts and inspire minds, not to break legs."

"Yeah. Thought it might be worth a try here, too."

I sighed. "I watched Queen Nimcha clap when Scimitar won races as a kid. The way she'd lift him up and tell him how proud she was. How he beamed at her praise. How could she—"

My voice couldn't carry on without breaking, without allowing my tears to flow, which wasn't an option.

"I don't understand it either," he said.

I rubbed my shoulder.

He released me from his grip. "Let's go for a run. I know shifting hurts, but it will heal your wound."

Even though I was exhausted, the lure of the woods was too strong.

With Drake by my side, I walked into the night, away from the castle, where my father's sad duty would see him charge his pack brother's wife with murder.

THIRTY-THREE

THE TREES LIT UP IN fireworks all around us. My wolf's hearing amplified each sound, yet I ran until my lungs threatened to burst. After half an hour, and feeling much more like myself, I shifted back into my human form. My clothes lay in the tree where I'd left them.

Getting dressed took time, though. Physically I was fine again, but my brain wouldn't let things alone. For once, it wasn't Clay who was in my thoughts, but Drake.

He'd proven over and over that he listened not just with his ears, but with his heart. Whether or not he'd once had dreams of being a pack leader, he'd largely approached his future without preconceived notions. This ability to keep an open mind made him the ideal consort to the first-ever alpha queen, but I owed him so much more.

He stepped out from behind his tree, wearing his shirt and dress pants and shoes so fancy, Jonah would tease him for days.

"You're one of a kind." I smiled so hard for fear my swelling chest would burst if I didn't release my love for him. "And although I call you my little bunny rabbit—"

"Which I find not at all emasculating, especially when you do so in front of Glendale and Delta."

"Even though I call you my bunny rabbit, you're a lion. Or, I guess, a wolf."

"I appreciate it."

"You know Dad will reschedule our confirmation, maybe as soon as next month. Are you sure this is still what you want?"

"Most definitely." He held his nose close to my neck, as he did so often to soak in my scent. "The past week has proven that power comes with sacrifices, and I want to be the one uncomplicated thing in your life. The one thing you don't have to worry about."

"And I'm telling you what Jonah and my dad have told you a million times. You didn't get your alpha genes to protect and follow, but to protect and lead. You may be okay with being a prince consort now, but what if one day you won't be?"

"Listen." He grabbed my waist. "If that day arrives, we'll deal with it. The Moon Promise will keep our love alive. The rest is about compromise. Besides, you know what happens when we disagree. Amazing make-up sex."

"Yes, but will it get us through the rough patches?"

He slid one hand down to squeeze my butt cheek. "Not a doubt in my mind."

"You're obsessed with sex." I sighed and happily leaned toward him.

"I'm obsessed with you." He kissed me, filling me with his warmth.

Keeping him as my king consort meant he'd forever play second fiddle. More than ever, I was convinced he was born for more.

While I'd been whining about the bad old times with Glendale or gushing about the good old times with Clay; plotting my revenge on those who'd wronged me and planning a bright and successful reign; I'd forgotten being queen wasn't about getting my own back or making my mark. Being queen wasn't about me at all.

A lesson Drake had learned long before me.

I put my mouth close to his ear. "Before I let you ravish me, let's check in with Dad."

Fireworks rained down on the castle, too, and the pops and distant 'aahs' from spectators held us in their spell. For a few minutes, we watched as Wildbach celebrated the end of the Black Forest Cup. The crackling lights infused the air with a tinge of burning sulfur and gunpowder.

"Wonder who won." Drake's gaze was aimed at the sky.

"Not us."

He pressed a kiss onto my hair, and we entered the castle's foyer. Tonight, all the guards were inside their rooms. Independently from each other, he and I raised a hand and waved into different cameras.

By the time we'd reached my dad's living room, Queen Nimcha had already confessed. The way Dad told it, it had taken them less than five minutes to get the truth out of her. She'd been weighed down by guilt and was almost glad it was over, especially once she'd found out Clay had been prepared to take responsibility for her crime.

Queen Nimcha hadn't excessively lavished either of her sons with affection over the years I'd known her. There had been indicators of pride and love, certainly. A clap to applaud a task well done, and a sly cookie before dinner, that kind of thing. Moments best defined as lapses in strictness rather than true maternal indulgence. Yet throughout I'd assumed she'd cared for the two boys equally.

"What's going to happen to her?" I lined up the peas on my plate to make an easy meal of them. Literally.

Today, Dad had insisted on serving up a good old Wiener Schnitzel, with peas, carrots, and fries. I slathered everything in thick gravy.

Dad lowered his fork and assessed me. "What would you do about Nimcha if you were me?"

I glanced at Drake.

He cocked his head. "He asked you."

I shifted my chair closer to ensure that, should the peas roll off my fork, they'd roll back onto the plate. "Put her in the dungeon and throw away the key."

"Come on." Dad seemed unconcerned by my battle with the food. "You can do better. What would Queen Kensington do?"

"Fine." I put down my fork and puffed out air.

Two sets of eyes stared from faces I loved so much it hurt. They were my family.

Clay's family, meanwhile, lay in tatters. He didn't deserve that. Maybe he wasn't the boy I remembered, but neither was he the monster I'd considered him to be for a few horrible minutes.

I took a sip of apple seltzer and slowly set the glass on the table. "Queen Kensington would allow her to go home with her husband and her son."

"Her mate, you mean." Dad gave me a funny look.

"Losing battle," Drake mumbled.

Damn it. When would I finally get this right?

"Yes, I'd let her go home with her mate and her *pup*." I stuck my tongue out at both of them. "King Lance won't go easy on her. He loved Scimitar. I imagine he'll put her under arrest, keep her locked up in comfortable surroundings, so Clay may visit her—provided he'd want to."

"I think so, too." Dad sounded satisfied with my answer. "They're preparing to leave now."

"Is King Lance finally going to confirm Clay as his heir to the throne?" I asked.

"Before Lance left, we had a talk. Not king-to-king, but man-to-man. I did my best to make him accept a portion of the blame for what happened. But how do you tell a man who's on the ground to stand up tall? How do you convince him that, now more than ever, he must lead and show fortitude?"

"In other words, we'll have to see what he does when, or if, he recovers from the shock. Blah blah blah." I showed him a talking hand. "Some people are so predictable."

"More or less." Dad gave a grim chuckle. "Puts you in the mood for your own confirmation tomorrow, doesn't it?"

"Tomorrow?" I gulped.

"Many of our royal and noble guests remained in town. For the gossip, I imagine. But as long as they're here, we might as well take advantage of it and put on a show. Stirling and Glendale are already greasing the propaganda machinery."

"My confirmation." I glanced at the ceiling. "Let's hope it'll be the last one."

For a while, we ate in silence.

"How did you put the clues together?" Dad asked.

"Me? Us?" I raised my eyebrows and waved the fork between Drake and myself. "We weren't allowed to investigate, remember? That was all Delta's doing."

"Funny. Come on. What gave her away?"

"Drake did most of the hard work. Once he'd discovered Scimitar and not Clay had been the presumptive crown prince, we realized Clay knew more than he was saying. It all came together once we talked to him."

"He confessed to protect his mother, but Kensi saw through it." Drake swallowed his last piece of food and laid his fork and knife on the plate. "It was a brilliant piece of deduction. A detective couldn't have done a better job."

I kicked him under the table. Hard.

My dad flinched.

"Oww. What was that for?" He leaned to the side to rub his leg.

I held my hand in front of my mouth. "I'm so sorry, Daddy. I didn't mean to hurt *you*."

"I was going to say, 'the things some parents do to their kids.'" Dad shook his head. "However, I'm finally getting it. Damn, that hurts."

"Do you want me to get you some ice?"

He sat up. "No. I'm good. But no more kicking, okay?"

"Yeah." I surged to my feet and poured a schnapps into a shot glass.

He accepted it with a smile.

I sat back down and set the bottle in front of him. Two more shots, and he'd be right as rain.

My gaze swiveled up to the wall behind him at a photo of my mother holding baby-me in her arms. In my teenage years, when I'd missed her the most, I'd looked at Queen Nimcha as a role model.

If Drake and I had kids, I'd make sure they never had to look outside our family for love.

Drake reached across to take my hand. "Sounds like we're having a big day tomorrow. Maybe it's time we turned in for the night?"

My heart literally skipped a beat. "That sounds like a good idea. I'm so tired, Stirling might not be able to wake me tomorrow."

We got up, and Drake and Dad shook hands. Their relationship was a little formal, but in a few weeks, they'd be old friends. I simply knew it. The two had too much in common to pussyfoot around each other.

As Drake and I prepared to leave Dad's living room, I stopped. "Can you head back without me?" I asked Drake. "I'll be right there."

"Okay." He frowned but accepted his kiss and left the room. "Don't be long."

"What is it, Schatz?" Dad asked. "Do you need anything?"

"It's about the confirmation ceremony." I gave an uncertain smile. "I have a favor to ask."

THIRTY-FOUR

"You claimed the throne for both of us." The ripples on Drake's forehead could mean many things, only a few of them good. "Crown Prince Drake, your father said. Not 'consort.' There was no 'consort' in his acceptance. Shit. And did you notice the audience's reaction?"

Here I thought he'd be happy. Maybe I should have consulted him before upending his life once again.

The midday sun shone through the large, open window, and music drifted up the castle wall. Our guests continued to celebrate, taking the warm day as an opportunity to gather outside.

"Hear that?" I raised a finger. "They're okay with it now. They were surprised, that's all. A throne has never been ruled equally by a pair of alphas."

He took off his robe and threw it onto a dining room chair. "I can't believe you made your dad agree to this."

"I didn't twist his arm or anything." Clothed in my oversized dress, I leaned against the door to my bedroom. "In fact, he seemed happy to give his blessing."

Drake undid the cufflinks on his shirt. "Despite your dad's bootcamp, what do I know about being a king?"

"When someone wrongs me, I want to punish them. You want to win them over. And if unity is the way to our kind's survival, we need more of you and less of me."

"Thank you." He broke eye contact. "I never expected this kind of happily ever after."

I turned my head to make him see my smile, kind of like a warning that I was about to get all gooey on his ass.

"You're my happily, and the Moon Promise takes care of the ever after." Then I took his hand with the care typically reserved for a precious jewel. "You make me a better person, and you will make me a better queen."

He gently touched the back of my hand with his lips. "And our arguments? Two alphas in charge are bound to disagree occasionally."

I winked demonstratively. "As you said: make-up sex."

"Sure. I did mention that."

"So, are you angry?"

He brushed my artistically created locks aside and cradled my face between both hands. "I'm awed by your generosity. Being queen has been your lifelong dream."

"My dreams have changed and invariably include you."

A naughty grin spread across his beautiful face. "That would explain why you drool in your sleep."

"We're having a moment here, idiot." I playfully punched his stomach.

He huffed, although his abs were too hard for him to be hurt. "We should get ready. Brent will be here in an hour to prepare us for the afternoon entertainment."

We entered the bedroom and fell exhausted onto my bed.

"Feel different, Crown Prince Drake?" I rolled onto my side to study him.

"Sure. I can do what I like. People bow and call me 'Your Royal Highness.' I never have to lift a hand again in my life." He raised one leg in the air. "Take my shoes off, woman."

"I would, but I'm a freaking crown princess. I too won't have to exert myself again. I won't even order people around."

"No?" He lowered his leg.

"No. I'll just point." I demonstrated this with a weak hand.

"Let me ask you this." He tiptoed a finger up my arm. "Are you still intent on locking up all the males and make them work for their female overlords?"

"Of course I want to lock them up." I watched his hand move up toward my neck. "That's why you need to keep me in check."

"Keep *you* in check? You must think I'm Superwolf or something."

"You are to me." I playfully snapped for his finger. "We'll need all your superpowers if we're to continue my father's work and ensure the survival of our species."

"Sure, but until then, we should do our part, too. Make new werewolves." He clicked his tongue. "Get my drift?"

"No, you're being real subtle. Hang on, you said you didn't want babies yet."

"Doesn't hurt to practice though, right?"

I stuck out my finger in his direction.

"What?" he asked.

I licked my lips, yet kept my finger aimed square at his chest.

"What's the matter?" His frown deepened.

"I told you. I just point at the things I want from now on. No more work for this princess."

He snatched me into his arms and rolled me onto my back. "Good thing I don't consider making love to you work."

"You'd better not. You're my mate, and satisfying me in every way is your job."

He gently brushed my hair aside. "You called me your mate."

I gave a contented sigh. "I know, Hasi. Now are you going to kiss me or what?"

He did.

The End

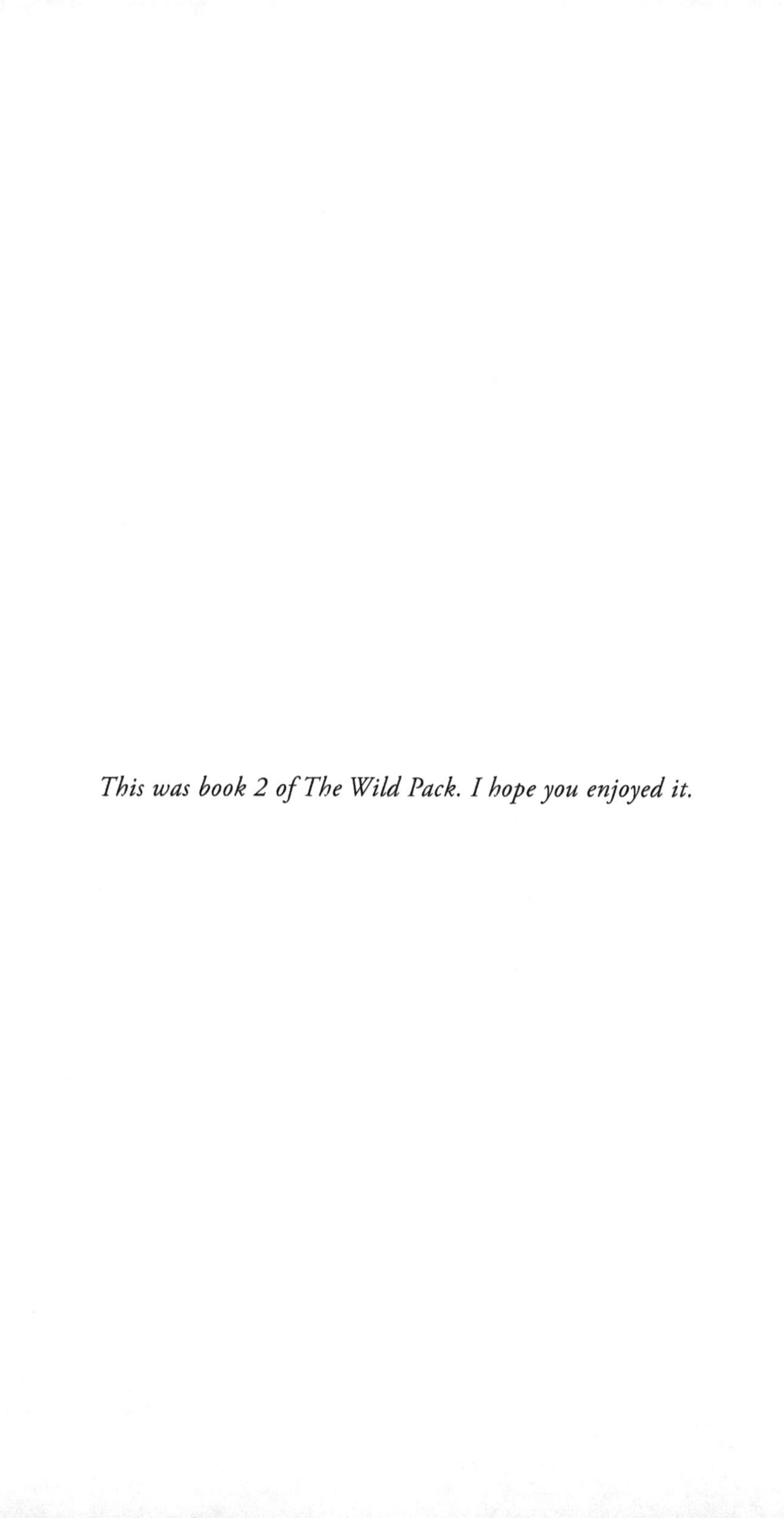

This was book 2 of The Wild Pack. I hope you enjoyed it.

Divide and Conquer

Champions of Elonia

Elonian warrior Nieve isn't thrilled about being asked to mentor a prophesied 'chosen one' who can't tell a sword from a hairbrush. Yet the king's command is absolute, and time's running short.

Unfortunately, physicist Lea, the reluctant 'chosen,' doesn't believe in fixed fates or wacky wizardry, and Nieve's warnings about the shadows fall on deaf ears.

An unprovoked attack at night finally convinces Lea that Nieve's not some raving lunatic. Soon, she throws herself into this new reality that hails her as a hero. A reality in which she can become invisible, light up like a torch, and fly with the birds.

But as the saying goes, all is fun and games until one of them dies…

GUARDED

THE SILVERTON CHRONICLES

IVY'S NEIGHBORS HAVE A SECRET. They aren't human. But Ivy has a secret, too. She knows. As long as everyone keeps quiet, she's happy working as a P.I. by day and chillaxing with her BFF Florian, a vampire, by night. When a routine pickup drops her in the middle of a murder, her two worlds collide. While Florian knows how to throw a punch, deep down he's a softie. His idea of scary? Running out of hair product. It's time Ivy faced facts. Even with a vampire on stand-by, one gal can only kick so many asses.

For help, she must put her faith in others. A human, who might just be the one. A demon, who will, for a price, open the doors to her heritage. And a werewolf, who wants to protect her from herself.

Torn between these men, Ivy must tread carefully, because one wants her heart, one wants her body, and one wants her dead.

Books by Carmen Fox

THE SILVERTON CHRONICLES
Guarded
Bound
Hidden
Trapped – Free download for newsletter
subscribers (https://dl.bookfunnel.com/pyzqppmb32)

THE WILD PACK
Moon Promise
Moon Dynasty

CHAMPIONS OF ELONIA
Divide and Conquer
Hide and Seek
Bait and Switch

ALSO AVAILABLE
Conversations with the Dead
A Knight's Quest

ABOUT THE AUTHOR

USA Today Bestselling Author Carmen Fox lives in the south of England with her beloved tea maker and a stuffed sheep called Fergus. She writes about smart women with sassitude and guys with an edge, and will chase that plot twist, no matter how elusive.

Facebook: www.facebook.com/authorcarmenfox
Twitter: twitter.com/authorcarmenfox
Website: www.carmen-fox.com